❧PRODIGAL❧
FATHER

PRODIGAL FATHER

A Father Dowling Mystery

Ralph [M.] McInerny

St. Martin's Minotaur
New York

www.minotaurbooks.com

Library of Congress Cataloging-in-Publication Data

McInerny, Ralph M.
    Prodigal father : a Father Dowling mystery / Ralph McInerny.—1st ed.
       p.   cm.
    ISBN 0-312-29129-9
    1. Dowling, Father (Fictitious character)—Fiction.   2. Catholic Church—Clergy—Fiction.   3. Land tenure—Fiction.   4. Illinois—Fiction.   I. Title.

PS3563.A31166 P76 2002
813'.54—dc21

2001058865

First Edition: July 2002

10 9 8 7 6 5 4 3 2 1

For Vaughn and Carole McKim

PRODIGAL FATHER

❧ Overture ❧

Moonlight softened the contours of the maintenance shed and lent an eerie opacity to the glass panels of the greenhouse. The line between nature and art blended, natural growth and the works of man fused in the altering light. Nocturnal life went on, a whirring racket emanating from the shadowed trees and hedges. An owl interrogated the night.

Paths reflecting the pale light, moons to the moon, linked shed and greenhouse with the lodge beyond. And with the grotto, where votive lights flickered in the hollowed rock. Our Lady opened her arms in a perpetual offer of help. All tenses seemed present there, permitting a glimpse into the future of these coordinates in space:

Strange primal sounds come from the maintenance shed, animal grunts, the toppling of tools that ring when they strike the concrete floor. The door of the shed bursts open. A single figure appears. He staggers along the path, nearly falling several times, righting himself, pushing on. When he comes to the grotto he all but collapses on the prie-dieu before the shrine. He falls forward as if in prayer. The ax handle emerging from his back glows in the moonlight.

Part One

There is one thing I ask of the Lord, for this I long, to live
in the house of the Lord, all the days of my life.

—Psalm 27

The old priest came slowly down the long drive from the main
building to a predestined point, then turned and looked back with
the eyes of youth. From where he stood, the veranda was visible,
and the great double doors of the main building above which the
grand facade rose four stories. Atop the dome, catching the morning sun, was the gilt statue of St. Athanasius. His creed had once
formed part of Sunday matins in the days when the Breviary
was still said in Latin, the language in which Father Boniface himself still said the daily prayer of the Church. This June day might
have been a long-ago summer, with classes over, the seminarians
dispersed, long indolent months stretching hot and humid before
him until September brought another school year, and the familiar
routine of teaching Virgil and Cicero. Birds twittered among the
trees. Except for the constant hum of traffic on the interstate, the
scene was as it had been when he was a boy here, learning rather
than teaching Latin, preparing as he had thought to take his part in
the far-flung work of the Order. But he had been destined to live

out his priestly life where it had begun, watching his classmates go off to their assignments at the two parishes in Chicago, the retreat band, the high school in Cicero, or the missions in far-off Africa and Central America. Generations of his students had also gone forth, but he had remained, witness of the decline and fall of the Order of St. Athanasius.

I alone have escaped to tell you. That recurrent line of the servant returned to tell Job of his losses—cattle, family, worldly goods—had become his motto. Or *I, Tiresias. . . .* T. S. Eliot. He had come almost to cherish the melancholy sense of dissolution. The church tower rang the half hour, two musical phrases, mechanically operated now as it had been for years. Once a student had been assigned as bell ringer and pulled with living arms the thick rope that measured out the hours and days and years. The bell seemed to toll for young Conrad, a fourth-year boy, who long ago had hung himself from that rope in a fit of adolescent despair, dying to the cacophonous clang that had awakened the school in the middle of the night. The lips of the old priest moved in prayer for his long-dead classmate. And for his dying Order.

The decline had begun in the late sixties, in the wake of Vatican II, the ecumenical council, that had been summoned by the saintly Pope John XXIII with effusive optimism in the early '60s, inveighing against the prophets of doom who could not, as he did, see the world and the Church with the eyes of hope. As a young priest, Boniface had felt his pulse stir to the pope's call for renewal, for a new springtime of the Church. Religious orders were to find anew the purpose for which they had been founded. But John XXIII died, the council went on for several years, and what had begun in hope soon took an unexpected turn. Religious men and women deserted the life they were meant to renew, priests were laicized, the student population of this place dwindled as the Order of St. Athanasius, like so many others, lost its moorings. The rector of the seminary ran off with his secretary, applications for laicization became more numerous than new vocations, soon Latin lost its central role in preparing young men for the priesthood, and a species of English reduced the liturgy to banality. Boniface had lived through all that. For several years he had been the caretaker of the Order. There was only a handful of priests left at Marygrove, all but one older than himself. In the 1970s, the American branch declared its independence of the mother house in Turin. The missions were abandoned, they no longer had the men to staff the parishes in Chicago, and soon all that remained was the seminary on its magnificent grounds west of Chicago. But thin wisps of hope had lately risen in Boniface's soul.

A half year ago a stranger had asked to see him, or so he was told, but the man who stepped into his office was no stranger to Boniface.

"Nathaniel?"

"No one has called me that in thirty years. When I asked Father Joachim who was in charge he didn't recognize me."

"I remember you as Richard Krause as well." A boy who had a gift for Latin but who was to become an angry advocate of the vernacular.

"Arma virumque cano," Richard said and the remembered words made him seem again the boy in the front row who was always ready with the day's passage and exchanged a pained and knowing look with Boniface when one of the others stumbled through the stirring lines of Virgil. Now they announced his own homecoming.

Later it seemed to Boniface that he had been apprehensive even then. It should have been an occasion for joy, a lost sheep returned, perhaps the harbinger of others.

"I want to come back."

"Didn't you marry?"

"My wife died."

"What have you been doing all these years?"

"I became a financial advisor."

"Many went into counseling."

"I was a counselor in a way."

Richard went on to say that he had lived on both coasts, he had prospered, there were no children of his marriage. Nor had the former Nathaniel come unprepared to plead his case. Boniface must have read of former priests wanting to return. Twenty percent, it was said. Nathaniel was full of such lore. He had made inquiries at the chancery downtown, had spoken to someone. The cardinal himself was a member of a religious order, as so many new bishops seemed to be. Good things had happened in the archdiocese in recent years, but the signs of restoration had nothing to do with the Order of St. Athanasius. Boniface in his capacity as superior had spoken not long ago with the cardinal, giving him a report on the Order.

"There are just seven of you?" the cardinal had asked.

"Yes, Your Eminence."

He was small, bald, and birdlike, a man of steel with a gentle manner. If he was shocked he did not show it.

"So what is your future?"

"God knows."

"Indeed."

Boniface had tried desperately to put a good face on the events he reported. They had kept the seminary in good repair, the grounds were as they had always been.

"No vocations at all?"

"There have been inquiries. Older men, in their thirties and forties. They had known our priests in the parishes. I am afraid the prospect did not look inviting to them."

"Do you have a plan?"

"A plan, Your Eminence?"

"For renewal. The Church has been through rocky times. Perhaps we are now at last ready for the Council to have its effect."

Boniface had gone back and talked with the others.

"The Council has already had its effect," Joachim said with sudden bitterness. "We were renewed right out of business."

Boniface did not encourage this reaction. Old Martin had looked at him quizzically, but then his hearing had now become so keen that, as he put it, he heard things that hadn't been said. And little that was. Ambrose had an artificial knee and had never learned to walk properly since the operation. Peter was wracked with arthritis, and Bartholomew had been asthmatic all his life, unfit for anything more demanding than looking after the books. John, the one priest younger than Boniface, had suggested they volunteer to help in parishes.

"How I miss pastoral work."

In the end that was the extent of the next report Boniface made to the cardinal. John had been made assistant—pastoral associate as it was now called—at an ethnic parish, putting to use his knowledge of Polish. And Boniface himself said Mass at St. Hilary's in Fox River whenever Father Roger Dowling needed him.

"You really want to come back after all these years?" Boniface had said to Richard Krause.

"If you'll have me."

Boniface worked out a plan. Richard would spend a trial year, after which the cardinal promised to restore his faculties. Richard actually wept at the news.

"But what will I do?"

"Think of it as a retreat. You said you were a financial advisor?"

"Yes."

"Perhaps you could help Bartholomew with the books."

And so he did. Boniface had expected resentment, resistance, an angry refusal to have Richard looking over his shoulder, but Bartholomew relished having an assistant, for that was Richard's designation. The lost sheep took more enthusiastically to helping Bartholomew than he did to the spiritual regimen Boniface put him under.

"What's the point?" Richard asked, when told to study the rule, reacquaint himself with the life of the founder, review the work of the Order. "It's a record of failure."

"If you believed that, you wouldn't have come back."

"No," Richard said, as if seeming to reject a number of possible rejoinders. "You're right."

Apparently Richard had dyed his hair in the world. Now he wore his gray hair dramatically long and when Boniface suggested a haircut Richard was ready with an answer.

"The founder did not believe in haircuts. Or in shaving."

"Ah. So you will grow a beard."

Richard grew a beard. "I want to say good-bye to everything I was."

It appeared that he had been many things, financial advisor only the last of a long line of pursuits. Perhaps when one deserted a life to which he had vowed himself, nothing else exerted a permanent claim.

"Tell me about your wife."

"She had been a nun. We were like two angry adolescents, though we were both in our forties. We blamed the Church instead of ourselves."

It was the surprising restatement of the Church's teaching on contraception that had decided them not to have children. Marriage was above all a relationship between two people.

"We were flower children."

They had lived in California, which was where they had met. She, it seemed, had become a psychological counselor.

"Her goal was to relieve people of their sense of guilt. For her, to be a Catholic was to be burdened with guilt. Especially about sex."

As Richard described it, his wife—Marilyn—had preached the obverse of the Christian ideal. The body was paramount, its needs to be embraced, pleasure was not a sin but fulfilment.

"You disagreed with her?"

"Oh, no. You would have had to have known her."

Was he slipping free of any responsibility for the life he had led?

"It all unraveled when she learned she had cancer, Boniface. All the fears and anxieties she had warned others against came back with a vengeance. She worried about her soul now that her body was moribund."

Eventually, Marilyn had dreamed of returning to the life she had led as a nun, but she had a husband. Besides, her species of Franciscan was nothing like it had been when she belonged.

"She was shocked at the changes."

"Did she try to go back?"

"She would have liked to lead the rest of them back. They laughed at her. She wouldn't have been allowed to come back. Her change of heart set me thinking."

"Did she have a good death?"

Richard looked at him. "You can't know how odd that would sound to most people. But yes, she died with all the consolations of religion. I saw to that."

"What do you mean?"

"In an emergency. *Tu es sacerdos in aeternum*. Even when you're laicized."

Richard had become a priest to his wife. That had made it easier for her.

"Imagine her explaining everything to a hospital chaplain. More than anything else, being with her at the end made me realize what I had thrown away."

It was Joachim who first wondered about what Richard would bring to them if he came back. Boniface was surprised by the suggestion, but he put it to Richard as his own.

"I divested myself of everything. It was like a repudiation of all that I had been. I come back empty-handed, Father Boniface."

It didn't matter. If nothing else, the Order of St. Athanasius had prospered financially. Not even the near dissolution of the Order altered the fact that they had no monetary worries.

"I had no idea how well off the order is," Richard said.

"Is it?"

"Don't you know?"

The truth was that he did not, not in any detail. From time to time, Bartholomew told him of the investments he had made. And old friends of the Order continued to send in donations as if they were hard at work in the various fields of the apostolate. The land they held in Fox River was coveted by developers, but what would they do with the profits if they sold? The question was Bartholomew's. Boniface found it sacriligeous even to suggest that they would do anything to diminish what remained of the Order. Changes in personnel and the work the Order did were one thing, but he did not intend to preside over the dissolution of the Athanasian empire. Winston Churchill. Of course the real reason was personal. He wanted the school and the grounds kept just as they were when he had first seen them at the age of thirteen.

"It makes sense," Richard had said. "Look at what has happened to Fox River."

When the order—the American branch, as it was then—settled in Illinois, Fox River was a sleepy little town that had lost its importance long ago when rivers ceased to be the principal avenues of commerce. By the end of the second millennium, it had become one of the burgeoning suburbs that accommodated the fleeing population of Chicago. Marygrove, the headquarters of the Athanasians, was located on hundreds of acres that had proved a buffer against this, though there was no way to stop the proliferation of new highways that enabled the new population of Fox River to travel back and forth to the Loop. Of course they had obligations beyond the Order itself.

"Andrew George's father was head of the maintenance crew, and his son will take over eventually. We have more to think of than ourselves, Richard."

"Did the Georges ever become Catholics?"

"No."

"You could pension them off and still save money."

"I am not interested in saving money!" said Boniface.

He should not have made it so personal. Richard's reaction told him that.

"You're against change."

"There have been too many changes."

"I wonder what the others think."

It had seemed a threat, almost. Richard had already won over Bartholomew.

"We're like the dog in the manger," Joachim said.

"Our Lord was laid in a manger."

"Because he was so poor."

He could of course have told the cardinal that he was unwilling for Richard to be reinstated. How easy it was to imagine the reasons he might give. Richard had returned because the world had disappointed him. The Order was the last port in the stormy life he had led since leaving. And he could imagine as well the cardinal's response. When a man takes final vows an order, too, takes on responsibilities. Did Richard's long absence dissolve those responsibilities? And then Richard won his heart.

"Why isn't saying the office a community devotion?"

"With so few . . ."

"Two would be enough. You and I could form a choir."

Richard had begun saying the office again, as part of the plan Boniface had devised for his rehabilitation. It turned out that he still had the breviaries he had once used.

"We can say it in Latin."

And so once more the hours were recited in the stalls of the church sanctuary, as they had been from time immemorial. Boniface accused himself for letting communal prayer fall into desuetude. The Liturgy of the Hours was in English now, but there was a revised Latin version.

"Can't we use the old office?"

Privately, yes. But in community? The cardinal was more than amenable.

"It may earn you the graces that will enable you to flourish again."

Others joined them, as if they had been waiting for this to happen. They became almost a monastic community, gathering in the church at the appointed hours. Richard, it appeared, was a musician and when there was a quorum in the choir he took his place at the organ. And such a voice he had. When he intoned the Nunc Dimittis at Compline, tears formed in Boniface's eyes. Was it possible that the worst was over and a new day was dawning? And then Richard asked him to speak with Mr. Anderson.

"Anderson?"

"He is responsible for most of the growth in this part of the state, Father."

"If it is about our property . . ."

"Just listen to him. That's all I ask."

This was on a Sunday evening. The opening psalm of Vespers still clung to the corners of Boniface's mind. *Dixit Dominus ad Dominum meum . . . "The Lord said to my lord, 'I will make your enemies a footstool to thy feet.' "* Boniface agreed to listen to Mr. Anderson.

And now on this June morning, he stood halfway down the drive, looking back at the main building, hearing the church bell toll the half hour. But it was the evening prayer that filled his mind. *Now dost thou dismiss thy servant, O Lord, according to Your word in peace.*

In the shadow of your wings I take refuge till the storms
of destruction pass by.

—*Psalm 57*

There had been a time in his priestly life, too long a time, when
Roger Dowling had almost begrudged making his annual retreat,
so full had his mind been of his work on the archdiocesan marriage tribunal. At first the tribunal had been a welcome assignment where he could make use of his training in canon law, but
gradually he had been weighed down with the burden of all those
couples looking for a legal loophole that would enable them to
claim that they had not really entered into a marriage after all.
Their general view seemed to be that a decision that had produced
such unwelcome results could not have been truly made. There
were those who had anticipated an annulment by getting a civil
divorce and regarded the tribunal as simply another court that
could undo the past. Whatever credence one gave to their tale of
a loveless marriage, however willing the couple to collude with
one another in the testimony given, each as eager as the other to
get the Church's sanction on their intention to marry again in the
hope that they would be luckier a second time, there was nothing
the tribunal could do for them. Friends and relatives might add

their testimony, but the fact remained that a valid marriage had been entered into and no tribunal could put asunder what God had joined together.

During his first years as defender of the bond, Roger Dowling had known only one case where it was possible to believe that no true marriage had taken place, the husband fully intending, as he pledged fidelity at the nuptial altar, to be unfaithful with the mistress he had no intention of giving up. How could such a man have made an authentic promise to plight his troth to the unsuspecting woman in her bridal gown, stars in her eyes, her imagination full of the life of bliss that lay before her? When eventually she learned of her husband's perfidy, when he and his friends acknowledged that he had not sincerely entered into a marriage, there was indeed the possibility that the case could be successfully sent to the Roman rota and a verdict of nullity eventually reached. Eventually. That had been the rub. But most cases were hopeless and brought before him men and women who expected the tribunal to do what not even God could do—make what had been not to have been.

A week's retreat was not long enough to cleanse the mind of all those sad stories. He felt almost self-indulgent, spending long, silent days in prayer and meditation, and in the evening listening to clerical gossip but not able to join in. His head was full of things he must not divulge any more than he could have chatted about what he heard in the confessional. It would not do to speak of Mr. A and Mrs. A since one of his classmates might know the couple, however algebraically he referred to them. With time the pressure grew too great, even his annual retreat did not relieve it, and be began to seek solace in drink. The habit had stolen upon him, an evening libation becoming two, then more, until increasingly it became his only solace in what he had come to think of as Bleak House. Finally his condition became known. All his prospects of promotion went aglimmering. Bishops were chosen from those with degrees in canon law as often as not, and Roger Dowling had been widely regarded as on track to be named an auxiliary of Chicago and eventually to have a diocese of his own. When all that came crashing down upon him, something like despair gave way to relief.

After rehabilitation he was told he was to be pastor of St. Hilary's in Fox River. Before taking up the post, he made a retreat at Marygrove which was near his future parish. His retreat master had been Father Boniface. It was the first genuine retreat in years and ever since, after he had settled in at St. Hilary's and come to see that what was universally regarded as his personal tragedy was a gift from God, he had returned each summer to that seminary and to Father Boniface.

"You saved my life," he often told the wise and gentle priest.

"Hardly that, Father."

In the evening, they would stroll the lovely grounds of Marygrove and Boniface would liken his own life to Father Dowling's.

"Without the happy ending, of course."

"I don't think I have ever known a man as contented with his lot as you are, Father Boniface."

"I dreamed of being a missionary when I was a boy here."

"How old were you when you first came here?"

"Just out of grade school."

"That came to be thought a mistake, taking a boy from his family at so early an age."

"In some cases that may have been true."

As Father Boniface recounted what had happened to his Order, the peace of the place seemed an illusion. Why had Father Dowling never realized the significance of the quiet that awaited him on such occasions? Perhaps he had thought that summer was merely a lull in the busy life of the place, that the handful of priests in evidence meant only that the rest were engaged in other work during the vacation months. Boniface had told him of the decline of the Order of St. Athanasius in a tone of wondering resignation.

"Life is a book in which we set out to write one story and end by writing another."

"Who said that?"

Boniface stopped and tried to frown the author from his memory but without success. It didn't matter. They resumed their walk.

"And now you bring consolation to me, Father Dowling."

Perhaps he did. Priests need priests, too, after all. Father Dowling had lived through some version of Boniface's story, watched men flee the priesthood and nuns doff their veils and head into another—and they hoped—more satisfying life.

"I have been told that some come back," Boniface said. "As many as twenty percent."

"One out of five?"

"Perhaps more want to but cannot."

"Married?"

"Yes."

For a time it had seemed far easier for a priest to be returned to the lay estate than for a couple to receive an annulment. The new code of canon law had altered the practice of many marriage tribunals. Judgments could now be made at the local level and, imitating the divorce courts, tribunals allowed psychological impediments to contracting a valid marriage supplement and then replace the older more stringent requirements. The results had often been scandalous, but a brake had been put on such abuses.

"Have any of your own men returned?"

"One."

"Not twenty percent?"

Boniface laughed ruefully. "I suppose it's not really a matter of numbers."

"Tell me about him."

And so Father Dowling had heard the story of Richard Krause. He had not realized that the distinguished bearded man in the choir when office was said was on probation. Nothing in his appearance suggested that he had spent his life differently than the other fathers trading verses of the psalms as they recited the hours in chapel. Father Dowling felt a kind of kinship with the man, another lost sheep returned. But it was by accident that he met the bearded prodigal one evening when the two of them happened to be making the outdoor stations of the cross together. After the fourteenth station, Father Dowling introduced himself.

"St. Hilary's? I said Mass there from time to time years ago. You're a Franciscan?"

"No. They had the parish for a time."

"We had parishes, too."

"Yes." Father Dowling had been filling his pipe and when he lit it Richard watched with amusement.

"We all smoked here. Almost all."

"And you quit."

"I never really acquired the habit. It was something we did during recreation. I was glad to give it up."

"When did you do that?"

The other man combed his beard with his fingers. "Has Father Boniface told you about me?"

Father Dowling nodded. "I was surprised at your name. Richard."

"My religious name is Nathaniel."

"And will you adopt it again?"

"First I have to be adopted."

"And has Father Boniface told you about me?"

"What would there be to tell?"

"Nothing dramatic."

"Like my own story?"

"No, nothing like that."

For some reason he had not wanted to confide in Richard. And he did not think of what had happened to himself as dramatic. Even so, like Richard's, his story had a happy ending.

"Some day I would like to say Mass at St. Hilary's once again."

"I think we could arrange that."

"Boniface tells me you sometimes rely on him."

"Not as often as I would like. St. Hilary's is not a demanding assignment."

That was all. Was he just imagining that Richard avoided him after that?

From deceitful and cunning men, rescue me, O God.

—*Psalm 43*

Marie Murkin would not take vacations and she did not go on retreat. Her role as housekeeper of the St. Hilary rectory was all she needed of restorative satisfaction in this Vale of Tears and more than she needed to keep a watch over her soul. There were pastors who gossiped with their housekeepers as if they were aunts or older sisters. When from time to time she got together with another housekeeper—Gretchen Carey of Mother of God was impossible to keep at bay—she listened with tolerant amusement to tales of the chatty domesticity of that sybaritic rectory with its two and a half priests (old Father Harrington was in residence, and good for a Sunday Mass, but otherwise Gretchen's foe at pinochle), and she was filled with contentment at her own lot.

Oh, there had been the years in the land of Egypt when the Franciscans were in charge. From day to day, she had never been sure how long she could abide those jolly, incompetent friars under whom St. Hilary's went into a financial nosedive. The exodus from the great old homes in the parish had begun and FOR SALE signs abounded as one ribbon of concrete after another cut off the parish from what had once been the surrounding countryside. With revenue down and parishioners melting away like wax, with the school only half full and run by suddenly discontented nuns, Marie would have thought that any pastor worth his salt would do his best to galvanize the parish and defend against the evil day that was upon it. But Father Felix, the last of the lot, was out of the rectory more often than he was in it, playing golf or having lunch elsewhere with important friends who never gave a dime to St. Hilary's. And then, as if to prove that novenas to St. Anthony were never in vain, everything changed and Marie was confirmed in her suspicion that the Franciscans had wrongly appropriated the saint of Padua as one of their own. Would any Franciscan have heeded her prayer that the parish be rid of Franciscans?

Almost over night they were gone and the cardinal sent Father Dowling to brighten her twilight years.

Marie was not that old, but she became a valetudinarian when her husband disappeared, going off without warning, not to be heard from again for years, as if all those hitches in the Navy had made dry land impossible for him. And so she had become a housekeeper.

"The grass widow's equivalent of joining the convent," Father Dowling had said with the dry humor that had taken some getting used to.

"The convent!" The nuns were gone then, the school closed, but Marie's memories of the disgruntled band in their silly pastel suits and veils the size of hankies over their permanents were fresh. They had abandoned the convent as cutting them off from the people, and took up residence in one of the larger houses on Dirksen Drive. A crafty developer named Anderson had talked Felix the Catholic, as she ironically thought of him, into converting the convent into posh apartments, causing the few remaining nuns to covet the place they had so cheerfully abandoned. But soon they and Felix were gone and Father Dowling was in place.

"It is the age of delayed vocations, Marie."

"You mean departed vocations." Two could play at that game, as she quickly learned.

"You're not thinking of leaving?"

"Is that what you would like?"

"Talk it over with your spiritual advisor."

The knack of getting along with Father Dowling lay in knowing when he was serious and when he was not. He had been through the mill, as Gretchen was only too eager to tell her, Marie nodding through the narrative as if it was not all news to her. It was difficult to think of Father Dowling as a man with elbow trouble. He drank nothing stronger than coffee now, and gallons of that, and he ate like a bird. Marie's cooking was legendary, but it was all lost on Father Dowling. She could have served him cereal at every meal and she doubted he would have noticed. But he had the wit of the Irish and kept her on her toes and she flourished under the new regime. And he was always on the job, so much so that his annual retreat and the monthly day of recollection that took him away were equivocal times for Marie Murkin. The days of recollection were not bad, but the weekly retreat in June was another matter.

The first two days, she went over the rectory, scrubbing, scouring, beating the carpets, waxing the floors, doing the downstairs windows, and putting Edna Hospers's boy Carl to work on those on the second floor. He was such a fearless acrobat at the work she couldn't watch him, but Edna told her not to worry.

"He leads a charmed life. And it gets him away from his computer."

Thank God, Father Dowling shared her disdain for such new contraptions. He had an old portable typewriter in his study on which he wrote his few letters; he kept the books by hand and could have been an accountant if he really cared about money, which he didn't. Not for himself.

"You haven't had a raise in years, Marie."

"What would I do with more money?"

"You could consult with your spiritual advisor."

Was he telling her she ought to have one? Once she hinted, after meeting Gretchen at the Crossed Tea, that she had taken his hint. He lowered his head and looked at her through a cloud of pipe smoke and she resolved never to try fooling him again. He did give her a raise and she sent it to Mother Teresa. She realized that she no longer felt like an employee. It was Marie's little secret that she was in her way a pastoral assistant. Don't get her started on the subject of women's ordination, it wasn't that, but for all Father Dowling's kidding manner she never felt patronized, or worse, ignored, as she had with the Franciscans. Phil Keegan, the Fox River captain of detectives, was a tougher article, but Marie accepted him as the pastor's friend since boyhood.

"I washed out of Quigley," Keegan said.

"I don't believe it."

"I'll take that as a compliment."

"As a priest, you would have made a good cop."

"I didn't have to know Latin to be a cop."

"You wouldn't have to know it now to become a priest," Father Dowling remarked.

"It's too late," Phil said, but without regret.

"Oh, I don't know. Marie is thinking of entering the convent."

"And exiting five minutes later."

"Oh, they might let *you* stay."

There were times when no reply was the best reply. It was good to have a layman in the house as often as Phil Keegan was. His wife had died, and his daughters lived at opposite ends of the country, but between his work and frequent visits to his old friend, he was more or less content with his lot.

"Or you might marry again," Father Dowling said with a straight face.

Marie harrumphed. "Once burned, twice shy."

"Is that St. Paul?"

"The epistle to the grass widows."

"Marie, you know you're eligible. And Keegan is willin'."

Phil Keegan was more embarrassed than she was by such sallies. Of course Father Dowling did not mean it. He was not an effusive man, but Marie was confident that he relied upon her and would act very differently indeed if she ever spoke of leaving.

On Wednesday of the pastor's annual retreat week, the house was spotless—all but the study; she had learned her lesson about touching anything there.

"Don't," he had said. "I use the Dewey decimated system. I know where everything is."

"Everything" was largely the books that lined the four walls of the study and were piled on the only windowsill as well. The first time Marie had smelled the aroma of pipe smoke she had wanted to cheer. The Franciscans had smoked malodorous cigars and the house was as full of ashes as a crematorium. But the smell of a pipe was a glorious thing and Father Dowling was a very neat smoker. He only smoked in the study and the room was redolent of sweet tobacco. But how quickly it dissipated. She went into the study now, but the smoky ghost of the pastor had gone with him. It was a sad thought that the signs of our passage are so quickly gone. She had aired the house for days after the Franciscans left, but the smell of cigars had lingered until it was replaced by the pleasant one of pipe tobacco. It seemed a metaphor of life that the effect of Father Dowling's smoking should be so quickly diluted. She would discuss that with her spiritual director. She had long since decided that living in the same house with Father Dowling was all her soul needed, and for special consultation she had herself. No need to confide in some stranger.

From the study window there was a view of the former school, now converted into a center for seniors of the parish to spend their days. Edna Hospers was in charge, something of a sore point with Marie, as Edna had formed the habit of reporting directly to the pastor rather than to Marie. She never said anything about it, not directly, but Father Dowling knew her views on the subject. He also knew Edna's. A truce was established, more or less friendly between the two women, but Marie longed to exercise the same authority at the Center as she did in the rectory. Not uncontested authority, of course—the line was very difficult to discern on occasion—and Marie did not want to be scolded by Father Dowling for interfering with his specifically pastoral work.

She saw Edna talking to a man on the sidewalk that connected school and rectory, a man not old enough to be one of her wards at the Center. Marie lowered her glasses to the tip of her nose, giving up on her bifocals, but her eyes were useless at a distance. She decided to go see who the man was. Perhaps he wanted the pastor and Edna was telling him to come back next week. That certainly was a decision for Marie to make.

"Oh, here's Mrs. Murkin," Edna said as Marie approached. "Maybe she can help you."

Maybe! But Marie's stern look vanished when the man turned and smiled at her. He was somewhere in his fifties, trim, tanned, wavy-haired, the kind of man who had been featured in magazine ads when Marie was susceptible to appeals to her lower nature.

"Stan Morgan," he said, taking her hand in his. Marie half expected to be pulled into an embrace and half hoped it, too, if only to be one up on Edna.

"I'll leave you, then," Edna said. "Sorry I couldn't be of help."

But Edna was now out of sight and out of mind for Stan Morgan. Marie asked him how she could be of help.

"And why don't we go to the rectory?"

"Mrs. Hospers said the pastor was away for the week."

"That doesn't mean I can't offer you tea."

On the back porch, he sprang forward to open the door for her and when they were in her kitchen he stopped, mouth open, hands extended, and sighed as he looked around.

"And this is your domain."

He lost points there, consigning her to the scullery, but he quickly recovered.

"And why would you want to be anywhere else but here?"

"I won't tell you how long I've been here."

He didn't ask how long, which was probably just as well. She would have been tempted to tell a fib to make herself seem younger than she was. She sat him at the kitchen table and put on the kettle.

"What kind of pie do you like?"

"Do I have a choice?"

"Cherry or apple."

He hesitated, smiled, shook his head. "Apple, I guess."

"How about a little slice of each?"

"Aren't you having any?" he said when, tea poured, she seated herself across from him.

She shook her head, the self-denial of a woman intent on retaining some semblance of her figure. "So how can I help you?"

"What is the pastor's name?"

Marie sat back. "You're not a salesman, are you?"

"Good God, no."

They both laughed. She told him Father Roger Dowling was pastor. He thought about it.

"I don't remember that name."

"Why would you? He worked in the chancery before coming here."

"I used to live in Chicago."

"And where do you live now?"

"Haven't you heard that everything not nailed down slides to California?"

"And you weren't nailed down."

He let a little laugh suffice for an answer. "Did you ever hear of a priest named Richards?"

Marie ran it through the Rolodex of her mind and came up blank. "There's a Father Ricardo."

Stan Morgan shook his head. "No. Richards. He mentioned Fox River several times so I'm just following a hunch."

"Is he missing?" Marie's mind went briefly to her husband.

"Let's just say I can't find him."

"You sound like a policeman."

"How would you know what a policeman sounds like?"

"I am thick as thieves with the captain of detectives of the Fox River police. Philip Keegan."

"Aha."

"No. It's not that. He's a lifelong friend of Father Dowling's. You didn't answer my question."

"Would you read back the transcript?" he said in a theatrical voice.

"I asked if you were a policeman."

"You're amending the record. You said I sounded like a policeman."

"It comes to the same thing."

"I am not a policeman."

"Maybe you ought to ask the police if they know your Father Richards."

"How could they if you don't?"

Marie's pleasure was displaced by a sudden realization. "Was he a Franciscan?"

"What's a Franciscan?"

"Don't ask. There are two kinds of priest, you know. Those that belong to dioceses, like Chicago, and those who belong to orders. The Franciscans are an order. St. Francis?"

"Are there many orders?"

So Marie told him about the Franciscans and Dominicans and Benedictines and then all the societies and congregations. "The priests at Notre Dame belong to the Congregation of Holy Cross."

"I thought they were Jesuits."

"Oh, they're not that bad." But Marie laughed when she said it. "The Jesuits are another order."

Stan Morgan shook his head. "You'd think I'd remember some of that, wouldn't you?"

"You're a Catholic, aren't you? I mean with a name like Morgan . . ."

"I suppose I am."

"That doesn't sound very certain." This was more like it. With Father Dowling on retreat, Marie felt no compunction at all in assuming the role of pastoral assistant.

"Living in California is different."

"But now you've decided to do something about it. Is that why you're searching for Father Richards?"

He dropped his chin, looking at her between the rims of his glasses and his silvery brows. "You sure you aren't the pastor?"

"Women can't be priests."

"I thought that had changed."

"Don't you believe it. It will never happen."

"Well, if it does I hope you're the first. You know, there was a kid in my class in grade school that went to the seminary." He closed his eyes and rubbed his chin. His eyes popped open. "The SVDs. We kidded him about those initials."

Marie ignored this. "Society of the Divine Word. They were in Techny, Illinois."

"How did they get SVD out of that?"

"Probably a translation from the Latin. Oh, there were scores of religious houses in the Chicago area in those days. Jesuits, Benedictines, Athanasians, Oblate of Mary Immaculate, you name it. Father Dowling is making his retreat at the Athanasian seminary. Marygrove."

"Retreat?"

"A time of prayer and meditation. A spiritual advisor might suggest you do something similar."

After a time, they went into the study where Marie got out the Catholic Directory to look up Richards.

"He was married when I knew him," Stan Morgan said.

"Married! Then he left the priesthood."

Stan Morgan nodded. "I would never have known he'd been a priest if he hadn't told me."

Marie closed the directory. "Well, then he wouldn't still be listed here."

When he left by the kitchen door, the way he had come, Marie assured him that she would make further inquiries. This seemed to alarm him.

"I assumed all this was confidential."

She put her hand on his arm. "If that is how you want it, that is the way it will be. Call next week. I may have information for you."

"I never tasted such delicious pie."

"Oh, get along."

He got along, and Marie watched him go. Only her spiritual

advisor would know the thoughts that briefly teased her then. But she turned and went inside and put the dishes in the sink and then went upstairs for forty winks.

Listen, O daughter, give ear to my words: forget your own people and your father's house.

—*Psalm 45*

Michael George had grown up in the house provided his father as maintenance man for the grounds of Marygrove, a house called the lodge. And hated it. His grandfather had worked for the Athanasians, his father had given them his life, and now when his turn loomed the whole outfit was going to hell.

"They've been good to us, Michael. And we're not even Catholics."

"What's that got to do with it?"

"You thinks Jews would hire a Christian? You think Lutherans would hire a Catholic?"

"I thought we were supposed to be Orthodox."

"We are Orthodox."

"Is that why we never go to church?"

"You've got a smart mouth, Michael. You think you won't go

to heaven because you don't put in three, four hours in church every Sunday?"

"No."

"All right, then."

"That isn't why I don't think I'll go to heaven."

Michael, if he had ever believed in heaven and hell and all the rest, hadn't given it a thought in years. He was now nineteen with the horror of high school behind him and would have rebelled against the suggestion that he carry on after his father as Andrew had done after his until it dawned on him that he might not have the choice.

"St. Athanasius was a Greek," Andrew said, as if he had just provided the key to the George presence at Marygrove.

"And the cardinal stole our name."

But his father was through arguing, giving his undivided attention to the *Sun-Times* sports page. He never went to a game, but he followed all the Chicago pro teams as if the millionaires playing for them were personal friends. All but the Latinos. What would the old man say if he knew about Rita?

"Sure we'll get married," Rita had said to Michael. "Right after you get a job."

"I'm in the family business."

"Well, I'm not going to get in the family way until I'm married."

He admired her for that, when he wasn't complaining of her coldness.

"Warmth has a price."

"What are you anyway, a hooker?"

"No, just a woman who wants a husband along with any babies."

"Rita, I'll be careful."

"Just shut your face, Michael." But she patted his cheek tenderly as she said it. "And another thing, I'll only marry a Catholic."

"Do you know who my father works for? Do you know where I live?"

Of course she knew. It was on the grounds of Marygrove that she had torn herself free just when he was certain he was going to score. Later, he was ashamed for thinking of it that way, as if they were wrestling and he wanted to pin her and win, but at the moment he was as angry as he got. "You think you got to be a Catholic to go to heaven?"

"No. Just to marry me."

Face it, the first time they hooked up after class, Rita had been just another Hispanic—"Say it quick and it spells spick"— one of *them*, matured early, hot to go. Little did he know. The Martinez home was like a church, holy pictures everywhere, Our Lady of Guadalupe over the couch in the living room, which was why he didn't try anything until he took Rita for a walk on the seminary grounds. He had begun thinking she was lucky to have a gringo like him interested in her, but he ended up like an outsider seeking entry to the castle where the fair maiden lived. What did he know about Hispanics? What did any of his friends? They had a singsong way of speaking English, but then Michael could remember his own grandfather's accent, too.

"Do I have to learn Spanish, too?"

"It would help."

He had flunked out of Spanish in high school. He had been told it was a snap course. Maybe it was for Hispanics who made up most of the class. Why the hell were they learning a language they already knew?

"Why do you take English?"

"So why go on speaking Spanish up here north of the Rio Grande?"

"It's a whole tradition and culture, Michael. There are things you can't say or feel in English."

She was up against him as she said it, her dark eyes imploring him to understand. The fold of her lower lip drove him crazy. He put his own lips on hers, gently, to show this wasn't like before. It would have been pretty soon if she hadn't freed herself and stepped back. Firm legs, great body, a great swish of coal black hair, the face of a doll.

"Rita, I've got a job."

"But for how long?" He had told her of the declining fortunes of the Athanasians.

"Growing things runs in my family. You think there isn't a demand for gardeners all over the Chicago area?"

"My cousin works for a lawn-care outfit."

"It's not the same thing! It's not mowing and trimming, for God's sake. Look at this place."

"I can't see in the dark."

He took her there in the daytime, surprising her by how much he knew about the seasonal timing of the flower beds, about the conifers and deciduous trees, about the grove of magnolias just behind the parking lot of the main building.

"Tulip trees," she said.

"Magnolias. Honest-to-God magnolias. My grandfather was told this was too far north for them to survive. Look at them. You should see them in April."

She was impressed by the grounds and Michael felt like he was showing her around the family estate.

"What kind of priests are they?"

"Athanasians."

She wrinkled her nose. "Never heard of them. They're Catholic?"

Once Michael had called them the Athanoccidents and his father had belted him. Andrew was loyal as a serf. That day they ran into the guy with the white beard who had just come back. He stopped as they approached, so there was no avoiding him.

"You're Andrew's son."

"That's right."

The man's eyes were on Rita in a way Michael didn't like. And then he spoke to her in Spanish, rattling it off, and she responded in low, respectable tones. To him she was sassy and bossy, but to this stranger she was humble because he was a priest and spoke her language.

"Looks like you'll be taking instructions, Michael."

"In Spanish?"

Rita answered him, in Spanish, and that was the end of that subject. Had she said something or had he just guessed?

"Who's the new man—Father Richard?" he asked his father.

A rustle of the *Sun-Times*, an angry noise. "The sonofabitch who thinks they ought to sell the grounds to Anderson the developer."

"Sell the grounds?"

"You paid any attention you might know what's been going on around here."

"Attention to what?"

"This place used to be full of kids, young plants. That's what seminary means, a seedbed. I took care of the real plants, the priests took care of them. One day they'd bloom and be priests themselves. Look at the place now."

But for him the place had always meant the grounds, that's where the family pride was.

"You think we got a guarantee? You think it's gospel truth you'll live in this house with your wife and kids?"

He hadn't introduced Rita to his father yet. That might take a little preparation. His father had hired some Mexican immigrants to work on his crew, but they all left one night, following some crop or another, bringing a raging prejudice from his gentle father.

"And Santa Claus wants to sell to Anderson." He meant the bearded priest.

Anderson was a label, not an individual. He stood for all the developers and contractors who had turned the Illinois countryside into acres of new homes, almost solid city from what had once had once been the Chicago limits to the Fox River.

"Father Richard?" Michael repeated.

"He used to be Nathaniel. I remember him when he was Nathaniel. I was your age. Caught him in the greenhouse with one of the girls worked in the kitchen."

"No kidding. And he was a priest?"

"Not yet."

Michael stored it away. Richard had emerged as the family enemy, come back to talk the old priests into selling their land to Anderson. Michael had never realized before how much he wanted to follow in his father's footsteps. The old man had taught him all he knew.

"You got the touch, son."

"That's what all the girls say."

His father shook his head, but he couldn't control the corners of his mouth.

You anoint my head with oil; my cup runs over.

—*Psalm 23*

A week without news, a week without newspapers, television, or radio had seemed to measure his life with real time. St. Augustine said he knew perfectly well what time is until someone asked him what it was. The difference between "What's the time?" and "What is time?"

Roger Dowling came back to the routine of St. Hilary's with the sense that he was slipping from reality into illusion. Until he walked into the house and was confronted by Marie Murkin.

"Has it been a week already?" A preemptive strike.

"And how were things in my absence?"

The housekeeper shrugged. "Only one visitor worth mentioning. He came to see you, but I gave him tea and we talked."

"Good."

Despite her world-weary air, Marie was dying to tell him of it, so he did not prompt her. She followed him into the study where he sat behind his desk. His two favorite books were on the desk where they always were. If she had moved them in his absence he would have known immediately.

The first part of the *Summa Theologiae* of Thomas Aquinas,

the portable BAC edition, which was the second edition he had owned, the first being the blue and typographically forbidding Ottawa edition with the Leonine variations in the footnotes. And *La Divina Commedia*. Old friends. The older he got the more he reread rather than read. The tried and true.

"He was looking for a priest he had known in California."

"He?"

"The visitor. Stan Morgan. I started to look him up in the Catholic Directory when he told me the man had left and married."

The Catholic Directory was back on the shelf. He could see now that it had been taken out and returned. He never kept things so neat.

"So he went away disappointed?"

"I told him to call back when I had a chance to ask you."

"What was the name?"

"Richards."

Marie was a woman without guile, or at least without any guile she could conceal. She was simply repeating what the man had asked.

"That was his last name?"

"I never heard Richards as a first name."

Even so it set his mind going. The bearded former Athanasian who was going through a period of testing before he could be reinstated. Could that be the priest Stan Morgan was seeking?

"What was it, nostalgia?"

"It emerged that he was a lapsed Catholic. I think he thought Richards could help him."

Marie recounted her own pastoral session at the kitchen table. She was self-effacing about her role, but he could imagine her in action. Marie had been here for some years when he arrived and had begun with the attitude that she was showing him the ropes.

Potential trouble, that, but within a week he was sure he wanted her to stay on. From what Marie said, it was possible the man had been in search of Richard Krause. He had been raised in a local parish, he had lived in California, where he had met Richards. Krause had told Boniface he had worked on both coasts, but latterly in California. It was possible. But he said nothing.

"He said he'd call?"

"Would you like to see him?"

"If he comes."

"I'll suggest that."

She filled his Mr. Coffee pot with water but left the making to him. The strength of his coffee did not meet with her approval.

"I don't know how you ever get to sleep."

"Lying down usually does it."

"Did you have a good week?"

"Yes."

"How are they?"

"The Athanasians? They may be coming out of their darkest days."

"What's the point of all these little orders?"

"They each have a slightly different purpose."

Marie was unconvinced. Of course she thought of the Franciscans as one of the little orders. "I like Father Boniface anyway."

"He sent his regards. And I asked him to come say one of the masses next Sunday."

Marie brightened under this. How could she not like Boniface? He was always lyrical about her cooking and ate like a trencherman when he was in the rectory.

.   .   .

"You might have come by to say hello at least," Marie said to Phil when he came to lunch after the noon Mass.

"And you all alone in the house, Marie? I have a reputation to consider."

"It's too late, Captain Keegan. Far too late."

Marie went off to her kitchen before Phil could reply. "So you're all rested and refreshed, Roger."

Roger Dowling nodded.

"I drove by Marygrove once during the week. What a sight it is to see those magnificent grounds the way they've always been. It must cost them a fortune to keep it up."

"Anderson is after them."

"I hope they have the good sense to ignore him." Phil gave him a sudden look. "They're not so hard up they'll jump at it, are they?"

"It isn't that."

Boniface had recounted the argument that it was selfishness on their part to live on that vast acreage when it might accommodate hundreds of families. It was clear the old man did not have a ready answer to that. Or rather he'd had one that was turned against him.

"A dog in the manger." He had shaken his head.

"I hope you won't be swayed by the thought of hypothetical houses and equally hypothetical occupants."

"Father, we take the vow of poverty, and look at how we live."

"Very modestly, I should say."

This was true. The food was plain if plentiful, there was no bar in the recreation room, which was where the only television in the place was located. Those well-tended grounds and handsome buildings seemed small compensation. The acreage wasn't the problem. More than ever before, Roger had felt that he was making his retreat in a rest home. Chanting the office was no doubt a good thing, but most of the Athanasians had not been blessed with voices and there was hesitation over the now-unfamiliar Latin.

"That might have been a mistake, Father Dowling. Not everyone is enthused."

"Richard obviously is."

Boniface agreed. "Sometimes I wonder if he wants to come back for aesthetic reasons. Gregorian chant, the liturgy properly done, the green grass of home."

After Phil left, Father Dowling went over to the parish center to find Edna chatting with a man in her office. They both stood up when he came in without knocking.

"This is Stan Morgan, Father."

"Roger Dowling. Marie is expecting your call."

"Marie?"

"Mrs. Murkin. My housekeeper. You can catch her now if you want."

The man looked at Edna, gave a little shrug. Edna looked away. "Can I talk to you, Father?"

"I'll be back before you leave," Father Dowling said.

He and Edna seemed to listen to the sound of his footsteps going downstairs. Father Dowling shut the door.

"And who is Stan Morgan?"

"He came by last week, asking for someone, and Marie came over and . . ." Edna stopped. "I sound like one of my kids."

It was of those kids and what must be Edna's loneliness that he had thought when he saw her with the very attractive man, not much older than she. Having heard Marie's story of how the man had captivated her, he had the impression that he was doing the same with Edna.

"I've seen him several times, Father."

He sat down. His wariness about Stan Morgan was irrational, he knew that. A stranger come to ask about a former priest he'd met in California who had mentioned Fox River, Illinois. From that he had jumped to wondering if it could be Richard Krause who wanted to be reinstated with the Athanasians. And what if Morgan, too, was a laicized priest? One thing was clear. Marie might have been just a lady to jolly, but Edna was an attractive young woman, forced by her husband's prison sentence to live a celibate life in her prime. He was sure that one of the reasons she gave so much of herself to the Center and her kids was to keep her mind off such things. There weren't many good-looking, smooth-talking men who stopped by the former principal's office where she now worked, and she was clearly susceptible.

"Edna, it's none of my business."

"He took me out to dinner once. And he took us all to a ball game."

She might have been going to confession. He wished he could back up the clock and make his entrance again, knocking this time. And not sending Morgan off to Marie as if he meant to scold Edna.

"Who is he?" he asked again.

"Father, I really don't know much about him. He can talk and talk and . . ." She shrugged her shoulders.

He had the uncomfortable feeling that he had returned to his days on the archdiocesan marriage tribunal. Of course Edna would be susceptible to the attentions of a fine-looking fellow like Stan Morgan, particularly when he seemed as interested in her family as in herself. The children could have only the vaguest memories of their father and Earl had been unbending in his wish that they should not be brought to see him at Joliet. One married for better or worse, and Edna had ended up with more worse than better, but that did not make her any less married.

"So how is Martha Vlasko doing?"

The abrupt change of subject brought an almost audible sigh from Edna.

"She has decided not to sue."

Martha, a busy and self-important woman who affected the air of just looking in at the old people when she came to the Center, which was nearly every day, had pushed through a small group at the door and stumbled outside onto the playground. A bruised knee and ego were the sum total of her injuries, but she decided to make a federal case out of it. The Center did not meet the minimum specifications for such an operation.

"Nonsense," said Amos Cadbury. Amos, the premier lawyer of Fix River, product of the Notre Dame Law School, took care of all the legal work of St. Hilary's parish—pro bono, of course. He and Father Dowling had become good friends over the years.

Martha asked where the handrails were, where the easy-access elevators, where the automatic door openers.

"Tell her to look at her membership agreement," Amos advised.

The majority of the seniors came in the door from the parking lot, spent their day in what had once been the school gym playing cards, shuffleboard, watching television, or just drinking coffee and talking. It was not a high-risk schedule. In any case, the old people agreed to take the place as is.

"She wanted a class-action suit, Father. That was her mistake. The others laughed her to scorn."

"Where do people learn all this legal jargon?" Father Dowling asked Amos Cadbury later when the lawyer dropped by the rectory. Amos's clear blue eyes lifted to implore the mercy of heaven.

"Everywhere. People can go to the library and receive legal advice from computers. They can buy handbooks in the drugstore. *Law For Idiots* or whatever it's called. I am told that new clients now explain to their lawyer the strategy they have mapped out for him."

Amos no longer took new clients himself. He was still a presence in the firm he had founded, and there were several things that he kept in his personal control, among them the affairs of St. Hilary Rectory. He had come out to have a little chat with Martha Vlasko, to make sure her discontent was behind her.

"She said she was only concerned for the old people," Amos said.

"Altruism unleashed."

"She will be no more trouble. I knew her husband . . ."

Sometimes Father Dowling wondered if there was anyone on whatever social level in Fox River that the patrician Amos Cadbury had not known. The circle of his acquaintances had shrunk in recent years, of course. He had been to many funerals, he made regular visits to rest homes to visit other undeparted friends. Casey Vlasko had been in plumbing and heating. Nothing big, but he had a good reputation and his business could have grown if he had wanted it to. When he retired he sold the business.

"To Anderson, of course."

"The developer."

"That suggests a dark room. Appropriately."

It was unusual for Amos to volunteer an opinion about anyone, let alone a negative one. But they were interrupted by the entry of Marie Murkin with a tea tray. No master of ceremonies to a cardinal archbishop could have been fussier than Marie when she served tea to Amos Cadbury. The lawyer had sincerely and often sung the praises of her scones, and Marie all but ignored the pastor when Amos was there to be waited upon. She dropped a slice of lemon in a cup and then poured as if she were measuring out some incredibly precious liquid, not a drop of which should be lost. She handed the cup to Amos. He took it with a bow, raised the cup to his lips, and tasted it with closed eyes. The purring began before he returned the cup to its saucer.

"Marie, Marie . . ."

She made an impatient gesture and turned to go. "Your coffee all right, Father?"

"I made it myself."

She hesitated, but no parting shot occurred to her and she was gone.

"So you were on retreat last week, Father Dowling."

"Yes. At the seminary of the Athanasians. Do you know it?"

"Oh, yes."

Blessed is he whom you choose and call to dwell in your courts.

—*Psalm 65*

The first time Amos Cadbury was consulted by the Order of St. Athanasius was in the early seventies. He had been highly recommended at the chancery, Father Geoffrey Skipton told him, watching with narrowed and interested eyes for his reaction to this.

"Bishop Baglio?"

A shake of the head. "No. Himself." Skipton said this in an unsuccessful brogue.

"Ah."

"You're a Knight of Malta."

Amos had not cared for this. Thirty years ago his reputation had been well-established and while he respected a potential client's wish to know what kind of lawyer he might be getting, he did not care to have it seem that he was bidding for business. The only reason he had come in response to Father Geoffrey's invitation was that he was a priest. What he would have assumed was that the man had learned he did work for the Church pro bono.

"And what might I do for you, Father?" His voice emphasized the subjunctive.

"It's an unusual matter. I thought it was just canon law at first, but that is unclear."

With great circumlocution, Father Geoffrey came to the point. Perhaps Mr. Cadbury had followed the sessions of Vatican II and the exciting events that were following on it. Religious orders were asked to renew themselves by returning to the charism of their founders, the purpose for which they initially began.

"That is where the difficulties lie."

The Athanasians had been founded in Turin in the middle of the nineteenth century by a saintly priest, Don Raffaello Schiavi, first as a community sanctioned by the diocese, then expanding into other parts of Italy. To say that the order had flourished would have been an exaggeration, but it had attracted vocations, it had been assigned an African mission, and it had established itself in the United States, in Fox River, Illinois. There had been semi-annual meetings of local superiors at the mother house in Turin since the close of the Council, but the sunny prospect that had seemed to lie before them at the outset of their meetings changed radically.

"Vocations are down everywhere," Geoffrey had said. "But we are losing priests."

The great exodus had begun and the Italians and the Americans could not agree on what the remedy was. In Turin, they wanted to abolish street clothes, the habit to be worn always and everywhere. They wanted the *novus ordo*, the new order of the Mass established after the Council, to be said only in Latin by Athanasians. They wanted to allow some men to live a hermetic life.

"What it comes down to is that they are really against the Council."

Amos waited.

"The only remedy is divorce, Cadbury. Believe me, I have far more sympathy with people caught in a bad marriage than I ever had before."

What was wanted was a new corporation that severed all ties with the mother house in Turin, and gave the Fox River institution full autonomy. Amos agreed to undertake the matter, reluctantly at first. He had not liked Geoffrey. He disliked his arrogance, his condescension to the "people in Turin," his certainty that he had an infallible sense of the spirit of Vatican II. And he had been full of the jargon of that time. The Church must read the signs of the time, which he apparently took to mean it should take its cue from the secular world. The windows were to be thrown open, apparently to let in the spirit of the age. Habits, clerical dress, fasting and abstinence, all the gloomy and negative attitudes toward sex were out. "Let's brighten up. Look at John XXIII, for heaven's sake." Amos might have found a way to avoid the task, but the more time he spent with the Athanasians, the less typical did Geoffrey seem. Bartholomew was a delight to work with; he knew to a dime what the assets were. Amos suggested a cash settlement to Turin.

"What for?" Geoffrey cried.

"Under the present legal setup, they arguably own everything here."

"They never provided a nickel."

"But everything you accomplished was as members of the Order, the assets, the buildings, the grounds, are community property. I suggest being very generous or this may be in the courts forever."

A lawyer wants to protect his client from future litigation, from any negative effects of what he does for him. Playing fast and loose with the Italian Athanasians could stir animosities that would not soon subside. Far better a generous parting gift. God knows the Americans could afford it. They had indeed prospered. They were situated on what had once been the estate of a Chicago banker whose second wife had been Catholic and brought him into the Church. Left a widower a second time, old Maurice Corbett's thoughts turned more decidedly to eternal things. He had arranged the loan for the first modest foundation of the Athanasians in Illinois and eventually he left them his estate. The mansion remained but was no longer visible as one came up the long drive from the county road. Amos would see the sun sparkle from the statue of Athanasius atop the main building. The chapel was exquisite, the whole nave a choir, with descending facing pews in which a sea of seminarians wearing snow-white surplices had knelt.

Within a year, Amos had completed the work. The Athanasians were established as a corporation according to the laws of the State of Illinois. All previous legal provisions for their presence in the state were superseded by the new arrangement. The archdiocese approved, as did the relevant cardinal in Rome.

"So that's that," Geoffrey had said after the signing of the papers in Amos's office. He was wearing a plaid sport coat and a shirt open at the neck. The spirit of Vatican II?

"That's that."

"I consider this my gift to the Order, Amos."

The question of his fee came up and Amos dismissed it.

"Don't be a fool," Geoffrey urged. "You know how well off we are. And you deserve a chunk."

Amos promised to give it thought, but, of course, he had no intention of profiting from the work he had done. He was not even sure that it had been the right thing for the Athanasians to do. Oh, he was all for American exuberance. The truth was that the American branch had operated in relative independence from Turin almost from the beginning. It had been Vatican II that had strengthened the sense that they were a single far-flung Order. The effort to define the new sense of unity had fragmented them. But the rhetoric of Geoffrey and the changes at the seminary during the months Amos was arranging the divorce from Turin were strikingly different. Renewal, the spirit of the Council, advancing into the modern world, were like clarion calls, but there was a precipitous drop in student applications for the next year and the student body was only a third the size it had been when the Council closed in 1965. An Athanasian at one of their Chicago parishes applied for laicization and was free and clear in a matter of months. Others followed.

A month after the signing of the corporation papers, Amos received a call from Father Boniface.

Boniface ushered him into Geoffrey's office and took the chair behind the desk. "I hope this doesn't sound odd, Mr. Cadbury. But I would like you to explain our exact legal status now."

"Well, as Father Geoffrey no doubt told you . . ."

"Father Geoffrey is no longer with us. He left."

He had exacted a sizeable severance package from Bartholomew.

I thought of the days of long ago and remembered the
years long past.

—Psalm 77

It wasn't just Father Dowling's reaction, it was the kids' as well. Edna felt that she had lost tons of moral credit with them, especially with Jane, the oldest. The boys had liked going to the Cubs game, no doubt about that, and they pigged out on Wrigley Field food, but they'd resisted Stan's attempts to be a good old buddy with them. The only one he made any headway with was Eric and that, predictably, involved electronics. Stan had a palmtop that seemed to do everything but contact the moon, and he handed it over to Eric without qualm, no warnings, no mention of how expensive it was. Not until Eric asked him how much it cost. And in the fourth inning his cell phone rang and he spoke enigmatically into it for half a minute and hung up.

"It's a convenience, but it's a nuisance, too."

And he let Eric look at the phone as well. The two of them huddled, ignoring the game, while he told Eric of all the things it did.

"Want to call someone?"

Eric looked at her and Edna gave him a noncommittal shrug. He called one of his friends and gave him a play by play of the inning. Sosa hit a home run and Eric described it as if he were Chip Carey. The Lord only knew how much that call had cost.

"Wait'll you see my laptop, Eric."

It was a slim little Toshiba, silver and gray, and once again Stan just turned it over and let Eric run it through its paces. When it was attached to the cell phone it had access to the Web. Eric was impressed with Stan's gadgetry if nothing else. But Jane and Carl never broke out of their wary silence until he was gone.

"Who is he, Mom?"

"Someone who came to see Father Dowling."

She might have been invoking a blessing on the day, on her susceptibility to a man who was so unthreateningly interested in her as a woman.

"They're wonderful kids, Edna."

"You and Eric hit it off."

"When I was his age I had trouble making old-fashioned phone calls."

"Do you have kids?"

"Not that I know of." But his smile absolved the remark of any serious meaning. "How long have you been separated?"

"Seven years." That was worse than a lie. She felt that she was being unfaithful to Earl. But what had she done, really? She had dinner with a man, she let him take her and the kids to a ball game. Not what you would confess, for heaven's sake. But somehow they felt like sins. She told herself she was dramatizing something that had no meaning at all.

"What's he do?" her son Eric asked her later.

"I'm surprised you didn't find out."

"He must be some kind of salesmen."

He based this on files he had seen on Ed's computer. A list of properties in the area. And religious orders.

"Religious orders?"

Eric nodded. "All of them in Illinois. Around Chicago. One in Fox River."

"He's a priest, isn't he, Mom?" Jane said.

This was much later. The boys were in their rooms, Edna was fresh from the shower and sitting in her bedroom looking at herself in the mirror, trying to figure out what she looked like to a stranger.

"A priest!"

"You said he was a friend of Father Dowling's."

"No. I said he came to see him."

"He acts like a priest."

"And how would that be?"

"I don't know. He just does."

"Maybe you're right." The suggestion had given her the strangest sensation, casting the dinner and ball game into a very different light, and she seized on it as a way to stop Jane's silent reproach. But it had been her girlish response to Stan that filled her mind, the too-easy laughter, the desire to please, the sense of being flattered out of her shoes by his interest.

"Didn't he say what he did?"

"No. And I didn't ask. Why would I?"

Putting the ball in Jane's court ended the conversation, but Edna lay awake reviewing the day, thinking again of the earlier dinner with Stan. She had called home and said that something had come up, she would be late, could Jane just make spaghetti and a salad and look after things. But she had not wanted to say what had come up. Now that Jane had mentioned it, she found it all too possible that she'd had a date with a priest.

After a sleepless night, she went to work and sat at her desk. Some time during the night she had resolved to put the question to Father Dowling. The pastor's reaction to her remark that she'd had dinner with Stan increased her doubt about the man. Finally, she decided to settle the matter.

She went over to the rectory without calling first and faced the formidable obstacle of Marie Murkin.

"Is Father in?"

"Oh, yes."

"In his study?"

She swept past Marie and went down the hall to the study. The door was open and Father Dowling looked up, surprised, then delighted.

"Edna. Come in."

She pulled the door shut, sat across from him, and suddenly did not know what to say. Father Dowling waited patiently, giving no sign that he found this visit unusual. Finally, he asked about the Center. She found her tongue and said that everything was fine. She was desperately trying to think of something about the

Center that she could use as an excuse for barging in on him like this, when he said, "Any more strange visitors?"

"Did you talk to him?"

"Yes."

"My Jane asked me a question about him."

This was so awfully like going to confession, something she had never done face to face, as was sometimes now done.

"About Stan Morgan?"

"Eric looked him up on one of those search engines, Google, and drew a blank." She inhaled. "Jane asked if he's a priest."

Father Dowling laughed. "No, he was looking for a priest. A former priest."

"And he isn't one himself?"

"I'm sure that would have come out in our conversation. It didn't. What made Jane think so?"

"Because I embarrassed her. She didn't like it at all that I let him take us to the ball game. She thought of it as a kind of date."

"But it wasn't?"

"Not in that sense. Oh, I don't know. Father, I feel awful."

"For accepting an invitation to dinner? For letting a man show his generosity and take you and your kids to a ball game?"

"Father, I was flattered."

"Perhaps he was, too. That you accepted. That's all it was, wasn't it?"

"Yes! Oh, Father, don't think—"

"Edna, what I think is that you are a wonderful wife and mother, that there wouldn't be a Senior Center if it weren't for you, and that you have a conscience as delicate as a Carmelite's."

His words brought all the relief of the formula of absolution after confession. Edna did not cry, she was not given to easy crying, but her eyes welled with tears. If she ever loved a priest it would be Father Dowling; she did love him—how could she not, after all he had done for her when Earl was arrested and then the awful trial and afterward, asking her what she thought of turning the school into a center for senior parishioners?

"It's just a big white elephant now, Edna," he had said. "The parish could save money by tearing it down, but I can't bring myself even to think of that. A center would be a way of justifying the expense of the building, not to mention what it might mean for the old folks. We're becoming a parish of old folks, Edna."

And so she had become the director of the Senior Center. It had enabled her to keep the family together and begin the long wait until Earl would be set free. Most important of all, it had lifted the cloud she and the kids were under because of what Earl had done—if he had really done anything, the thing of which he was accused. But he had felt guilty and he had been found guilty and she and the kids shared in it. Yet as director of the Center she had received the endorsement of Father Dowling and now, all these years later, she doubted that many people even wondered where her husband was.

"Why don't *I* take you and the kids to the ball game?"

"Oh, Father."

"How about Saturday? Phil Keegan could come along, if you wouldn't mind."

"But it's an afternoon game and you have confessions."

"Father Boniface is coming this weekend. He can take confessions for me."

She felt that she was on a cloud when she left. In the kitchen, she stopped and talked with Marie and accepted the offer of tea.

"Father said that he has a helper this weekend."

"Father Boniface." Marie stirred her tea. "He's all right. Did I ever tell you about the Franciscans?"

She had, many times; it was Marie's way of establishing her seniority in the parish, her long suffering, illustrating the moral that no matter how bad things look they can get better in a minute.

"Boniface is no Franciscan, Edna."

"He seems nice."

"He's a saint," Marie said emphatically, as if she were presiding at a consistory in St. Peter's. But then she changed gears. "Do you remember that man who came looking for Father Dowling when he was on retreat?"

There seemed to be no ulterior intent in the question, but Edna preserved a receptive silence.

"A wonderful man. He sat right where you're sitting and we had the nicest conversation. I only wished I could have helped him. He came back, but Father Dowling wasn't any help."

"He was looking for someone?"

"Some former priest as it turned out. God knows why."

"Maybe he's one, too."

Marie's laughter was merry. "Edna, when you've known as many priests as I have you can tell them a mile off. And he sat right at this table. No, he was no priest nor ever had been."

Added to her talk with Father Dowling, this assurance sent Edna back to her office with a sense that she had been shriven several times over.

My vows to the Lord I will fulfill before all my people.

—Psalm 116

On Saturday morning, Father Dowling awoke to find it raining. But it had stopped by the time Phil Keegan arrived.

"It's over, Roger. Have no fear. The game is on."

After saying his Mass, with Phil behind the wheel of the Center minibus they drove to Edna's where she and the kids piled in, the boys full of excitement.

"This is our second game this year," Eric said.

"There's nothing like Wrigley Field," Phil said. "Win or lose, it's always a treat to be there."

"You working on any murders?" Eric asked him.

"Ah, murders," Phil said. He was on the interstate now and happy to pontificate about the blood and gore that filled his days. "The trouble with interesting murders, you almost never solve them. Does that surprise you?"

"You've got a small department," Eric said.

Phil didn't like that. Edna told Eric not to bother Captain Keegan while he was driving. A sound suggestion, given the abandon with which Phil was switching lanes and exceeding the speed limit.

"Can a policeman get a ticket?" Jane asked.

"Only if he breaks the law." Phil let up on the gas and settled into one lane.

"Had Father Boniface come before you left?" Edna asked.

"No. But he'll be in good hands with Marie. She was miffed that Phil and I didn't stay for lunch. I told her we'd have all we could eat at the game. Marie will have a most appreciative diner in Father Boniface."

"She told me you-know-who is definitely not a priest."

"That settles it, then."

Jane seemed intent on making up for her sullenness on the previous trip to the ball game. She sat next to Father Dowling and they fell into a deep conversation that Edna made a point of not overhearing. How much more joyous an occasion this was. For all of them. She was thoroughly ashamed of herself at having been flattered by Stan Morgan's attention. This game would sweep memories of it from her children's minds. Jane had heard her appeal to Marie Murkin's authority on who was a priest and who was not. She did not want her daughter to think that it had been a former priest who showed such interest in her mother.

Now that it was safely in the past, Edna could take innocent pleasure from the fact that Stan Morgan had found her attractive. She had tried to convince herself that his attention had only the purpose of pumping her about the man he was looking for. There was some of that, no doubt, but it hadn't been all and she knew it. Having emerged from the fire unscathed, she could enjoy the boost to her self-esteem. She had told Earl that Father Dowling was taking them all to the game.

"I'll be watching it," he said.

"Oh, how I wish we were all going together."

"We will. We will."

How often it was she who needed cheering up when she visited him. Earl was resigned to serve out his sentence. He had killed no one, no matter what the court had found, but it was just luck that he had not and that did change the appearance of the evidence. To Edna he seemed like a soul in purgatory, being punished but certain that the day would come when his troubles would cease and he could return to his family. She kept him supplied with recent photographs, but the kids knew him only from the wedding picture on her dresser. How young they both had been, squinting into the sunlight, not knowing what lay before them.

Jane enjoyed the game as much as the boys. And Phil Keegan. He was up and down, cheering, groaning, shouting at the umpire, constantly flagging down anyone selling food.

Phil amazed Father Dowling. He could watch a game in the rectory and never raise his voice, but he was an active participant today. They had hot dogs and peanuts and popcorn and soft drinks, but when Phil waved down the kid selling Frosty Malts, Father Dowling begged to be excused. So did Edna. Jane sat between them, as knowledgeable about the game as her brothers, explaining everything to Edna, and giving Father Dowling a look at her mother's lack of knowledge. But that certainly didn't diminish Edna's enjoyment. What a good woman she was and how well she was raising her children in difficult circumstances. But then the moral resources of ordinary folk never ceased to amaze him. Tragedy struck without warning—an unexpected death, a daughter in trouble, an intractable son—and people rose to the occasion and saw it through. Who would suspect the burdens

Edna bore seeing the calm efficiency with which she ran the Senior Center? And there was not an ounce of condescension in her treatment of the old people, even when foolish little romances flared up among septuagenarians and elderly men and women acted like children on the school grounds of their youth. Edna might have been anticipating her own innocent susceptibility.

On the way home, Eric sat next to Father Dowling on the back seat of the little bus, reviewing the game and analyzing why the Cubs had lost despite two home runs by Sammy Sosa. Like Phil, he regarded any loss as the result of bad calls and lucky hits by the opposing team. But finally they all fell silent, weary from the outing. They were nearly at the Fox River exit when Eric roused himself.

"Mom, you know that guy that took us to a game? The reason my Google search didn't work was I got the name wrong."

"How so?"

"I thought it was Moran. But it's Morgan. I remembered that and got a pile of stuff."

"Did you print it out?" Father Dowling asked.

"I could."

"I'd like to see what you found."

Give me again the joy of your help, with a spirit of fervor
sustain me.

—*Psalm 51*

Marie Murkin continued to sing the praises of Stan Morgan. "I
wish he'd come back, Father."

"I'm surprised he hasn't."

"The way you treated him?"

"I was thinking of the way you did."

"Oh, for heaven's sake."

At least Marie had no inkling of Morgan's interest in Edna.
What a thing she would have made of that. It was one thing for
her to have tea in her kitchen with the attentive young man, but
if she knew Edna had had dinner with him, that he had taken her
and the kids to a ball game . . . Roger Dowling did not like to
think what she would have said.

"Why do you call him a young man?"

"Because he is."

"You mean younger."

"I mean young," Marie said and tromped down the hall. The
kitchen door banged shut behind her.

. . .

In the old days, they had had nuns who took care of the laundry and refectory, a community of German nuns who chattered away in their native tongue and had only an imperfect grasp of English, much to the delight of the seminarians who were always trying to get them to commit spoonerisms. But Marie Murkin was something entirely different. Boniface had had two sisters, one a nun, the other married, both dead now, and he supposed he had heard female chatter as a boy before he went off to the Athanasians. But Marie Murkin's loquaciousness was a marvel. There was some respite while she was at work in the kitchen, but she sat at the dining room table while he ate, watching each mouthful, anxious for his reaction. But mainly she just talked. Little response was required of him and Boniface considered it a small price to pay for the delicious meal. But he was looking ahead to the solitude of Father Dowling's study before he went over to the church for confessions. And then she mentioned Stan Morgan.

"I'm sure Father Dowling told you of him."

"No."

So Marie did. "It shows you the influence a priest can have, doesn't it?"

Was there any secret of St. Hilary's parish that Mrs. Murkin would not divulge to a priest she trusted? When she began about the man who had come looking for a runaway priest, Boniface quelled his conscience and asked her to continue.

"Can you imagine? Now he was as nice a man as you could expect to meet, Father. I gave him tea and we had a good talk. You never know when something you say will strike the proper note. You know what I mean."

"And you struck the proper note?"

"Oh, I tried to help him. Father Dowling was spending the week with you, and I do what I can."

"He wanted a priest?"

"Not just any priest. This was someone in particular. A man he had met in California and who had mentioned Fox River . . . so, of course, he came here to ask."

"To ask?"

"If I knew the man. Now what was his name . . . ? Richards. Yes, Richards."

Boniface managed not to express the surprise he felt. "He was looking for a man named Richards who said he was a priest?"

"That was his story. Do you know what I thought? Well, I was right. It turned out he himself was a lapsed Catholic. It didn't take a genius to figure out that was just a story. He wanted help."

"Ah."

She chattered on. The man said he had come from California, but Marie would not vouch for that. Boniface would know what subterfuges people use when they are in need of help.

"Did he say why he wanted this particular priest?"

"When I got out the Catholic Directory, he told me the man was no longer a priest. I think he was afraid I would find someone and the whole point of his coming by would be lost."

"Of course."

"Anyway, we had a good talk and I hope I did some good."

"I'm sure you did."

Eventually he escaped to the study. He sat at Father Dowling's desk and noted the volume of the *Summa* and Dante sitting on it, as if for ready reference. The First Part of the Second Part. What a marvel the *Summa* was, particularly perhaps in its moral part. He opened the book without moving it. Question 16. A bad conscience binds but does not excuse. A difficult doctrine, though Boniface was sure it was true. Medieval Latin grated on his inner ear, but he was willing to acknowledge this as a fault. In the medieval schools, Latin had been a living language, not a nostalgic return to classical times as it had been during the Renaissance. It was the Renaissance revival of classical Latin that had made it a dead language. C. S. Lewis. This was true. Aquinas wrote in Latin as in his mother tongue, a contemporary idiom, which was as it should be.

But Boniface's mind was full of Father Richards.

Richard Krause? It was not impossible. He got down the Catholic Directory and found several Richards, none of them from Illinois. He admitted to himself that in his heart of hearts he did not want Richard reinstated as an Athanasian. His years away from the Order represented a vast *terra incognita*. What Boniface had learned of it did not inspire confidence in the prodigal returned. And yet there was much in his favor, not least his role in restoring the communal recitation of the office in choir. Richard had been the best Latinist Boniface had ever taught. He remembered the sadness he had felt when he learned that Richard was among the many who had decided to return to the lay estate. Of course one was always a priest, *tu es sacerdos in aeternum*, an indelible mark that lasted into eternity, but a priest could be laicized. And so many had been. They had rushed like lemmings to the sea, in Richard's case to California. Stout Cortez, wasn't it? A financial advisor. It would be quite in order to ask Richard for a detailed account of his life in the world, places, dates, occupation. And to learn more about his marriage, and the former nun he had married who had since died.

How sad any life is when summed up in a sentence or two. A life sentence. He imagined a young girl becoming a postulant, passing through the novitiate, taking her vows. And then? Boniface had never understood what prompted men to leave the religious life, let alone women. They had come to regard being faithful to the vocation to which they had been called a weakness. Did they want the security of a predictable life? Well, that could be the case. All the spiritual writers warned against it. They had been instructed about such dangers from their first years in the Order. The right deed for the wrong reason. But one could strive to do the right deed for the right reason. Wasn't that the task of a lifetime? Security did not seem quite the word for that lifelong quest of perfection. Why was abandoning the task preferable?

Just before three, he went over to the church and took up his post in the visitor's confessional. And then they came, one after the other, with their little menus of sins, their fear of punishment, so often a calculating attitude as they argued with themselves and with God whether they had really done anything wrong at all. Boniface listened patiently. The fact that a person was in the confessional was prima facie evidence of repentance. It was one of the rules he had learned. And it was true. He accepted the recitation of sins and tried to direct the penitent to sorrow and a firm resolution to amend his life. Or her life. His or her life, as the phrase now was. The different genders did not seem so different in the confessional. Boniface assumed the role of an *alter Christus*, welcoming the sinner, whispering encouragement. Between penitents, he prayed for them all, the ones who came and the ones who feared to come, certain their deeds were unprecedented in their depravity. A species of pride, that. Who has not sinned? Who is not capable of any imaginable sin?

Between penitents, thoughts of Richard returned, negative thoughts. Richard had lobbied the community on the matter of working out some sort of deal with Anderson. It now looked deadlocked, half for, half against, and, of course, opponents were thought of as antiprogressive, conservative, stuck in the mud. When had change as change come to seem unquestionably good? Most changes brought both good and bad. Sticking with the tried and true doubtless did the same. Yet it was the nature of such division that the opposite side had to be seen as benighted. Surely there were persuasive reasons to sit down with Anderson and talk.

The most powerful argument turned on the greed and selfishness involved in so small a community, a community that would dwindle before it ever grew large again, if it grew at all, possessing a vast piece of real estate. The main building was closed off on all its upper floors, floors that contained the dormitories and rooms that had once housed the student body. The whole second floor had been allotted to members of the community then, but now they all lived in the mansion, each with a suite—bedroom, sitting room, private bath. Boniface had been told that all the new houses going up in the area around them contained multiple bathrooms, six, seven, even more. He thought of his own home with its one bathroom on the second floor, more than enough for his parents and sisters and himself. Mention of the new trend in bathrooms had been meant to cushion the guilt they all seemed to feel to some degree at taking up residence in a house that truly deserved the name mansion.

It had a horseshoe form, the wide front made to appear smaller because of the overhanging eaves and the front porch whose descending roof seemed to take the house with it. Large, fat pillars supported the porch roof, green-tiled as was the roof above, the sides of stucco. The irony of the house was that when old Corbett could afford to build it he had few years left to live in it. Can a man in his sixties build with thoughts of only his own future? Boniface did not know. In any case, Maurice Corbett had unwittingly been building a house for a religious community he would not have heard of at the time of the house's construction. The entry from the county road gave little sense of what awaited as one came up the driveway. The unimpressive little woods through which the driveway wended soon gave way to an expanse of lawn on both sides that rose in broad terraces to the house. The trees became more numerous as one neared the house, decorous trees, trees selected for their variety and beauty. And, of course, the magnolias, their pride and joy.

The chapel was the first addition when the Athanasians took possession, and then what came to be called the main building, one designed to house every aspect of the Order's work. That building had gone up the year before Boniface's entry. When he first came up the drive what he saw had a look of permanency, of having been there forever yet he had seen it in its first years. Was he seeing it all now in its last? It was an odd thought that institutions, too, have lifetimes, a natural inevitable cycle from infancy through childhood to maturity and finally decline. But other orders had lasted for centuries and were still around. It would have been unthinkable to him as a young man that he had boarded a sinking ship. Well, all ships are sinking, nothing is forever in this world, we have here no lasting city.

There was the creak of the kneeler as a penitent settled in. Boniface slid the little panel aside to open the grill.

"Bless me, Father, for I have sinned."

You could guess the age of penitents by the way they confessed. Once nuns had drilled such formulas into children and they remained for a lifetime. Very likely the same sins had been confessed over the years as well, with every now and again some great eruption of misbehavior, but then settling down again into the uneasy mediocrity that marked most lives.

. . .

Father Dowling seemed refreshed rather than exhausted by his outing, though Captain Keegan soon went yawning into the night, leaving the two priests alone. Marie had finally accepted their refusal of a snack, a drink, tea, coffee.

"Good night, Marie."

"Well, if you're sure."

And she retreated to the kitchen and then up the back stairs to her apartment.

"*Mulier fortis,*" Boniface murmured.

"*Fortissima.* Do you use the Web, Father?"

"Only when first I practiced to deceive."

Father Dowling smiled appreciatively. "Neither do I. The young are all adepts now, of course. Certainly Edna Hospers's son Eric is. This is something he found and, as he put it, downloaded."

The pages on Stan Morgan contained news stories from various California papers, accusations, complaints of peculation, fraud, misleading of clients. There were half a dozen pictures of Stanley Morgan, the object of all these accusations. Boniface looked at Father Dowling.

"It's buried in the story."

And so it was, mention of a silent and suddenly absent partner in the firm that was the object of such obloquy. Richard Krause.

Search me, O God, and know my heart: try me, and know
my anxieties.

—Psalm 139

On Monday evening, when Father Dowling showed him the stuff
that Eric Hospers had downloaded from the Internet, Phil read
through it with a scowl.

"This is the nice guy you were telling me about, Marie?"

"Let me see that."

Phil handed her the papers. Father Dowling went on puffing
at his pipe, giving no indication of what he thought Phil's reaction
to the California machinations of Stanley Morgan would be. Marie
rattled the pages as she skimmed them, her expression one of
indignation.

"The man was accused and acquitted, that's the long and short
of it. He is as innocent as you or I."

"He got off on a technicality."

"What else is law but technicalities? He was acquitted."

"That's right," Father Dowling said.

Phil was relieved. He had feared that the pastor of St. Hilary's
expected his old friend the cop to run Morgan out of town on the
basis of these shenanigans on the West Coast.

"What's he doing here?"

"Searching for his flown partner, apparently."

Marie sat forward. "A man he said had been a priest!"

"He wasn't even indicted, Marie."

"So why did he disappear?"

"That's Morgan's story. He didn't accuse his partner of any-thing."

Marie was having none of that. She had found Stanley Morgan to be a fine man and swiftly developed her version of what must have happened in California. It was clear as a bell. This renegade priest had left Morgan in the lurch, Morgan was indicted, and the Judas Iscariot probably thought Morgan would be out of circulation for a good long time, courtesy of the California penitentiary system.

"Wasting away in Alcatraz."

"Alcatraz is closed, Marie," Phil said. "It's become a movie set."

"I just wish Stan Morgan was here to defend himself."

"He could plead guilty to a lesser offence. Again."

"That's right!"

"His partner does seem like a skunk, Roger."

The pastor sent a wobbly smoke ring sailing over his desk. "Have another beer, Phil. Marie?"

Marie got to her feet. "You can drink a toast to Stan Morgan."

After she brought the beer, Marie did not stay, and when they were alone, Father Dowling asked Phil to close the door.

"I think I know where Marie's villain is."

"The runaway priest?"

"He has returned. He was an Athanasian."

"So what is there for him to return to?"

"They're still a community, Phil. With the return of Father Nathaniel, there are six."

"Nathaniel?"

"Richard Krause."

"Aha. Who found him? Morgan?"

"No. I don't know that Morgan realizes where the man he is looking for is. Boniface made the connection when I showed him those pages. Eric gave them to me Saturday, Boniface was here, and I showed them to him. It seemed a cruel thing to do, but it would have been more cruel to keep the information from him."

Roger described the prodigal's return to the Order of St. Athanasius, where he was spending a period of probation before he could be reinstated.

"So you already suspected?"

"It was Boniface who saw the connection."

"What will he do?"

"I don't know. He is not enthralled with Richard's return."

"And this could blackball him?"

"We'll see."

Phil shuffled through the pages young Hospers had printed out. "All this stuff was there for the asking?"

"If you know how to ask. There was something about a search engine."

Phil did not even pretend to understand, but the printouts provided a spooky sense of the Web, everyone's secrets available to anyone with a computer anywhere on the globe.

"Cy Horvath has gotten into that. Sometimes it's quicker than going through regular channels."

"Have Cy put through a search on you, Phil."

"He better not."

"Boniface told me that something like twenty percent of those who left the priesthood have come back."

"And they let them in?"

"What would you suggest?"

"Drawing and quartering. Think of the scandal they caused, and the scandal their just coming back would cause."

"There is that danger, I suppose. But not with an Athanasian."

"I hope Boniface gives him the heave-ho."

"Well, that's two strikes against him."

"Did you advise Boniface to send him packing?"

"I was thinking of Marie."

"She's just infatuated with this guy Morgan."

"Is that a note of jealousy in your voice?"

"Roger, the idea of marrying again never so much as enters my mind. I am celibate as you are."

"And you might have been in the same way as I am."

"Latin," Phil groaned. "But don't get me wrong. I will never regret marrying and having my daughters, being grandfather to their children."

"That's not an impediment, Phil."

"To what?"

"Maybe you should return to the dreams of your youth. Talk to the cardinal."

Father Dowling's little joke. But driving home, the suggestion lingered. How unattractive it was. Yet how many times had he sat in Roger Dowling's rectory nursing the unexpressed illusion that they were just two priests, having a chat, watching a game on TV. But that was the allure of the might have been and never could be. Father Dowling's kidding suggestion confirmed Phil in the conviction that his inability to learn Latin had been providential.

He wasn't meant to be a priest. He was a cop and that was the way he would end up. And he didn't regret it a bit. He could still have his semiclerical evenings with Roger Dowling.

Let the field be joyful, and all that is in it.
—Psalm 96

Michael George awoke with a twinge of conscience to the sound of a mower, the latter the cause of the former. He scrambled out of bed and went to the open window of the lodge, the building that had housed his family since before the Athanasians had come into possession of the estate. All this was family lore. His grandfather had been employed by the Corbetts and when with his second marriage Maurice Corbett had returned to the faith of his fathers it had seemed to threaten the security of the George family. But the second Mrs. Corbett had been a paragon of ecumenism—Father Boniface had supplied the phrase—and it was largely due to her counsel that the estate was deeded to the Athanasians, with the proviso that the Georges went with the land.

"Serfs," Michael had said, shocking his grandfather and getting a belt on the ear from his father.

The sense that he and his family were part of the property persisted until he saw it all as Rita did, she of the dark flashing eyes and firm, trim body who had been unable to conceal her envy at the way Michael and his family lived.

"We head the maintenance crew," he said.

"And you should thank God for it." The lodge was mansion enough for her. Had she already formed the dream of living here? Michael had grown up scheming on how to escape his humbling heritage. At school, he had been identified with the estate. It was difficult to see their situation as demeaning, the way they were treated by Boniface and the other Athanasians. It was because of Boniface that he had passed three years following the course of the minor seminary, learning Latin and Greek and the great works of literature until he rebelled and was permitted to attend the local high school in his senior year. That was where he had met Rita. It was as if there was a plan laid down for his life and all he had to do was enact it. After years of language, he had put his mind to failing at Spanish.

"I'll tutor you," Rita had said, in Spanish, a species of Spanish, one that had crossed the Rio Grande with her family and then traveled north to Illinois where they settled, sending money home to their extended family near Guadalajara. He nodded.

"You understood me."

"You speak so clearly." Small white teeth peeked out beneath the upper lip, resting between outbursts on the plush lower lip he longed to touch with his own.

Rita had reminded his father of the immigrants who had always proved so undependable when he hired them onto the crew, but her deferential manner, her virginal composure, soon won over his parents.

"She is a good girl," his father said, and it might have been a warning.

He saw the estate and his home with her eyes and, compared

with the modest rented home in which her family lived, it did seem palatial. Her father called him *hidalgo* with a smile that showed his goldedged incisors.

"And this is where you'll live?" Rita mused.

"Of course."

"I would live with you in a hut," she said with more fervor now that it was clear that no hut awaited them if, as Michael insisted, they married.

"Not for years," his father said.

"Now. After we graduate."

"You're nineteen years old."

"Did you think I have to go to college in order to learn how to work with you?"

The point was taken. Boniface had remained unenthusiastic.

"I thought you might have a vocation."

"We're not Catholics, Father."

"Greek Catholics."

"Orthodox."

Their priest had told them the difference, insistently, considering where they lived and who they worked for. He came to see Boniface, ready for war, but the result was a truce.

"He is a good man," Father Maximilian said.

"They all are."

"I know only him. But you must be faithful to your own religion."

That would have been no problem if it hadn't been for Rita. She came with him to his church one Sunday and was put with the other women, wearing her mantilla, following it all with wary curiosity.

"When did the Mass part happen? I didn't understand it at all."

Michael could not explain it to her. His own understanding of the Orthodox liturgy was imperfect. She insisted that they must marry before her priest.

"If you're serious," she added.

He would have repudiated his family for her sake, but he knew his family and the lodge was a large part of the attraction he held for her. He tried to resent this, but found he could not. She seemed to think he was heir to the estate because he could follow in his father's footsteps, carrying the family tradition into a third generation.

"You have the touch," his father said, when he saw what Michael had done with the hibiscus bed. Were such things inherited, passed along like Original Sin from father to son? He instinctively understood the relation between the earth and growing things. It was not a theory, not knowledge in that sense. He had worked beside his father since he was a mere boy, an unconscious apprenticeship, one in which he felt a deep, wordless satisfaction when the various flowers bloomed in sequence from spring through early autumn.

"Is it okay with your parents, Rita?" He meant their marrying. He had planted things around the Martinez house, the wisteria bringing delighted cries from Mrs. Martinez.

"It is up to me."

"That's good."

"You're too sure of yourself."

Was it possible that he dissembled the fear he had that one day the bubble would burst and Rita would go off with one of the dark-haired young men with the premature mustaches and swaggers that swaggered over nothing?

"I want to be sure of you."

"We'll see," she said teasingly.

"You said yes."

"I wasn't thinking clearly."

"Thinking clearly is for strangers. I don't want you thinking clearly with me."

"There are months before graduation."

But now it was a week away and still she had not repeated her Yes as she had when her mind was unclear. When he held her she felt fragile, warm, nothing he dared press to himself with the urgency he felt. No talking then, no promises exacted or given, a mute understanding—that was what he had to settle for. He was mad with desire but told himself it was holy. He wanted her as his wife. When he imagined her naked beside him in bed, her warm brown body in his arms, his thoughts were not holy. But it could never happen unless they were married.

The car was several years old but it was a convertible and the man behind the wheel looked out of place. He was fat and thirty at least and beckoned to Michael to come to the side of the parked car.

"What do you want?"

"To talk. You one of the Georges?"

"Is that why you stopped?"

"It is. It is. You work on the Corbett estate."

"It hasn't been that for years."

"My grandfather built it."

"Yeah?"

"He's the one who gave it away."

"My grandfather worked for him."

"There. See how much we have in common?"

They had nothing in common, Michael saw that at a glance.

Sweat stood out on the broad, pasty forehead, and the eyes were small and bloodshot.

"You want to look around just go in the driveway. No one will stop you."

"I have your permission?" Spoken with a snarl, but then he tried to smile again.

"Go to hell," Michael said.

That was the first time. In the following weeks, he saw the car several other times. Once the guy did come up the drive, but he kept the car moving, never stopped or got out. Michael was in the greenhouse where he could watch him without being seen. Why did such a fat, sweaty bastard seem a menace?

Restore us, O God of our salvation, and cause your anger toward us to cease.

—Psalm 85

Being snubbed by the son of the gardener on his grandfather's estate was only the latest in a string of humiliations and disappointments that had defined Leo Corbett's life. He was twenty-nine years old and did not amount to a damn as anyone with the right to say so was quick to tell him. He accepted the burden. But he had developed a theory to account for it. He had been robbed of the family patrimony. His idiot of a grandfather had handed over to a bunch of yo-yo priests the estate he had spent so much time building he never himself had the pleasure of enjoying it. His second wife, Leo's grandmother, died two years after they moved into the house, with work on the west wing still going on. His grandfather developed the irrational conviction that it was the estate that killed her, that the whole vast ostentatious thing was a judgment on him. Leo's dying grandmother had told him what to do. The whole thing, kit and caboodle, was deeded over to the Order of St. Athanasius.

"Who was the lawyer?" Tuttle asked Leo.

"You wouldn't know him." Leo felt contempt for Tuttle as he did for anyone who took him seriously. He had met the little lawyer in a bar near the courthouse where Leo had been trying to get access to the transaction that had put his grandfather's estate into the hands of the Athanasians. Tuttle had said he could help. Leo gave him a retainer.

"Who was the lawyer?"

"Amos Cadbury."

"Cadbury!" Tuttle cried, then dramatically clapped a hand over his mouth. His tweed hat was out of season and he wore it low over his eyes as if he feared recognition. Leo had asked him who the other Tuttle in Tuttle and Tuttle was and was told that he would meet him some day. When Leo learned that Tuttle's partner was his deceased father who had never been a lawyer, he teased him mercilessly. Teasing was the only sure way he knew of establishing superiority, having been on the receiving end of the process often enough.

"I suppose everyone knows Cadbury."

"Not the way I do," Tuttle said. "I've been checking out the transfer. You should have known that only lawyers have access to such records."

"What about the Freedom of Information Act?"

"Nothing's free," Tuttle said pointedly. "This is going to take time."

"I'm not a bottomless pit of money, Tuttle."

"Much depends on what you want to know. And what you intend to do about it."

"I just want to know—how much there was." Leo's voice broke. This was masochistic, wanting an exact account of the money that was not his. The trouble with dealing with Tuttle was that it was like looking into a mirror.

His father had called himself an orphan. An annuity had been arranged for him and it supported him during his geological studies and he had been raised by an aunt. Leo's father was fascinated with rocks, the strata of the earth.

"It's all there," he would say with missionary fervor at table. Leo's mother drank rosé by the bottle, and drifted through life without registering what was going on. She was provided all the comfort she needed and was impervious to Leo's efforts to raise resentment in her.

"Look at the way we live, Mom."

She looked around the room that had been furnished out of discount stores. Awful padded couch and matching chairs, a coffee table with a glass top that wore the rings of his mother's wineglass for weeks before his father wiped them away. Leo left them so his father would know what she did all day. But his father seemed not to care. He had rocks in his head.

"It's all there beneath our feet, Leo. The history of the planet, the history of the solar system, more. I was never tempted by archeology. Man is too recent an arrival to matter much, digging up the residue of his past is to barely scrape the surface. Leo, the ages of the earth are still there, recorded in stone, all we have to do is dig it out and read it properly."

A man that interested in the zillions of years the earth had been around did not have much enthusiasm left for his own family. If the human race was insignificant, what were his wife and son in the scales of geological time?

"Tell me about your father."

"I never knew him."

"Your Aunt Genevieve must have told you about him."

"She hated him. They all did. For turning Catholic. Which is odd. They were all Catholics when they came to this country, the Corbetts. I was baptized Catholic myself, but Genevieve wouldn't let me near a church."

"We were married in the courthouse." His mother's voice seemed to emerge from one of those remote eras that so fascinated his father.

"That's right," his father said, as if he had need of the reminder.

One of his Leo's failures was the effort to become a Catholic to spite his parents. He talked to a priest at the Newman Chapel at the University of Illinois at Fox River.

"What are you now?"

"What religion? None."

"Your name is Corbett."

Leo said yes eagerly, hoping the man would say something of the legendary Maurice Corbett who had made a fortune and become a benefactor of the Church he had joined.

"That's Irish, isn't it?"

"I guess so."

"You from Belfast or something?"

Were the Corbetts kings in Belfast? "Why do you ask?"

"With that name I assumed you were Catholic."

Here was a new line of thought. His grandfather had returned to the faith of his fathers. Was Catholicism too part of his lost patrimony? Leo found this confusing. As misfortune piled on misfortune, he had taught himself to point the accusing finger at a rapacious Church that had taken advantage of an old man in his hour of grief. The truth was that Leo was well on the way to seeing himself the victim of unknown forces before he developed any interest in his grandfather. His father, groveling in rocks and dust, of the earth earthy, never spoke of his father and Leo had learned almost by accident that he was the descendant of one of the wealthiest men in northern Illinois. The Corbett museum in Fox River was not just an odd coincidence of nomenclature. It had been endowed by his grandfather. Leo stood before the huge oil painting of the benefactor in the lobby of the museum and sought in it traces of his father and of himself. But it was impossible to see in the lineaments of that complacent Croesus any semblance of his father's vague precision, the half-open mouth always ready to lecture his son on the formation of the planet. He had gained access, if not to rocks brought back to the moon, to everything written about it.

"So it is true," he had cried, as if Leo and his mother represented intransigent opposition to a theory of which they knew nothing. A meteor had sliced through the earth, sending a great chunk into orbit around it. "The moon! Daughter of the earth."

His father had trembled with enthusiasm. He had never shown similar pride in his personal pedigree. Leo could not begin to imagine his parents begetting him, but he was not tempted by the usual adolescent fantasy of having been left on their doorstep.

That was no more probable than that he had been found under a cabbage leaf. In any case, his father would have stepped absent-mindedly over the bundle on his way to the university museum. Approaching fifty, his father was still a candidate for the doctorate at the University of Chicago. He had so lost himself in the pursuit of truth that he had neglected the requisite exams. He was not even an ABD, one who had completed all requirements but the dissertation. His father remained enrolled as a part-time student, thirty years after matriculating, thus having access to the library and the student union.

"How do we live?" a confused Leo had asked his mother.

"On the annuity." She emerged from vagueness to pronounce the word as if it were a verbal talisman.

"What annuity?"

"Your father's inheritance."

"From whom?"

She thought he was being irreverent. That her son should not share her memories, know what she knew, was incomprehensible to her. But somehow, Leo extracted the bare bones of the story from her. He was the grandson of the great Maurice Corbett, dead when Leo's father, Matthew, was a child and anathema to the aunt who had taken him in as the daughter of pharaoh had rescued the Israelite baby from abandonment. Leo had acquired from his father an interest in the Bible; for his father it was an unwitting source book of clues about the past. The flood? Of course there had been a flood. How else could fossils be found thousands of feet above sea level, embedded in mountains? The ostensible purpose of the narrative of all those different books did not detain his father, but Leo pored over those accounts. He went into exile in Israel, leaving his father behind with Moses as he entered the promised land. He had fed on the manna of Scripture as a child, had been fascinated with David and Saul, had triumphed over Goliath, had read uncomprehendingly of the fragilities of the flesh. On the flyleaf of the Bible, unaccountably the King James version, was written in narrow strokes his grandmother's name. Priscilla Walsh Corbett. Leo passed his fingers lightly over the signature. He lowered his dry lips to it. He felt closer to the grandmother he had never seen, never heard tell of, than he did to his own parents.

He and his father became fellow students at the University of Chicago, where Leo read widely, developed the mandatory arrogance of the Chicago undergraduate, became contemptuous of the uncultivated masses, and flunked out. He took a job in the university library, a menial who returned books to their appropriate locations on the shelves. But he could not get through a day without hearing his father in whispered argument with some librarian or professor, or seeing him huddled over his books in the great reading room, his mounting years as nothing compared to the ages of the earth. Leo quit, he took a job with a fraudulent enterprise dedicated to placing encyclopedias in the homes of the illiterate, bought on installment plans beyond the dreams of usury. He was now a clerk in the pro shop of the Fox River Country Club in whose dining room another portrait of Leo's paternal grandparent was hung, smiling benevolently over the diners. And there was a plaque in the golf shop commemorating a hole in one by the great man, as a result of which he had settled a special fund on the golf shop in honor of the pro who had given him golfing instructions. Leo waited in vain for the current pro, Barfield, to notice the similarity of names.

One thing became clear. His grandfather had early acquired the habit of scattering his wealth far and wide. The museum and the country club were among the beneficiaries of his munificence during his first marriage, a fruitless union that did not interest Leo. Grandfather Corbett's penchant had merely been redirected when he married his Catholic wife, became a Catholic himself, begat a son, and, in his bereavement, signed over to the Order of St. Athanasius an estate that eclipsed the country club in acreage and natural beauty.

A year ago Leo's parents had set off in their ancient Volkswagen bus for the deserts of the southwest and their virginal rocks. They never returned. The Volkswagen was found in the petrified forest, the bodies in the canyon below. As he plummeted to his death, Corbett had gone past layer after layer of the earth's formation until he reached ultimate ground zero. In lieu of mourning, Leo raged at the newly learned fact that his father's annuity had not been passed on to him. It was granted for the lifetime of the otherworldly geologist. It was after learning this crushing truth that Leo had encountered Tuttle and accepted his offer of coffee. Tuttle, it emerged, knew of what had brought Leo to the courthouse.

"Such things happen," Tuttle said philosophically, but then added hastily, "no matter how unjust."

"It's not the money—" Leo began, but Tuttle laid a hand on his arm.

"It's always the money. And it should be yours. Imagine, the grandson of the Daddy Warbucks of Fox River without a penny."

"Can anything be done?"

"It damned sure ought to be."

Tuttle was not a prepossessing man. He had led Leo into the room reserved for journalists where he helped himself to a cup of syrupy coffee. "I'm an honorary member," Tuttle explained.

"Aren't you a lawyer?"

"Yes. And the best friend the press ever had. You'll need a lawyer."

Having said it, Tuttle pushed back the brim of his tweed hat and looked disinterestedly around the room.

"Could I afford it?"

"Are you employed?"

Tuttle did not show any sign of surprise when Leo told him of his present employment. Leo added, "In a menial job at the country club that was one of my grandfather's greatest benefactions."

"He golfed?"

Leo dismissed the question as irrelevant. "Don't you understand? I am reduced to the status caddies once had. I, the grandson of Maurice Corbett."

"Give me a token sum and I will be your lawyer and you shall be my client."

It had a nice biblical ring to it. Leo passed a dollar bill to Tuttle who made it disappear into his hat like a sorcerer.

"Be at my office at ten tomorrow morning," Tuttle said. "And don't mind Hazel."

Blessed are those who dwell in your house.

—*Psalm 84*

Marie, her eyes searching the ceiling as she said it, told Father Dowling that Martha Vlasko had come to see him.

"How's her knee?"

"I didn't ask."

"Show her in."

Martha was scarcely more than five feet tall and despite the weather clutched a coat sweater to her narrow torso. She looked accusingly around the study, took note of the books, of the simmering Mr. Coffee, sniffed the tobacco-laden air. This affected her.

"Casey smoked a pipe."

"Your husband."

"It never smelled as sweet as this. He smoked Prince Albert. There were little red cans everywhere. He put them to different purposes—to hold change, for bills, everything."

The bane of the nonbiodegradable container.

"You're feeling better, Martha?"

"At my age better isn't much. I came to talk about my lawsuit against the parish."

"I thought you dropped that."

"I did. I wanted you to know that I was put up to it by Joseph Novak. He told me that fall was my fortune."

"It certainly was a misfortune. Like the first fall."

"That was my first. I may be seventy-seven years old, but I am not helpless."

"No one would ever think so."

"I told Joe what I think of his advice. It has made me a pariah. No one will talk to me. They think I'm a traitor, and they're right. It was a bad thing to do, Father, and I'm sorry."

"Just thank God you weren't really injured."

"I twisted my knee. I wasn't pretending. But if it hadn't been for Joe . . ."

Martha and Joe were, in Edna Hospers's term, an item at the

Center, one of the twilight pairings-off that enlivened the scene in Edna's domain.

"I'm sure he meant well."

"Meaning well never does. He refused to come here with me."

"No need for that, Martha. No need for you to say you're sorry, for that matter. We live in a litigious age."

"Well, I don't know about that."

"Everyone suing everyone else."

"That's what Joe said. He made it sound as if I had an obligation."

"I hope there hasn't been a falling out between you and Joe."

Martha bristled. "That's another thing. They talk about us as if we were . . . well, never mind. I pray every day for the repose of Casey's soul."

"If you'd like, I'll say a Mass for him."

"Would you, Father? That would be so nice." She opened her purse and he shook his head.

"No. It will be my privilege."

"He wasn't as bad as people thought," she said enigmatically. As far as Father Dowling knew, Casey Vlasko hadn't been bad at all, no worse than the general run of the sons of Adam. But wives always know so much more. "I wish you had been here when he died."

"Was it that long ago?"

"He didn't like the friars. All they talked about was money, them with their vow of poverty."

No need to encourage that line of conversation. He got all of that he needed from Marie. "He died a good death?"

"Father Felix wouldn't say. He just patted my arm and said that God is merciful."

"And so he is," Father Dowling said, standing. "I'll say that Mass for Casey at noon tomorrow. I hope you'll be there."

"You're sure . . ." She was fiddling with the clasp her purse again.

He came around the desk and took her arm. "I'll show you out."

"Can we use the front door?"

She must have come by way of the kitchen, by way of Marie Murkin.

"Of course."

It was nearly time for his noon Mass. When he went through the kitchen, Marie said, "It's not yet eleven-thirty."

He looked at his watch, he looked at the kitchen clock. "You're right."

Since his retreat, he had been trying to recapture the old habit of making his preparation for Mass in the church whenever he was not prevented. Marie was opposed. She wanted a good pastor, but not a pious one. Why, there had been a friar . . . He had long since thought that Marie invented friars for purposes of some lesson she sought to give him. Her job induced cynicism, but cynicism was the mask of the naive wish that things should be as they seemed. Marie wanted a world where priests, even friars, were saints, where all religious people were close to God, where even housekeepers were patterns of Christian perfection. If only everyone were like Father Boniface.

"Skipping present company, of course."

"Marie, I am one of your long-standing defenders."

"Defenders?"

"You were speaking of Father Boniface."

"When his Order closes down you should ask him to move in here permanently."

"His Order is not closing down, Marie."

"Uh-huh."

Did she have sources of information closed to him? But his was Father Boniface, and the old priest admitted decline but not a final fall.

"For one thing," he said, "we can afford to keep the place. For another, there are signs of better times."

"Father Nathaniel."

"There are others, too."

"Ah. Vocations?"

"Of a sort."

Boniface was not to be drawn and Father Dowling had no desire to pump him for information about the Athanasians. The Order had not received a five-star rating in its best days, maybe three or even just two. As the hotel metaphor suggested, such rankings were often based on the hospitality one might expect as a guest of an order. The Athanasians had been generous but somewhat ascetic. They all seemed to be teetotalers, save for a glass of wine at the evening meal, and it didn't occur to them that a visiting cleric, parched from the dusty road, might want scotch instead of weak beer as a restorative. But they got high marks from priests who made their retreats there.

Father Dowling wondered what Boniface might have meant by a "sort of" vocation. Perhaps another returnee like Richard Krause. If they got their twenty percent there could be many prodigals trooping back to Marygrove in their twilight years. But they would all be of an age, not much promise for the future. What the Athanasians needed, and seemed no more likely to get than other such communities, was an influx of young men to fill up the rooms and chapels and make it seem like old times.

In the midst of these distracting thoughts, Art Hessian shuffled into the sacristy, there to act as altar boy for Father Dowling's Mass. His was help Father Dowling would have been willing to forgo, but he knew what it meant to Art. Art groaned audibly whenever he genuflected, he made going down the altar steps when the gifts were brought forward by equally old but more agile worshippers a *via crucis*, huffing and puffing at Father Dowling's side.

"Any chance of being made an extraordinary minister, Father?" Art had wheezed a week before.

"No need for that here, Art. The ordinary minister can handle the distribution of communion."

"I was thinking of the honor."

"That's not the point of it, Art."

Insofar as the point was much adhered to in many parishes, that is. At communion time on Sundays the priest was surrounded by a platoon of Eucharistic ministers, there to dispense Holy Communion under both species, to bless the children who came forward with their parents as if they had priestly faculties, smiling and demanding eye contact before giving the host. Phil Keegan had seen it all. Even Amos Cadbury had commented on it.

"The line between priests and laity is being smudged, Father. Smudged. The priest has become *primus inter pares*. No wonder boys don't think of the priesthood. They can marry and become Eucharistic ministers."

"Or permanent deacons."

"God forbid." Amos was a Knight of Malta as well as of St. Gregory, accepting such pomp as a loyal son of the Church, appearing in full regalia on special occasions at the cathedral. But these were unequivocally lay honors. As for Phil, he had become an infrequent presence at the Knights of Columbus.

"They're all guardhouse theologians now," he grumbled. "Go for a beer and some idiot wants to tell you what's wrong with the Church."

"We have known better days, Phil."

"But that's what they deny!"

How shall we sing the Lord's song in a foreign land?
—*Psalm 137*

When Richard Krause first met the woman he would marry, he felt sure she had been a nun. They were having a drink in the lobby of the hotel where he was staying and she was attending a conference of psychological counselors. He had been prowling the conference area and popped in on a talk about "The Guilt Edge." Marilyn was the speaker, her message was ways and means to move clients past the barriers of guilt and self-doubt into the happier climes of self-fulfillment. She was articulating thoughts that Richard felt he himself had developed in his days since leaving the Order. The trouble with having the past he did, all those memories and resentments, was that he couldn't discuss it with anyone. Imagine, telling some woman you used to be a priest! If she was Catholic she would be either shocked or interested for the wrong reasons, sure to tell him of some Father So-and-so who had tried to make a move on her. He tended to think that such moves existed largely in the receptive eye of the movee. He himself had been careful never to identify himself as a priest when he was testing the waters of the lay estate before making the big move and applying to be laicized. Something in Marilyn's intonations, even her vocabulary, suggested a kindred soul.

"Wonderful presentation," he told her afterward, waiting to be the last to get to her of those who had come forward. "Just wonderful."

"I'm afraid we have to get out of here. Another talk is scheduled to begin."

"Just what I was going to suggest. After yours, anything else would be a letdown."

"Flattery will get you everywhere."

"How about to a drink in the lobby?"

She was good-looking without being beautiful, squarish face with ash-blond hair she was rightly proud of. No ring on the relevant finger of her left hand, but a pretty gaudy emerald on her right.

"It was my mother's," she said, when he remarked on it.

"For the Emerald Isle?" The name on the tag pasted above her breast was Marilyn Daly.

"I never asked."

When the waiter came, acting like a prince in exile, bored out of his loafers, Richard said, "I'm going to have a Manhattan."

"Sounds perfect."

Two Manhattans later, they moved to the dining room, where wine seemed appropriate to celebrate the way they were hitting it off. He had been telling her that her talk reminded him in some ways of a retreat.

"What would you know about retreats?"

"I used to give them."

She sat back, tucked in her chin, looked him over with her light brown eyes. "Who were you with?"

"The Athanasians."

She thought a bit, then nodded. "The Midwest."

"That's Marygrove. And you?"

"OHM. Right here in Los Angeles. We're dissolved now."

It was a fascinating story. They'd had a big fight with Rome and the cardinal and then sold the whole thing, kit and caboodle, and distributed the funds. Each share turned into a pretty penny.

"So I finished my degree and set up shop in La Jolla."

"I live in San Diego."

Two weeks later, he moved into her apartment in La Jolla, mountains to the east, sea to the west, an impossibly beautiful setting that they justified to one another in terms of the thwarted lives they had lived during those wasted years. They deserved this, they were entitled. That was Marilyn's mantra, which he was happy to repeat. Marry? It would have seemed a repetition of the vows they had repudiated, and he was male enough to welcome the apparent impermanency of it all. Until the first clouds of jealousy began to gather.

"The men are the worst," she said. She was speaking of her clients.

"In what way."

"The hang-ups. You would think the body is their enemy. They have to see it as the glove with which they grasp the world."

"I hope they don't get too graspy."

"I wish they would. It is terrible to see people imprisoned by beliefs they no longer hold, if they ever did."

Any restraint was an illusion, one had to remain open, flexible, free. But it was more theory than practice with Marilyn. She had developed, or adopted, her own creed, the California creed as he thought of it, and its accompanying ritual, too. They spent hours at the beach, offering themselves as unclothed as decency permitted to the sea. It had been in the hour after sundown, on a blanket with the melancholy withdrawal of the sea, that they first made love. For all her theory, she was shy and clumsy. Her inexperience belied the houri she professed to be. Afterward she clung to him and whispered wetly in his ear.

"How long I have awaited you." Late have I loved thee? But it was his mention of the melancholy roar she asked about.

"Dover Beach. The receding tide of religious belief. Matthew Arnold watched it ebbing away with sadness."

"I envy you your education. I majored in pyschology. I got my degree after I was professed. It was like trying to subscribe to two creeds, what I learned in class, what was said in conferences. Of course, all that changed."

Under the influence of Carl Rogers who was brought in to help them renew. He helped them get in touch with themselves, Bocaccio scenes ensued. It was only a matter of time until they realized they had adopted a new religion, the religion of pleasure.

"The prudence of the flesh."

"Prudence was not our virtue, believe me."

It had seemed simple honesty when her order declared its independence of the cardinal, then of the Church, finally of their vows.

"At first it was spooky, you know? It is easy to talk about the silliness of all the taboos, but it is something else really to reject them. The woman I lived with when I first left became a mental case. The more affairs she had, the more guilt she felt. She was a warning."

Marilyn resolved to lead a disciplined life even in the new order of things. She opened her office in La Jolla and helped others rid themselves of inhibitions, but she herself . . .

"Richard, I was still a nun, essentially, when we met."

"Physician, heal thyself."

"Isn't it odd how all those phrases stick. I still love Jesus."

"How so?"

"How ridiculous it was to think of oneself as the bride of Christ. Think of the implications. In repudiating that I found him."

"As your personal savior?"

"Don't mock. He was a great man, a good man."

She probably had a theory to explain such a transfer. It helped, it was necessary to think that in her new life she was actually fulfilling the old. Theirs was a very cerebral affair. Only he did not want an affair, not after he began to wonder how participative counseling might become. They were married in front of a woman judge in San Diego and spent their honeymoon in the great Coronado hotel. It was when he undertook to invest her money that he discovered his gift for finance.

"Feel that," she said, offering him her breast.

"Gladly."

"I'm serious." She guided his fingers. "Is that a lump?"

It was a lump, discovered too late. He thought of himself, kneading that lovely breast, his only thought that it represented all the pleasures he had forgone. They had resolved not to have children, their reaction to the nonsense of *Humanae Vitae*. They were not the instrument of the species, their union aimed at something beyond itself. When she was told that the cancer had already invaded the lymph nodes, she was filled with terror. He held her tightly throughout the first night of the dreadful knowledge. She told him of the operations, of the ambiguous prognosis, of radiation and chemotherapy, and he held her more tightly. A true lover would have wished that he could offer his life for hers, but in his heart of hearts he felt the enormous separating relief of one still in possession of his health. She had the operation, the treatments made her bald, and the champagne-colored wig could not remove the tragic resignation from her soft brown eyes.

"I always thought I would die young. I think that is one of the reasons I entered the convent."

"Nonsense. You're going to be well."

"I thank God for you, Richard."

Not simply a familiar locution, as became clear. With the prospect of death, religion returned. "I would go back, if it was still there to go back to."

He rocked her in his arms. Some remarks were better left alone.

"At least I'm certain to have a priest with me when I die."

And he did give her the last rites, validly if illicitly, considering his severed status, but once a priest always a priest. She knew that as well as he did. Nor was it necessary that he believe it all as she clearly did. *Ex opere operato.* The efficacy of the sacraments does not depend on the sanctity or even the belief of the priest who administers them. Marilyn left him everything in her will.

One day within your courts is better than a thousand
elsewhere.

—Psalm 84

Hazel had come to Tuttle as part-time help, hired by the day, but
she swiftly brought order out of chaos, computerized his records,
such as they were, and nagged him into more vigorous ambulance
chasing. It had not helped to tell her that television ads had never
worked for him.

"Where did you run them, on a public-access channel?"

She made an appointment at a studio, acted as director and
script writer, and the commercial was shown at inexpensive hours
on local television, much to the delight of Tuttle's friends in the
press room at the court house.

"Let them eat their hearts out," Hazel snorted when he told
her of his ordeal in the press room.

"They're not lawyers."

"That's what I mean."

If Hazel ever lost an argument, Tuttle would like to be there.
She had turned his office into a model of efficiency, she had gotten
him into divorces, despite his principles and vow to his departed
father who was the second Tuttle in Tuttle & Tuttle. His father

had never lost faith in him, had continued to bankroll him as he repeated course after course in law school until he qualified to fail the bar exams. He got through the fourth time, by cheating, and his father, content, was gathered to his ancestors with his only son an attorney-at-law. Tuttle commemorated the paternal confidence in the title of the firm. Hazel had worked her mouth as he explained it to her but did not comment. Good thing. Tuttle was oriental in his devotion to his parents and any crack from Hazel would have filled him with the courage necessary to drive her from the office. But it was her amorous propensities Tuttle feared more. She had all but driven his closest friend, Peanuts Pianone, from his life; now he and the ungifted member of the Pianone clan, for whom a sinecure on the police force had been a family perk, met at the Great Wall or various pizza parlors. Peanuts had all he could take of Hazel.

"She's my secretary," Tuttle pleaded. Peanuts wasn't much of a buffer, but he needed an ally at the office.

"And what's that make you?"

A confused question, but a good one. What is the employer equivalent of the henpecked husband? But that was the direction in which Hazel's intentions seemed to point.

"No regular secretary would work in this pig sty."

"I'll give you a handsome severance payment."

She snorted. "You forget that I keep the books."

Perhaps when he ran out of funds, she would leave. But he no longer knew the status of his bank balance. Sometimes he feared that Hazel was working pro bono, amassing a debt he would be expected to pay off in the only honorable way.

"That'll help," she said sarcastically when he slapped Leo Corbett's dollar on her desk.

But she perked up as he told her of his new client. A Corbett of the Corbetts? She was visibly impressed. She urged him to have Leo come to the office.

"He'll be here at ten."

But it was after eleven before she finished with Leo and ushered him into the office where Tuttle had been awaiting the dreaded news that she had scared Leo away.

"Paper work," she explained, and closed the door on them.

"Not much of a building, but I'm impressed with the office," Leo said.

"Why throw money away in overhead?"

"So what's the plan?"

Tuttle glanced at the notes before him, prepared by Hazel. "We'll start with the annuity."

"That still leaves us with Amos Cadbury."

"Leave Cadbury to me."

The premier lawyer of Fox River had not succeeded in three attempts to have Tuttle disbarred. Tuttle had come to regard Cadbury with the camaraderie of the old adversary, whatever Cadbury's attitude toward him. Since his last meeting with Leo, Tuttle had learned that Cadbury had not only overseen the transfer of the Corbett estate to the Athanasians, he was the lawyer of the Corbett estate in the wider sense. It was he who had fulfilled Maurice Corbett's wish that his son Matthew should have an annuity. Tuttle asked Leo a few questions.

"I already told your partner."

Hazel. "Right. You get the benefit of the whole team here." Tuttle angled back in his chair. "Trust me, Leo, and you will repossess your grandfather's estate."

"You make it sound like an automobile."

Tuttle laughed, but Leo hadn't meant it as a joke. Best to get him out of here and see how much Hazel had learned. He got up and clapped Leo on the shoulder.

"How are things at the country club?"

"I work in the golf shop, Tuttle."

"Not for long. We'll have you out of there and on the first tee with the other members before you know it."

He showed him to the door, he stood in the doorway and watched him onto the elevator with a final wave.

"Fine young man, Hazel."

"What do you know about annuities?"

"Hazel, I'm a lawyer."

"What do you know about wills and estates?"

"What is this, a bar exam?"

"If it were you'd probably order a beer. Why don't I put Denise on it."

"You think a paralegal knows more than a lawyer?"

"What we need is the basic laws, precedents."

"Now you're a law professor?"

"You need help on this."

"I can't afford it."

"I'll be the judge of that. Anyway, Tuttle, if necessary I'd bankroll this myself. I think you've stumbled onto something."

He ducked out of the way when she ducked to kiss him. She wouldn't let him wear his tweed hat in the office and this left him naked to his enemies.

"I'll interview her."

"We'll interview her."

"You could get arrested for practicing law without a license."

"You could get arrested for practicing law with one."

It kept him on his toes, such banter with Hazel, when it didn't knock him back on his heels. The problem was she had been here long enough to make it difficult to think of life without her. Professional life, that is. The IRS didn't have to upgrade its computers, but he was doing better than he ever had, to the degree that Hazel let him in on the secret. The beauty of the stuff she brought in just answering the phone—she could sell an AT&T salesperson MCI long-distance service—was that it was so routine he could leave the details to her. Sign a few papers, a token appearance in court, cash the checks. Smooth, but it made one rusty.

Denise, the paralegal, was six feet tall and would have looked over both Tuttle and Hazel if she did not have such a pronounced stoop. When she stood up she could have done credit to the bow of a ship, the body of an Amazon, the long blond hair that hid her face when she stooped cascading over her shoulders, her breasts those of an undoubted mammalian, clear blue eyes. Only Denise did not know this. She was color-blind and this had kept her out of the Navy. She offered to get a cornea transplant, she tried to memorize all the variations in the eye test, nothing got her past the tests. An all-man Navy would have shanghaied her, but in the newer, fairer world she washed out, lost her self-esteem, became a paralegal because research kept her away from people.

She nodded at her knees as Hazel briefed her on the case.

"Leo Corbett?"

Were her ears going, too? "Leo Corbett."

"I went to school with him."

"This could be an asset," Tuttle said to Hazel.

"He always was." Denise snickered at her lap. "I don't have to meet him, do I?"

"There are no present plans," Tuttle said. He was signaling to Hazel—bringing a finger across his throat, shaking his head, pointing to the door—all this over Denise's head. He didn't care how good she was, this girl was weird. There was no way in the world he was going to hire her.

"You're hired," Hazel said.

The two women went into the outer office, where Hazel explained to Denise the kind of things that Mr. Tuttle would want. Tuttle felt like Oz concealed in his office, listening.

"We're lucky she was free," Hazel said when Denise had left.

"She's pretty cool to me."

"She better be."

"I won't be fought over."

"Don't worry; I told her about your STDs."

"What's that?"

"It's your naïveté that makes you so dangerous, Tuttle." She managed to tweak his cheek before he escaped.

The wicked prowl on every side.

—*Psalm 12*

As he was walking past the greenhouse, Father Boniface was hailed by Andrew George. The head gardener's face never lost its tan, but it had become more leathery with the advent of summer. The gardener tugged at the bill of the baseball cap he wore.

"So is it true, Father?"

"And what is *it*?"

"One hears that you are about to sell all this to Anderson so he can tear down the buildings, knock down the trees, and build hundreds of ugly houses."

"And who does one hear this from?"

"Is it false?"

He could condescend to George, put him off as a child is put off, and the gardener would not complain. But he could not so treat a man whose life, whose family's life, had been so intertwined with that of the community.

"There are no such plans."

"Are you speaking carefully?" Wild brows grew every which way above the horn-rimmed glasses George had worn as long as Boniface could remember. Did his eyes never get worse?

"If there were, you can be sure that you would be told."

"I hope I never hear such a thing."

"That is my hope as well."

It was not the complete reassurance that George wanted. Why hadn't he told him that the Order would sell to Anderson over his dead body? That would have expressed his sentiments. But he was only one man in a community, albeit the superior. One man is never in complete charge of the present or of the future. Yet he felt more comradeship with the gardener than he did with some of his fellow Athanasians. Richard had proved an adroit and effective apostle for change. He had come into command of arguments so disarming they could not be directly countered, describing their possession of these wonderful grounds as a species of institutional selfishness, arguably contrary to the spirit of poverty that supposedly governed their lives. What is poverty? Boniface felt like Pilate posing the question about truth. The first generations of Franciscans had divided into two camps on the questions, the Spirituals wanting a total absence of ownership, communal or personal. But the aspiration to be an angel, not a man, was the subtlest temptation, and one they were all susceptible to. Richard had managed to make some feel guilty about the life of abnegation they had lived, yet he himself had spent decades in the pursuit of wealth in the neopagan culture of California. Did he feel no awkwardness impersonating *Il Poverello*?

By affirmation or denial, Richard's life seemed defined in terms of money. Now he pursued communal poverty with the same zeal he had sought to amass a fortune, for himself and for his clients. But what did he really want? Selling the property to Anderson would only increase their wealth, not diminish it. What on earth would they do with the proceeds? Where would they go?

"One problem at a time, Boniface," Joachim said. He had become the spokesman for Richard, who sat silent in the rec room when the matter was discussed. It had become the only item on the agenda of their continuing informal chapter. Still the question remained at a stand-off, there were two who sided with Richard, and two who sided with Boniface. The one sure way victory could be achieved was by telling Richard that his probation had convinced the community that he was not ready to rejoin them. Perhaps later . . .

But Richard would appeal. How swiftly the petitioner had become a rival. Richard had returned, it seemed, to sow discord. He was hardly unpacked when he began to raise questions about the property on which Marygrove stood, the land, the mansion. Wouldn't it be more appropriate to their vocation to sell it, to give Mr. Anderson the opportunity to create a whole village on the site? You would have thought he was pleading for the homeless. But it was Boniface's inner life that was under threat. Dark thoughts occurred. Who did this renegade priest think he was to return after decades in the world to preach to them about the demands of their vocation? The prodigal returned to moralize the older brother who had remained faithful to his father. It was an unsettling parallel, putting Boniface is the position of the pusillanimous son. Hadn't Our Lord told the story in such a way that it was the wastrel who was the hero of the parable? The elder son's reaction was condemned. Boniface spent an extra hour in the chapel, praying to be rid of the uncharitable thoughts that surged up in him whenever he thought of Richard. (Only rarely could he bring himself to call him Father Nathaniel.) Sometimes he thought that getting the property sold had been Richard's motive for returning, but why would he want to do that?

Whenever Boniface returned from Marygrove after an absence of even a few days, his heart leapt within him as he came up the drive and the statue of St. Athanasius rose into view. Did he have true poverty of spirit if he was so attached to this place, these buildings, and all the lifetime of memories they invoked? Amos Cadbury's visit added to his unease, in a way he was sure the Fox River lawyer had never intended.

"I wonder if any records were kept of the discussion that preceded the deeding of this property to the Order. And letters from Mr. Corbett, any memoranda?"

"I am old, Mr. Cadbury, but that was before my time."

"Surely not. I was the lawyer in the case."

Meaning, of course, that they were the same age, which was likely true. The Order had come into the property in stages. And those stages were recorded. Boniface and Amos, with Joachim's excited assistance, found the files in the basement of the main building, in a warm, dry room behind the furnace room. Its lock gave way reluctantly, it had been so long since the room had been opened. Boniface had the sense that he and the other two old men were entering an innermost room in a pyramid.

"I drew up only the final transfer," Amos said, "but these other documents make clear that it was anything but an impulsive act."

"Some members of the community think we ought to sell the land to Anderson."

"Sell! To Anderson!"

Amos Cadbury looked more than shocked. His face was always pale, as if the circulation of his blood after all the years now made minimum demands on his heart, supplying the main arteries but letting the capillaries fall into desuetude. But there are degrees of white as there are shades of paper. Boniface himself was unaccountably ruddy of complexion, a full and jolly face that belied his tendency to melancholy. If Amos paled, he blushed.

"The buildings? The chapel? All of it?"

"Amos, the argument is made that we are preventing choice real estate from being put to a better use."

"There could be no better use, Father. Surely you are not among those favoring delivery of this wonderful property over to— Anderson."

"No."

Amos leaned against the table that held the boxes of old documents and closed his eyes. When he opened them, their sparkle had returned.

"I'm not sure you would have the right to sell, Father Boniface." Amos turned and picked up one of the letters from Maurice Corbett he had been reading. "While initially, it was simply an open-ended use, with the right to build, of course, the transfer is to the Order in perpetuity."

"But if the Order decides to sell . . ."

"Such things have happened, I know. Perhaps it can be done

in civil law, but there is canon law as well. It could be construed to be alienation of Church property. Do your opponents propose using the money to build an alternative Marygrove elsewhere?"

"The discussion has not advanced to that point."

"Perhaps that could be justified, legally. But I must tell you, as a lawyer who now spends much of his time administering estates, that there are insurmountable obstacles to acting contrary to the will of the deceased. I consider it a sacred obligation to execute a will exactly as it was written. Of course, they are wills I myself wrote, so I am in that sense an expert on the intent of the testator."

Boniface could not have been more pleased if Maurice Corbett himself had put in an appearance and warned the community against any thought of selling what he had given them. Would Richard and his allies be willing to confront the prospect of replicating Marygrove elsewhere? Had they looked into construction costs? Had they any idea what comparable land would cost? What new land might not become with the passage of time as valuable as the land they occupied now? Amos was warming to the subject.

"I will look into instances where religious communities acted with what I consider demonstrable irregularity. Monsignor George Kelly's *The Battle for the American Church* provides any number of examples. There were nuns in California who sold their college and other property and distributed the gains to members of the community as personal wealth. Most of them left the religious life and took their bonanza with them. I am not a canon lawyer, but that seems to me to be a clear case of alienation of Church property. A religious community does not consist simply of its current members; in any case, its current members hold in trust what the community over time has acquired. With your permission, I will consult a canon lawyer about the matter."

"Oh, you mustn't make this public, Mr. Cadbury. I cherish the hope that the whole thing will blow over. We do not need a scandal and your remarks certainly suggest how such a proposal could be construed."

"I was thinking of Father Dowling. His degree is in canon law."

Boniface actually sighed with relief. "I would rely entirely on Father Dowling's discretion."

Amos Cadbury had moved with stately dignity when he first arrived, but he came up out of the basement of the main building with vigorous step and fire in his eye. His car was brought round and Father Boniface shook hands with the lawyer before he disappeared into the capacious backseat.

For my soul is full of troubles.
—*Psalm 88*

"Boniface did mention to me that there was a discussion underway, and I know it troubled him, but I had the impression that nothing would come of it."

"Father Dowling, nothing must come of it." Amos had come directly to the St. Hilary rectory from his conversation with Boniface and he was clearly ready for combat. "Do you have Monsignor Kelly's book here?"

"Which one?"

"The one with the word 'battle' in the title."

"Ah." Father Dowling drew the hefty tome from the shelf. In it, the feisty monsignor from New York had recounted the history of the outrageous things that had been done in the alleged spirit of Vatican II.

"I think you mean the nuns in California. Los Angeles, I believe it was. They had a quarrel with the cardinal there. . . . Here it is."

"Read it," Amos asked.

"It's quite long."

"If you wouldn't mind, I want to hear every word."

When Father Dowling had read the account, Amos shook his head. "Bocaccio, thou shouldst be living at this hour." A lifetime in law had left him prepared for anything in the secular world, but ecclesiastical flaws found him an ingenue.

"Apparently a laicized member of the Athanasians who wants to be readmitted is behind all this. His name in religion was Nathaniel, but he was born and then reborn as Richard Krause."

"A troublemaker," Amos said. "He is the one who decamped to California?"

"And is being pursued by a man with whom he had business dealings. Let me show you this." Father Dowling passed to Amos the information Eric Hospers had downloaded from Google.com. "It's the name of a search engine."

Amos nodded. "It is the rare law office now that is not equipped to tap into the data base of such companies as Westlaw. Once a lawyer needed a memory. Now all he needs is a computer."

Amos browsed through the pages.

"Who is this man Morgan?"

"He has been here in this house. Boniface agrees with me that it is Father Nathaniel he is seeking."

Amos hummed. "Do we have here an explanation as to why the prodigal returned is so interested in raising money on the sale of Marygrove?"

"Phil Keegan has seen those pages. As he pointed out, the man Morgan, while tried for peculation, was found innocent. That leaves unaddressed all those poor witnesses who testified to the amount of money they had lost. Often what they had counted on to provide them security in retirement. Where does money go when it goes, Amos?"

"A good question, Father. Consider the fluctuations of the market. You buy a hundred shares at ten dollars apiece. The market goes wild and your thousand dollars becomes ten thousand. And then the market falls and your investment may be worth five hundred dollars. What happened to the nine and a half thousand? What reality did it really have?"

"I suppose I could have sold the shares."

"Yes, and then the money would be real however variable its purchasing power. But the ups and downs of the market create and destroy imaginary wealth. Those poor investors simply took a chance with this man Morgan. And, as the judge seems to have said, losing is no more punishable than winning."

"They said he promised them they would win."

"As any broker does, but carefully. By predicting the past, telling you what has happened, and counting on you to project that record into the future. But back to the other things. I got a call from my office on my way here. Now the grandchild of Maurice Corbett is apparently arguing that the Athanasians should at least share with him some of the Corbett wealth. Corbett's son Matthew was given an annuity, but he is dead and it is gone. The grandson, who had not been born when the grandfather was still alive, now feels that he has been cheated."

"Does he have a case?"

"He has hired a lawyer."

"Really."

"Tuttle."

"Good Lord. So much for his chances, if he had any."

"Dog will have his day, Father Dowling. Dog will have his day. If a returned confrere can make the good fathers feel guilty for living where they have always lived, who knows what their reaction to the grandson's plea may be?"

Father Dowling did not mention to Amos yet another factor, the uneasiness of the family that had been caretakers of the Marygrove grounds. Of course they had heard of the discussion within the community and felt threatened by the possibility that soon Anderson homes would spring up on the soil they had nurtured into the third generation.

Would the children of light become wise as the children of darkness, the Athanasians, were tempted to cash in on the value their land now had? When Maurice Corbett had bought those acres and built his mansion he had paid a risible amount for the property. Then it had been simply nowhere and nothing like what it has become. Its present beauty was the result of decades of effort, first by Corbett then by the Athanasians and the George family. Now, thanks to the westward drift of the greater Chicago area, nowhere had become a somewhere coveted by many, most notably by the king of suburbia, Anderson. And there was a Romeo and Juliet saga as well. Juan Martinez had come to the rectory and been kept waiting on the back porch by Marie until

Father Dowling rescued him and brought him into the study.

"Are Greek Catholics Catholics, Father?"

"That depends. Why do you ask?"

He asked because his daughter wanted to marry an Orthodox boy. Then he wouldn't be Catholic, Father Dowling said, and Martinez groaned.

"I said I'd ask, but I knew what the answer would be. My Rita will only marry him here but his parents will not permit it. Another girl might run off to the courthouse with the boy, but not Rita. The boy, his name is George, his family name, says he will defy his father and become a Catholic if that is what it takes."

"George?"

"The family are gardeners for a group of priests. Catholics."

"The Athanasians?"

Juan Martinez nodded. "They sound Greek, too, but they're not."

"No, they're not."

"I don't want him pretending to be a Catholic in order to marry Rita. You know what will happen afterward."

"Not always." He could not help but think of Maurice Corbett, whose conversion had gone deep and outlasted the marriage that had occasioned it.

"I offered to talk to the boy's father, but Rita says it would do no good. I talked to the boy." Martinez fell silent. And then he said, his voice heavy with disbelief, "Maybe he is as Rita says."

"Maybe I should talk with his priest."

Martinez displayed gold-edged teeth when he smiled. "I was hoping you would."

"Don't expect anything."

"I want Rita to be happy, if it is possible."

A little more than a week before, Roger Dowling had enjoyed

the unreal tranquillity of Marygrove. Boniface had introduced him to George, a man very much like Juan Martinez. Now that he was aware of all the subterranean troubles of the Athanasians and of many others connected with them, his retreat could seem almost self-indulgent. Now he felt swept up in conflicting currents, conflicts which promised to be standoffs, incapable of resolution. The promise of tragedy seemed everywhere.

In the day of my trouble I will call upon you, O Lord.
                                                    —*Psalm 86*

Hazel made him leave his tweed hat in the car when she pulled up in front of the building that housed the prestigious law firm of which Amos Cadbury was the patriarch.

"If I'm going to be in the same car as you, I want to be at the wheel," she had announced, bumping him out of the driver's seat with an authoritative hip.

"You got a chauffeur's license?"

"I'm surprised they gave you tags for this heap. I think we can afford something more impressive than a twenty-year-old Ford."

"It's paid for."

Tuttle almost welcomed the ongoing quarrel as they drove; it kept his mind off the interview ahead. At least it did until Hazel began to tell him how to act and what to say when he confronted Amos Cadbury.

"Maybe you should talk to him."

"He'd listen if I did."

Tuttle turned and smiled out the side window. That was one meeting he wouldn't mind arranging. He doubted that Cadbury would have any more control over Hazel than he did. Sometimes at night, he would awake from a dream about what his office had become and wonder how she had managed to take over as decisively as she had. She had dumped the folder prepared by Denise on his lap and now he opened it, glanced at the neat little index that made up the front page, and was about to close it when he saw that the paralegal had scared up a copy of Maurice Corbett's will.

"I hope you studied that last night."

"My mind is like a steel trap."

"Nothing sticks to stainless steel."

He would flip through the will in the lobby before going up. "I wish I'd brought Leo along."

"That creep."

"He's my client. He's my ticket to unimaginable wealth."

"That whelp doesn't deserve a nickel. What a whiner. You'd think the world owed him a living. Knocking his father, trying to cash in on his grandfather." She made an obscene noise with her lips, then honked back at a driver who thought she was addressing him.

"I thought you were on my side."

"On your side? I shouldn't even be in bed with you." She jabbed at his ribs, but he had become practiced in avoiding her. He didn't like it when she made raunchy jokes. You expect that sort of thing from men, but Tuttle wanted women on a pedestal, pure as the driven snow. Hazel had the sense of humor of those jerks in the press room at the courthouse. "Don't get me wrong. I'm with you all the way, pal. It's just a shame that we have to benefit Leo to make a bundle ourselves."

Those "we's" and "ours" were getting to be a habit. Tuttle wished that he and Peanuts Pianone could disappear into Wisconsin for a week, do a little fishing, drink beer, and have all the pizza they wanted. It seemed an impossibly attractive dream. Once he had been free and he gnawed at his chains when he remembered how it had been, he and Peanuts having Chinese in his office, then napping afterward, garbage all over the place . . . it had been heaven. Now the office looked like it was awaiting inspection by the attorney general. His desk was clean, the books had been straightened on the shelves, every morning there was a typed agenda waiting for him on his desk. She even reminded him to get haircuts. Made the appointments. He would learn this when he read the sheet. *10:45 Luigi. Don't be late, he has a perm at 11.* It was a unisex shop and Luigi was someone Tuttle wouldn't want to be alone with in an elevator. Every two weeks Hazel sent him to Luigi.

"You're beginning to look like a lawyer."

There was only the slightest trace of sarcasm in her voice. What did she know of lawyers, TV aside? She had a set going all day in the outer office, the constant murmurs of voices caught in artificial dilemmas. The plight of the wronged woman in daytime dramas brought tears to Hazel's eyes, alongside a snarl for the malignant male.

"What happened to your head?" Peanuts asked during a stolen lunch at the Great Wall. Hazel thought he was checking for himself the data Denise had gathered. He wouldn't have known how.

"Haircut."

"You insult the barber or what? He skinned you."

"A guy named Luigi."

"Yeah?" Peanuts trusted all Italians.

"You should get an appointment."

"She still there?" He meant Hazel.

"A lawyer needs a secretary."

"She's your partner."

"She takes a burden off my shoulders."

"Ha."

Lunch at the Great Wall reminded Tuttle of the free and easy, if hand-to-mouth, existence he missed. Getting rid of Hazel was a project that was with him night and day, but lately it caused anxiety. He no longer understood the procedures of his own office, so little did he have to do with them. What did she get out of it, except to nag the hell out of him? He thought of asking Farniente the PI to check her out, find out her background. There had to be something. Probably a husband or two buried in the backyard. He could do it himself on the computer, if he knew how. Hazel was always running searches on people. It was amazing what was floating around in what she called cyberspace.

"You know Google?" Tuttle asked Farniente.

"Barney?"

Tuttle laughed. Another reminder of childhood innocence. His father had loved Barney Google and Snuffy Smith, cartoon characters more real than Hazel's daytime television.

"Ever hear of Hazel Barnes?"

"What strip she in?"

"She works for me."

"Now I've heard of her."

"I want to get rid of her."

Farniente sat back, foam on his bearded face. He pushed the glass of beer a few inches from him. "I don't do that sort of thing. Try the Pianones."

"I want to fire her."

"So what's the problem?"

"You'd have to know her to know."

Farniente came by the office two days later. Tuttle, barricaded in the inner office, heard him out there talking with Hazel. They seemed to hit it off. A knock on the door fifteen minutes later and she brought Farniente in.

"Mr. Farniente is here about the Corbett matter." She beamed at Tuttle. Saying he had been asked to check out Leo Corbett had been the ruse he and Farniente had hit upon. Hazel was obviously impressed by his initiative and enterprise. He could imagine the report card she would give him.

She left them alone. Farniente looked around the office. "Tuttle, you're nuts."

"How so?"

"That woman is a gold mine. You're transformed, your office is transformed, thank your lucky stars."

Hazel always won. That was the moral. After Farniente left Hazel said how much she liked him. "For a man, that is." Maybe if Peanuts had hung around she would have turned him into her friend rather than his.

In the lobby of Cadbury's building, Tuttle sat behind a potted lemon tree and looked through the folder Denise had prepared, concentrating on Maurice Corbett's will and the transfer of his estate to the Athanasians. Nothing Cadbury put together could be put asunder by another lawyer, Tuttle was sure of it. He went up in the elevator with the sense that he was on a fool's errand, but whether he was the fool or Leo he wasn't sure. He had to cool his heels until ten minutes after the scheduled appointment, but then he was shown into the great man's office.

"Mr. Tuttle."

"Mr. Cadbury. Thank you for giving me this time. Leo Corbett of the Corbett family has come to me with a sad story."

Cadbury nodded but said nothing.

"His complaint may seem to have no merit from a legal point of view," Tuttle said disarmingly.

"But from some other point of view?"

"Blood is thicker than water."

Cadbury sat there like a judge while Tuttle told him of the life the young man had led. A brilliant father, it ran in the family, but he was now reduced to working in the golf shop of the country club. Cadbury showed interest.

"Tall, overweight, glasses that won't stay in place?"

Of course. Cadbury belonged to the country club. "That's him."

"He seems remarkably content with his work."

"He is seething with indignation. His father had an annuity . . ."

"I remember that."

He should. Cadbury had taken care of that, too. "Leo has nothing."

"He has a job that pays reasonably well for someone without skills or ambition."

"He's been beaten down by adversity. Think of it, working in the golf shop at the club where his grandfather was a charter member, seeing those priests in possession of his grandfather's estate."

"Does he imagine getting the estate for himself?"

"I have told him that he hasn't a leg to stand on, legally. But is it fair?"

"What are you asking of me, Mr. Tuttle?"

"Leo is the only Corbett left. He can't appeal to the family. He is the family. Now, you're the lawyer for the Athanasian priests. Good men, I'm sure. What would they think if they knew what the grandson of their benefactor had been reduced to?"

"That is a question you might put to Father Boniface."

"How do you spell that?"

"But I wouldn't recommend it, Mr Tuttle."

"What would you recommend?

Amos Cadbury gave him a wintry smile. "You're asking me for advice?"

"Not legal advice, certainly not. Would you mention Leo to the good fathers?"

He didn't say yes, and he didn't say no. He got up from behind his desk and accompanied Tuttle to the door. "I am glad that you realize that there is no legal basis for any complaint by Leo Corbett."

Another good grade on his report card. Tuttle was almost euphoric when he got into the elevator, but his good spirits did not survive the descent. How could he convince Hazel that the visit had been a big success? Not getting thrown out of Cadbury's office was a first for Tuttle.

19

In his riches, man lacks wisdom:
He is like the beasts that are destroyed.
—Psalm 49

Several times Stan Morgan drove his rental car up the long driveway that wended through trees until a vast lawn opened up. You
could hit a three wood from there and not hit any of the buildings.
Morgan moved at twenty miles an hour, drinking the place in. He
had been away from the Midwest so long before coming in search
of Richards that he was struck by how different the trees and
bushes and flowers were. He couldn't have named any of them,
but then there were few trees in California he could name. At first
the absence of mountains got to him. Flying to Chicago, there had
been mountains for hours and then suddenly just a pattern of
rectangles on the unbroken plain. Coming into O'Hare with the
lake in view was a lot like LAX but Chicago was not L.A. Morgan
had passed his childhood here, but he now felt that he was in a
foreign land.

The first night he stayed at the O'Hare Hilton, studying a map
of the greater Chicago area. Then he rented a car and for days
just drove around, staying at one motel after another, getting the
lay of the land. He was certain Richards was here somewhere,

probably in the Fox River he had mentioned from time to time. Fox River was the first place he located on the map, but a week went by before he went there. He got off the interstate and suddenly he was in a small town, preserved by the frame of highways that enclosed it. This seemed more like the Midwest of his imagination. When he came upon St. Hilary's parish and saw the school playground filled with elderly people, he parked and got out. The attractive young woman palmed him off on the parish housekeeper who happened along, but he had an interesting chat with her over tea in the rectory kitchen. She was full of parish gossip and for a moment he thought he had found his prey. But when Mrs. Murkin got out the Catholic Directory in the pastor's study, a comfortable scholarly room, he knew she would draw a blank. So he told her Richards had stopped being a priest. Her manner changed and it was clear she had no sympathy with priests who returned to the lay estate.

Richards had explained it all to Morgan, with something of a chip on his shoulder. He blamed it all on Vatican II.

"They dug in their heels, Stan. They were no more interested in change in the Church than they were in the collection basket."

When he first met him, before he knew he had been a priest, Richards had seemed just another smoothie. Morgan had tried to sell him an insurance policy, but their roles were soon reversed.

"Don't tell me, but I'll be there's not much money in what you're doing," Richards had said.

"I do all right."

"Look, this is a state where a great percentage of the people are either in therapy or retired. They're living on Social Security and whatever plan their company had."

"Are you retired?"

"Only in a sense." The sense was explained later, when he

told Morgan that he had been a priest, but on that first occasion, Richards—"Nathaniel Richards, but don't call me that. Or Nate. My surname will do."—became lyrical about the possibilities of helping all those retired people make their money go further. A day or so later, he met Marilyn, a good-looking ash-blonde who provided guidance for the perplexed. So that meant the Richards—though she didn't use his name; even the apartment was in her name—already covered half the target he had described for Morgan.

"So why don't you get into financial management yourself?"

"I already am. But I am my sole client." A pause while he let Morgan grasp the significance of this. "I manage my own portfolio and I am making notes for a book. One Marilyn and I intend to write together."

"Well, that takes care of you."

"Have you thought about my proposition?"

"What proposition?"

It was too good to believe. Richards would set Morgan up, send him through a crash course on investments, and let him run the office. "Of course, you'll have to bring on more people as you prosper."

"Why are you doing this?"

"Because I nearly bought an insurance policy from you. You've got the perfect manner for it. You obviously like people."

Within a year, Morgan had opened an office in Coronado, paying an astronomical rent, but Richards insisted that appearance is reality when you are offering to help others do better with what they have. Licensed, franchised, computerized, a reassuring woman of middle age, Mildred, as receptionist, Stanley Morgan waited for the clients to come. And they did. A tasteful ad announcing the opening of the office and soon people who had prepared for a carefree retirement and spent most of their time keeping an eye on the market drifted in.

"Think of it as one of the corporal works of mercy," Richards said. It was the first clue he had that Richards was, or had been, Catholic.

"I don't remember financial advising on the list."

"Hey, this is the postconciliar world."

Morgan hadn't really believed that his silent partner would remain silent, but he did. There was never any suggestion that their fifty-fifty deal be made formal. A handshake had done it. The arrangement seemed more than justified when it became clear that he was not expected to pay back any of the money Richards had invested in setting him up in business. Richards was content to be treasurer and keep the books.

Stanley Morgan had been twenty-eight at the time, nine years ago. A dropout from the University of San Diego, he had been in sales until he went into insurance, always with the sense that what he did was temporary. He might have been preparing himself for the fateful day when he met Nathaniel Richards. He became close to both of them, but Marilyn was a little relentless in talking about sex. She assumed that he had a string of girlfriends.

"No doubt it has its attractions," she allowed. "And unlike serial killing, it isn't against the law. But sexual maturity and fidelity go hand in hand. You want someone for the long run."

"I'm in no hurry." The truth was that he had been all but celibate since breaking up with the girl that had led to his leaving the university as well. He might have been leaving to spite her.

"With casual partners, you can never develop a fully meaningful sex life. You have to know one another, body and soul, in order to realize your full potential as a sexual being."

Surprisingly, Marilyn was the religious one of the two, though her religion seemed to revolve around sex. Richards just sat there smiling when his wife lectured Morgan. The implication was that he and his wife had what all the world wanted. Maybe they did. Until Marilyn was diagnosed with cancer. What does sex have to do with death?

"Shouldn't she see a priest?" Morgan suggested.

"I'll take care of that." Another remark whose significance he had missed at the time.

They had weekly conferences about Morgan's clients. Richards wanted to make available what he had learned looking after his own money. He was big on savings-and-loans. "Money making money from money making money," he explained. And he found an outfit in Arizona that he touted highly. Morgan directed many of his clients in that direction.

Marilyn's death changed Richards. He became moody and thoughtful.

"She died well."

"The grace of a happy death?"

"Do you practice your faith, Stanley?"

"Did I say I had one?"

"Oh, come on. It's written all over you. And you went to the University of San Diego. The Notre Dame of the West."

"Not the way I used to."

"It's the story of our times."

Six months later the Arizona savings-and-loan went belly-up and Morgan had an office full of angry clients. He told them he had lost money himself, investment is a risk, they knew that.

"But that money is what we lived on, for God's sake."

If too many of them had all their eggs in one basket, it was due to his advice, but where else could they find an outfit like the one in Arizona? Paper profits had soared and there had been many expressions of heartfelt gratitude until the bubble burst. Happy investors had brought in their friends. Stan Morgan had acquired the reputation of being a magician of the market. And he had sunk everything he could lay his hands on personally into the Arizona outfit.

"It was bound to happen," Richards said philosophically.

"Wasn't your money there, too?"

"Some. Diversification is everything, as I shouldn't have to tell you."

Smug, that was how he seemed. He dipped his head and just looked at Morgan when he asked if Richards could do anything to help him out of this mess.

"The next thing you'll be telling me is that this is all my fault for not leaving you to selling insurance."

At the moment he would have given anything to be just an insurance salesman again. His clients were important people and they went to the media. Morgan was filmed leaving his office as if trying to escape. Finally he agreed to an interview as the only way to stop the adverse publicity. It had the opposite effect, as he should have known. He read the story in disbelief, trying to remember if he had said anything like the words attributed to him. Overnight he became the symbol of the shrewd financial con man preying on the gullible rich. Under cover of darkness, he drove to Richards's apartment, wanting camaraderie at all costs, to hell with the smugness. Richards was not there. His car was not in his parking space. Stan waited in his parked car for his silent partner to return. After two days of fruitless efforts, he realized that Richards was gone.

Why? Did he fear being connected with the debacle now that a police investigation had begun? That couldn't have been it. Morgan went over the accounting records on the computer Richards had used in the office. Suddenly he realized how silent his partner had been. There was no recorded involvement of Nathaniel Richards in the firm. His fifty-percent share? There were quarterly payments to a bank in Zurich. In the trial underway in Yuma, Stanley Morgan's name came up as in collusion with the savings-and-loan to defraud their investors. Faxes from his office were produced, faxes he had never sent. But California wanted him for its own. He was indicted and put on trial.

How could he explain the incriminating faxes? He knew nothing of them. And what of the mysterious Swiss account? Again he knew nothing. His only advantage was that his former clients began to be portrayed as wealthy old geezers who had been greedy for more. His lawyer persuaded him to plead guilty to questionable business practices and the charge of fraud was withdrawn. In the posh facility in which he served out his year with other white-collar criminals, he came to a full realization of what a dupe he had been. From the first meeting, it seemed in retrospect, Richards had been sizing him up for a patsy. What an ass he was to think that someone hitherto a stranger would offer to set him up as financial advisor, would pay for his training, establish him in an impressive office simply out of benevolence. Why hadn't he seen that there had to be a reason behind all that. Everything about Richards was fake—except for the death of Marilyn. And Stan Morgan resolved that he would track Richards down if it was the last thing he did. And then? His thoughts didn't go much beyond telling the bastard what he thought of him.

There is hot anger and there is cold anger. There are impulsive acts and there are cool and calculating ones. Stan Morgan developed a cold anger and from the time he set out to act on it his every move was considered and dispassionate. Had Richards really been a priest? He knew his moments of doubt, but what else did he have to go on? Someone who had been ordained, who had served for a time in the active ministry, should have left some kind of trail. The only clue Stan Morgan had was Fox River, Illinois. There was no more trace of Richards in the apartment where he had lived than anywhere else. Marilyn had rented it before they married. A marriage record? There are no central marriage records. The archdiocese of Los Angeles could find no record of a marriage between Nathanel Richards and Marilyn Daly.

And so he had come to Fox River. Taking Edna Hospers to dinner, taking her family to a Cubs game, had not been part of the plan. The old people that frequented the Senior Center reminded Morgan of his clients. Maybe he had imagined they could trade stories on how difficult it is to deal with people that age. He had liked her boy Eric, but the kid was too curious. Prudence dictated that he keep his distance from her. So on the basis of something Marie Murkin had said, he drove through the grounds of the Athanasian headquarters called Marygrove. Could such a peaceful setting hatch the kind of traitor Richards was? The third visit there, he saw him.

Morgan stopped the car immediately, pulling slowly over to the side of the road, and watched the bearded figure wearing some kind of habit. It all might have been a disguise, but Morgan remembered the odd hitching movement Richards made when he walked. He was not alone. He was bending the ear of an older man similarly dressed. Morgan watched them out of sight with a grim smile. He had found Father Richards at last.

When he is judged, let him be found guilty, and let his
prayer become sin.

—Psalm 109

"You probably haven't noticed, Father, but several times I have
driven onto the grounds and then lost courage."

This was a disarming remark from the man who had been
shown into his office by a glowing Father Joachim. Boniface had
heard a conversation going on in the outer office. The voices al-
ternated as the voices of the community did when they said the
office together in chapel. Boniface had made community office
optional, but now everyone came and at least during that time
when they were together the continuing disagreement among them
about their property was forgotten. The young man's voice from
the outer office had not seemed that of a frightened man.

"John Sullivan." He put out his hand and Boniface took it
with the sinking feeling that Joachim had let a salesman into his
office.

"I am Father Boniface."

"Yes, I was told."

"Mr. Sullivan—" he began, but he was interrupted.

"I want to make a retreat."

"A retreat!"

"Father, I haven't practiced my faith in years. I want to come back."

This was hardly a request that Father Boniface could refuse. Not that he was in the least inclined to. The small taste of pastoral work he'd had made him all the more eager to seize on the opportunities that came his way.

He took the young man for a walk on the grounds, listening to the story of the life he wanted to put behind him. They ended at the grotto, often taken to be a replica of Lourdes where Our Lady appeared to Bernadette.

"Her body has been preserved uncorrupted. I saw it myself at Nevers in France. A beautiful girl. Of course she had become a nun. The world is full of such signs that most people choose to ignore. Some years ago, the mayor of that city committed suicide. Imagine, living in a city where one could see daily the body of a woman who had died a century ago. We do not have eyes to see. But seeing this should be enough for us." Boniface gestured toward the grounds.

"It is a beautiful place, Father. That is what attracted me to it. Will you let me stay?"

"For a retreat?"

The young man's story was heartrending. First, a tragic love affair, the girl dying before they could marry. He then threw himself into a life of dissipation. He did not spare himself. *Why don't I quite trust him?* Boniface wondered.

"I would like to spend my life here. But just let me have a few days . . ."

When priests like Father Dowling came to make their retreat, there was no problem, even with the buildings other than the Corbett mansion all but out of use. A priest could just become a temporary member of the community, following his own regimen, of course. But a layman, under present conditions?

"The gardener and his family live in a lodge on the grounds. You could stay there."

"Anywhere."

"And did you want me to act as your retreat master?"

"Would that be possible?"

Boniface nodded. "Come."

They went to the maintenance shed behind the greenhouse where Andrew and his son were attaching the mower to the tractor. "Andrew, this is John Sullivan. He has come to make a retreat, and I wonder if you have room for him in the lodge."

"Father, the third floor is unused."

"Is it habitable?"

"It can be made so in a minute."

And so it was arranged. Andrew introduced the visitor to his son, and asked him to take Mr. Sullivan to the lodge.

"Should I get my car? My things are in it."

Michael and the penitent went back toward the main building. The road would take them around to the lodge.

"Is he a priest?" Andrew asked.

"No. Just a sinner."

Andrew blessed himself in the reverse manner of the Orthodox. "We all are."

"I was not exempting priests."

"Is there any further news?"

There was no need to say of what. "Nothing."

"How long will he be here?"

"He says he would like to spend the rest of his life here."

"So would I."

"In that, we are of one mind."

. . .

When Boniface climbed the steps of the main building, Nathaniel was standing on the veranda.

"Do we have a visitor, Father Boniface?"

"A man who wants to make a retreat."

"And you are letting him stay?"

How could he tell Richard that he felt the same misgivings about the man as he did about him. "Yes."

"And you will lead the retreat?"

"Now I have two penitents."

Richard looked startled, but then he subsided. It was well to remind him that he was still on probation. How quickly he had shaken off the years during which he had lived in the world, married, drifted from the faith as he had from the priesthood. And now, a few months back, he had become a dominant figure in the community. No doubt it spoke well of the community that they had not treated Richard like a pariah, but Boniface almost wished they had. A man should not spend much of life outside the life he had vowed to live and then return as if he had been out for a walk.

"Where will he stay?"

"The Georges are putting him up in the lodge."

"There are rooms in the mansion."

"He's not a priest. I don't think he would be comfortable with us."

"And maybe vice versa?"

"Maybe." Boniface paused. He was about to voice his uneasiness with Sullivan but then decided against it. What a gossip he was becoming. Maybe that was an effect of pastoral work. But he felt he should say more. "A tragic story. He lost his fiancée to cancer and then fell apart. I hope his stay here will help him."

The trouble with a bearded man is that it is difficult to know what he is thinking unless you read his eyes and Richard insisted on wearing sunglasses at all hours. A California habit, apparently.

In the office Boniface noticed that the visitor had left his briefcase there. A handsome item, with initials embossed in gold: S. M. ODD. But it could not belong to anyone but the visitor.

They reel to and fro, and stagger like a drunken man.

—*Psalm 107*

"If it isn't a legal matter, why do I need a lawyer?"

"Do you want your dollar back?"

Leo looked at him abjectly. "I'm sorry. I know you've gone to a great deal of trouble."

"Imagine what two dollars would get you."

Leo cheered up. Tuttle was inclined to take his side because Hazel thought so little of Leo.

"Look, Leo. I had a very good session with Amos Cadbury. He is the lawyer that drew up your grandfather's will."

"I know who Amos Cadbury is. I'd like to sue him. I think

he's the one who gave my grandfather all these ideas."

Whatever influence Cadbury had had, and no doubt it was a lot, old Corbett had been in a giving mood long before he became Amos Cadbury's client.

"I have a better idea."

"What?"

"Meet me at the courthouse tomorrow at ten."

"But I have to go to work."

"What's more important to you, having a chance to live like a Corbett or sell a few golf balls? Call in sick."

"I'm never sick."

"Don't tell them that."

"That's crazy," Hazel said when he told her. He had promised himself not to, but how often did he have a stroke of genius?

"I'm glad you like it."

"If your meeting with Cadbury was so successful why would you want to antagonize him like that?"

"It's the sort of thing he expects of me."

"Maybe you can work as a paralegal when you get disbarred."

"I only worry about what will happen to you."

Hazel's expression was one he had never seen before. Her face went utterly blank. Then she burst into tears and ran into the outer office. Geez.

The pressroom at the courthouse at ten in the morning had the look of an emergency ward, with representatives of the media trying to work off last night's hangover. Tetzel was banging away at his computer the way some people hit themselves on the head with a hammer.

"Get lost," he growled when Tuttle tapped his shoulder. But he stopped typing.

"Tetzel, this is Leo Corbett." And Tuttle stepped aside like a magician to show that it was indeed so. Tetzel turned his tormented expression on Leo.

"So?"

"Corbett. Leo Corbett. As in filthy rich. The benefactor?"

It would be too much to say that he had Tetzel's interest, but the reporter's disinterest diminished to a degree. The chair Tuttle pulled up made a scraping sound, and Tetzel's hands went to his head.

"Don't do that!"

"Sorry. Tetzel, you are about to become the toast of Fox River journalism. When you are through those two Watergate guys will be history."

"They already are."

"Sit down, Leo. And be careful with the chair."

Leo had been complaining since they met on the steps of the courthouse, saying that he should be at work. "Gasper, the pro, didn't believe me, I know he didn't. I never could lie."

"Neither can sleeping dogs."

"Huh?"

"Forget about the golf course. You know what George Eliot said about them. A thousand lost golf balls," said Tuttle.

"You mean T. S."

"Don't be vulgar. And remember why we are here."

"You haven't told me."

"Come on."

But Leo had worn his worried, petulant expression into the press room and it was clear that Tetzel did not find him prepossessing, as he would have put it. The first time he used the word

Tuttle thought he was talking about insurance against having the finance company take your car.

"What crazy idea you got this time, Tuttle?"

Tetzel glanced at Leo as Tuttle spoke because the object of the conversation kept trying to break in and correct the account his lawyer was giving the reporter. Leo had a weak appreciation of the need to dramatize, select, emphasize, if so jaded a journalist as Tetzel was to show a spark of interest, let alone the enthusiasm with which Tuttle spoke.

"Why didn't his daddy leave him no money?"

"Everything he got stopped when he died."

"Money his daddy gave him?"

"Right. Did he ever work for a living, save anything?" He put this question to Leo, who took umbrage at it.

"My father was a distinguished geologist." This was the first time Tuttle had heard Leo speak well of any of his ancestors.

"Aren't they paid?"

Leo made a moue and shut his eyes. When he opened them, he was looking over Tetzel's head. "My father gave his life to science. The stone marking his grave is one that he himself—"

"You hear the one about the guy who left his body to science and they refused it?"

Tuttle got out of the way of the jab Tetzel aimed at his ribs; Hazel was keeping him in training.

"Tetzel, this young man has been reduced to working at the country club, in the golf shop."

"That a year-round job?"

"I've only been there since late March."

Tetzel was shaking his head. "It's all wrong. Tuttle, you have to put him into a soup kitchen, into a shelter for the homeless."

He meant as a volunteer. What Tetzel thought the public

wanted was the spectacle of an altruistic young man, robbed of his inheritance, devoting himself to helping those even less fortunate than himself.

"I won't do it," Leo announced.

Tetzel looked at him with interest for the first time. "You wearing contacts or something?"

"I am not."

"Your eyes look glassy."

Suddenly the puffy, whining, disinherited creampuff was transformed. He rose and took Tetzel by the lapels and lifted him out of his chair and began to shake him as if he were a doll. The reporter spluttered and cursed and began to kick. Leo dropped him into his chair, Tetzel's arm hit his keyboard and it clattered to the floor. The computer might have followed if Tuttle hadn't steadied it. Then he turned and stared at his client.

"Where do you work out?"

"I run ten miles every morning." Leo lied. He looked down in every sense at Tetzel. "I'll take that as an apology."

"You'll take what?" Tetzel had bent over, intending to retrieve his keyboard, but straightened with a great cry, his hand going to his head. He made as if to rise, but Tuttle had only to put a hand on his shoulder to subdue him.

"Let's continue."

"All right," Tetzel said, glaring at Leo. "This lethal weapon takes a job in a soup kitchen. I discover him there, with my photographer." He paused. "If I wrote like that I'd be fired. A photographer will happen to be with me, in search of human interest stories we come upon the grandson of Corbett, how did he end up here? We toy with the idea that he sold all he had and gave to the poor . . . I like it."

"It's a great idea," Tuttle agreed.

So it was that Leo Corbett bade good-bye to the golf shop and the country club and found himself ladling soup into the bowls of shuffling men and women far worse off than himself. Such a spectacle of misfortune did not dull his own sense of the injustice that had been done him, which was just as well, since it was only the utilitarian aspect of his volunteer work that had induced him to take it up. He would wander for some time in this desert of poverty on the understanding that it would lead on to the promised land. His situation had the further advantage that those whom he served did not connect him with the object of the passionate series that soon commenced in the *Fox River Tribune,* nor did they wonder at the commotion involved in photographing the putative heir behind the food line. They were used to the equivocal concern of the wider society and had lost any egoism that might have objected to being photographed in the most heartrending of attitudes—a grizzled old man, wearing his baseball cap rakishly in reverse, daubing with a piece of bread the last drops from his bowl; a woman gnawing with the only teeth left her the resisting drumstick that had been put upon her tray; a little boy with a bowl who might have been Oliver Twist saying, "More." It was to the credit of Tetzel's photographer that these were not posed scenes, but authentically drawn from life as it was lived in and about the soup kitchen where Leo Corbett was depicted as the goodest of Samaritans.

Tetzel reached deep into his rhetorical resources, the boy with the bowl inspired a Dickensian passion and there was danger, in the second story of his series, that he would go off on a tangent, making the plight of the homeless his theme. But there was art in this. The more undeserving to the suburban eye the objects of Leo's compassion, the more surely would he engage that of his reader. Had it come to this that the grandchildren of yesterday's plutocrats were to be found in shelters for the homeless, and who knew for how long Leo would remain on the right side of the food line?

"If I didn't know better, I'd think that young whelp was a saint."

"Hazel, you have no heart."

"Wanna bet?"

With phase one of his plan well under way, Tuttle called Farniente to his office. His instructions were terse and clear. Tuttle wanted the private investigator to see if there was anything at all unsavory about the Lucases who directed the shelter where Leo was now covering himself with glory.

"Unsavory?"

"If I knew what I meant I wouldn't need you."

"That's true."

Call it instinct, call it luck. Glen Lucas and his wife Celia had previously run a day-care center that had come under a cloud. Children had come home with odd stories; Glen Lucas was accused of an excess of loving care to the little girls. He lay down with them at nap time, he held them on his lap until Celia tore his burden from him and cuffed him on the ear. She in her turn showed more than maternal interest in the genitalia of little boys. They were shut down. All this had been in Milwaukee. They migrated south, ingratiated themselves with the local United Fund, and lamented the absence of a homeless shelter in the otherwise progressive community.

"No peculation?"

"You mean sheep?" Farniente's misunderstanding owed something to his residual knowledge of his parents' native tongue.

"I mean money. How close an accounting does United Way receive of the operation of the homeless shelter?"

"Ah."

The results were ambiguous, but that was enough for Tetzel. Sometimes it suffices to raise questions. And then hints of improprieties in Milwaukee strengthened suspicion of the Lucases. The director of the United Way, the object of wrath from Planned Parenthood from whom he withheld public funding, acted with dispatch. The shutting down of the shelter added poignancy to the plight of the altruistic young man whose grandfather had shamelessly lavished his wealth on a religious order in decline while his should-be heir had lost even his volunteer position healing the needy and destitute. As to what would now happen to those who had daily come to the shelter, the many who had established all but permanent residence there, Tetzel's series did not inquire. The victim was Leo Corbett and no other.

Mention of the Athanasians was by no means a grace note in Tetzel's account.

"I'm going after them," he told Tuttle.

"Of course."

"I warn you, I'm not Catholic."

"In my Father's house there are many mansions," Tuttle said unctuously.

"Well, those fathers live in a mansion. They have moved out of the buildings they put up and are all living in Corbett's mansion!"

But Tetzel saved his indignation for phase three of Tuttle's plan. The beneficiaries of Corbett's wealth were to be depicted as unworthy of it, men ostensibly vowed to poverty living in the lap of luxury because of the foolish sentimentality of an old man in his dotage. The bearded father who provided Tetzel with his most damning quotations was Nathaniel.

Unless the Lord builds the house, they labor in vain who
build it.

                             —Psalm 127

Lars Anderson had started in cement, contracting to replace the
sidewalks for which the residents of Fox River were personally
responsible. And liable. Broken pavement and pocked surfaces
making footing unsure opened the possibility of lawsuits of an
annoying kind. Anderson had prospered. There had been a pop-
ular tune at the time whose recurrent line was, "Cement mixer,
putsy putsy," and it had become his theme song. A voice was not
among the few gifts God had given him, but he sang nonetheless,
repeating that line as if it were a mantra. He had been drafted
into the Korean War, and ended up in the Sea Bees where construction in its various forms became known to him and suggested
his postwar career. Throwing up overnight dozens of temporary
dwellings for servicemen inspired him.

He began small, Roosevelt Heights, put up in a former corn-
field two miles outside Aurora. The houses were built on slabs,
had no attics, and might have been intended for the Army. But
they were inexpensive, convenient, and sold like popcorn. Anderson became the darling of the banks. Loans were his for the

asking. With success, he aimed higher. In his middle period, what might have been called the mansard roof phase, he had put up dwellings for dentists and rising young salesmen and teachers. The billboards announcing new sites, as well as the notices in the metropolitan newspapers, called them Bedrooms for Chicago. And white Chicagoans, fleeing the social engineering that was turning the cities of the nation into war zones, snapped up Lars Anderson's houses. In this third and final phase, he catered to the affluent. He built great brick castles with four-car garages around artificial lakes. The earth was shaped and undulated by bulldozers and, when the carpenters and plumbers and electricians and all the other tradesmen who sang Anderson's praises moved on to his next site, the bleak setting was transformed overnight—sod was laid, trees planted, ducks set afloat on the lake, and at the entrance to the development, in a castellated building that would house security and control entry, salesmen greeted the prospects, many of whom were moving up from another Anderson settlement.

A lesser man would have rested on his laurels, retired to his seaside place in Baja California and watched the waves come in, satisfied with a long and productive life. Anderson was now seventy-one years old. But the juices still flowed in his old veins. He had had open-heart surgery and though some joked that the purpose of the operation had been to see if he had one, he had emerged from it with the sense that his life was beginning anew. For he had acquired enemies as well as grateful (more or less) occupants of his homes. Environmentalists regarded him as a menace. They spoke of the wet lands he had despoiled, how flora and fauna once indigenous to the area had been ruthlessly extinguished by the greed and avarice of Lars Anderson. The great man took little notice of this. He longed to undertake the final and crowning phase of his career. And that required his getting possession of the land occupied by the Athanasians, the erstwhile estate of Maurice Corbett in whom Lars saw a prefiguring of himself.

Anderson had himself flown by helicopter over the grounds, photographs in abundance had been taken, his architects had presented him with a multitude of plans, he had settled on one. The Corbett mansion would be left untouched. The architecture of this ultimate effort would be inspired by that of the Corbett mansion. Anderson himself intended to take possession of the mansion and thus seal the continuity of his career and Corbett's. But the Athanasians had reacted to his overtures with horror. They had no intention of selling their property. The satisfaction with which Lars Anderson read the Tetzel series in the *Fox River Tribune* was immense! His one regret was that he had not thought of the idea himself. He instructed his administrative assistant, a disarmingly petite thirty-year-old named Charlotte, to locate Leo Corbett and bring him to headquarters. Charlotte all but saluted when she went on her mission.

Charlotte Priebe had been a slattern as an undergraduate at Chicago, a woman of the left, a Green on every day but March 17 when the Chicago River was contaminated and turned into one of the lime drinks Walgreen's had once been noted for. In an earlier day, she might have become a Communist. There was little left now but environmentalism and antiglobalism. In her senior year, Charlotte was mugged by reality when her father lost his job thanks to a successful campaign in which she had participated. She sat in Rockefeller Chapel one afternoon and reviewed her life. Were bugs and birds and plants and trees more important than her father? In any case, this was a false choice. It was that heretical realization that began her conversion. People were compatible with the environment. Industry was compatible with the environment. She gave her kindred spirits credit for having raised the consciousness of capital. For whatever motive, companies now considered themselves the custodians of the environment in which they located their plants. Of course there were laws and federal agencies. Too many laws, as Charlotte came to think, and agencies run by zealots such as she herself had been. She had her hair shampooed and cut. She began to wear skirts. She made a heroic effort in her senior year, changing her major to economics, fulfilling all the requirements in a marathon effort to retool herself for what she now saw to be the true crusade of the modern world. She began to listen to Rush Limbaugh, albeit with a headset, and laughed aloud to the surprise of fellow passengers on the bus when he spoke of wacko environmentalists. She read with interest and admiration of the career of Lars Anderson and, upon graduation, she presented herself to him and won his heart with a completely sincere recitation of her new creed. He put her in his office, within a year she was his private secretary, now she was his administrative assistant. Among her many assets was the fact that the register of her voice was perfectly audible to his hearing, which had long ago succumbed to the assault of cement mixer, putsy putsy. This was the emissary Lars Anderson sent to Leo Corbett.

"Your grandfather was one of the giants of this area," she told him on the veranda of the country club where they sipped iced tea. Leo had been taken back into the golf shop at the insistence of a majority of the members. His grandfather's membership in the club was bestowed on him in reparation for the indignities he had suffered and the prospects that now seemed his.

"He cut me off without a dime."

"That must be rectified."

Charlotte was dispassionately sensible of the attraction her feminine endowments exercised on the male of the species. That these had played their role in her swift rise at Anderson Ltd. had not been lost on her, nor had she been beneath showing a little leg for the benefit of her admiring but harmless employer. Her skirts were dangerously short, and when she crossed her legs on the veranda of the country club, Leo Corbett all but gasped in alarmed admiration. But the operation was accomplished without any pornographic display. She brought her iced tea to her mouth; plush red lips closed around the straw. Her cheeks hollowed as she drank. Half the battle was already won. An hour later, they were on their way to the corporate offices in Barrington in Charlotte's olive-green Mercedes.

Deliver me from my enemies, O my God.
—*Psalm 59*

The man named John Sullivan who had been placed in the third floor of the lodge in which the Georges lived was said to be on retreat, but he seemed to do little other than show himself about the grounds and sit at the laptop computer he had installed in his room. And speak Spanish to Rita. And not just *Como esta usted?* He rattled away in a manner that brought Rita's milk-white teeth on display in her warmest smile, the smile Michael had imagined only he elicited.

"What did he say?"

"Oh, nothing." But she smiled shyly when she said it and turned away.

This distraction slowed Michael's appreciation of his father's concern at the stories in the local paper about Leo Corbett and, the culminating blow, the description of the former Corbett estate with the interview with Father Nathaniel, the bearded deserter who had returned to sow discord among his former confreres.

"He is in the employ of Anderson," Andrew George decided. "He is a Trojan horse in the community."

Father Nathaniel had certainly proved a godsend to the journalist Tetzel, mocking the pretensions of Leo Corbett, talking of how the Athanasians had taken a promising site and turned it into a garden spot.

"Does he propose to come back here and live in the selfish luxury his grandfather did?"

"But he was your benefactor."

"And his benefaction has served its purpose."

"What do you mean?"

"Let me tell you about the present condition of the Athanasian Order."

MORIBUND COMMUNITY CLINGS TO ESTATE ran the leader over Tetzel's story detailing the amazing revelations of Father Nathaniel. A once-thriving Order had, in the manner of so many religious communities in recent years, gone into decline. Buildings that had once burst with candidates for the priesthood, from high school through novitiate and on to philosophy, theology, and ordination, men who had played a significant role in the work of the Catholic Church, even taking responsibility for several parishes in the Chicago Archdiocese, were now the echoing habitat of a handful of aging priests. Buildings were entirely or partly shut up. The community, whose members took the vows of poverty, chastity, and obedience, were now living in the gorgeous mansion Maurice Corbett had built for his second wife. Under her influence, Corbett had become a Catholic and in his waning years had deeded the property over to the Athanasians. Whatever merit there had been in that idea—and the noble history of the Order sketched by Father Nathaniel told how much—the Athanasians were not what they had been, nor were they likely to become so again. Meanwhile, the property was there, attractive, extensive, all but useless.

"No one need tell us of our obligations," Nathaniel had said.

"Meaning what?"

"Some of us are willing to talk to Lars Anderson about his hope to develop the property into a tasteful new community, mindful of the environment."

"How many?"

"Not yet a majority."

"More than there were?"

Nathaniel nodded.

"Because of my articles."

"But you are the champion of Leo Corbett."

"Surely he has a claim."

"A claim to enjoy these acres by himself, to stand in the path of progress? Nonsense."

Andrew George cried out with pain as he read this account, as he did several times, always aloud, as if he wanted God to hear and do something about it. Mr. Martinez heard about the series and Michael was shaken by Rita's account of his reaction.

"He wants to know what kind of work you'll do now."

"All this will blow over. The Georges have lived here for years and aren't going anywhere."

"But if the priests sell?"

"Tell your father that Nathaniel ran away years ago and married in California. He came back just to cause trouble. But they won't listen to him." Michael said this with such conviction that he almost believed himself.

"He ran away and got married?" She was deeply shocked.

"That's right. Ask my father."

Michael decided that he had to marry Rita before anything further happened. He would marry her in front of a priest, maybe Father Boniface would do it in the community chapel; that would cushion the blow to his father.

"He would regard it as the deepest betrayal," Boniface said, almost in alarm.

"Can you promise me that I will live here as my father and his father did?" Michael asked, adding, "Father?"

Gone was the round and merry face that Michael had known all his life. He remembered when he had been enrolled in the dwindling Latin class that Father Boniface taught. He had surprised the priest with an aptitude for classical tongues that Michael himself had been too young—thirteen—to find surprising and which had led him, at fifteen, to pagan poet Catullus, much to the old priest's dismay. Boniface had given him Augustine to read that his mind might be cleared of the pagan hedonism, which could be redeemed only by the love poem addressed to his dead brother, *Ave atque vale*.

"That might be Nathaniel's motto. He has come back to greet us with a final farewell."

"Now, now. Everything is in God's hands."

How could he explain, without sounding like Catullus singing of his Lesbia, that he wanted to be in Rita's hands and have her in his. Even in the sanctum sanctorum of Father Boniface's office his breath caught at the prospect. He had respected Rita too much to take advantage of those moments when she as well as he found postponement a physical pain, but such restraint had been an investment, proof that he wanted her in the only way that would leave her conscience untroubled. And his? There was Mediterranean blood in his veins, as there had been in Augustine's, and it was the early Augustine that tempted him now: Make me chaste, Lord, but not yet.

"You were meant to be more than a gardener, son."

"Horace and his villa."

"He had slaves to take care of the farm at Tivoli."

"Is my father your slave?"

"You know he isn't. Oh, Michael, I wish I could promise you that things will go as your father and I wish. I am the superior here, but in such matters I have but one vote."

"There was no need to take a vote until he came back."

"No."

"Send him away."

He could see that he touched the deepest desire in the old priest. And why not? Nathaniel, as he insisted on being called again, was a renegade. He did not deserve to have a vote equal to the others. He was on probation. And that meant that his staying was still undecided.

"Send him away, Father. He is destroying us all. What he said to the reporter . . ."

The old priest winced.

"My father read it aloud, again and again."

And Michael remembered his father only that morning, trimming the hedge when Nathaniel passed and when his back was to him, gesturing at him with the whirring blade, as if he would like to trim his beard, and his head as well.

"The poor man."

"My father?"

"Of course. Michael, let me promise you this. No matter what happens, you will be taken care of. Perhaps this is God's way of insuring that your talents will be developed. The order will finance your education, you can continue your study of the classics, become a teacher."

"No."

"It has been the consolation of my own life, son."

But it was the prospect of living in the lodge after they were married, to have it to themselves eventually, filled with their children, that had removed all resistance Rita had previously shown to his impetuous desire that they marry. Now, waiting was a sin if their love need be no sin. Her response to the man Sullivan, with his Spanish fluency, made him see how tenuous his hold on her was.

"I want to be a gardener here and Nathaniel won't stop me."

And he stormed out of the office as if his dilemma was of Boniface's doing.

Rescue me, Lord, from my enemies, I have fled to You for
refuge.

—Psalm 143

The dark wood choir stalls filled the sanctuary of the chapel, and
in the summer evening a polychrome shaft of light descended from
a stained-glass window high above them, falling on the just and
unjust alike, making Nathaniel's beard look like the dyed hair of
a young delinquent. Back and forth between the stalls the verses
of the psalm were traded, the words of David that had defined
Jewish and Christian worship for millennia, sung in a way that
also had its origins in Israel and had been modified in the mon-
asteries to carry the prayer of the Church, the *opus Dei*, up to
God, hour after hour, day after day, year after year, century after
century . . . Boniface never felt more a part of the long history of
the faith than when he said or sang the office, his voice blending
with those of long-dead Jews and monks, the choirs of angels
harmonizing with them, solving the great mystery of Israel, the
covenant and the cross at last in concord. And the recovery of
this practice among them they owed to Nathaniel.

A church remains cool in summer, in shadows, the invisible
ceiling above with the great arches making them safe as Jonah in

the belly of the whale, old men with their reedy voices finding in the mesmerizing monotone of chant the purpose of their lives as they moved toward the little variation at the middle of the verse and the greater one at the end. And then the other side picked it up. At the end of the psalm, the deep bow as they sang the doxology. Oh, dear God, how he loved it, and how he hated the man who had made it possible again, Nathaniel at the organ, Nathaniel with his golden voice, Nathaniel the Judas among them.

Boniface realized that the community was split along the lines of their opposite views on the proposal that Nathaniel had put before them. How could those men be so insensible of the sanctity of this place that they could imagine putting it on the block for a mess of pottage? But they would go from the church to the common room where the by now all-too-familiar discussion would go on. But tonight it would go on with a difference.

He opened the meeting with a statement.

"I am told that canon law prevents us from selling, even if we were agreed," Boniface said. He had wanted to hold back this precious information, but noticing the wavering among his allies, he could not restrain himself.

"Whoever told you that is wrong," Nathaniel said.

"My informant has a degree in canon law."

"But law is a matter of precedents, even Church law. Other communities have sold their property."

"But not licitly, I have been informed. It amounts to the alienation of Church property."

"Are you saying that the Church has never sold a piece of land in two thousand years?"

Old Martin piped up. "During the Reformation, churches were confiscated, the heads of statues knocked off, terrible sacrileges committed."

"Don't forget the goddess of Reason on the main altar of Notre Dame," Ambrose said, and a moment of silence ensued when the rest of them tried to remember.

"Of course it all would depend on what we did with any money gained from the sale of the property," Boniface said.

What did he mean?

"If it were used to establish another Marygrove elsewhere, the goods of the Church would not be alienated, but put to a different sacred use."

Boniface watched Nathaniel as he said this. It proved to be far more of a trump than his first invocation of canon law. Father Dowling had described for Boniface the precedent that had so pained Amos Cadbury and himself, the nuns in Los Angeles who had enriched themselves personally with money gained from the sale of their property, each one pocketing her share and heading into the world. Hadn't Nathaniel said that the woman he married had been a nun of that community? Boniface felt that he had indeed hit upon the precedent that motivated Nathaniel, and if that was so it cast his return to the community in the darkest of lights. In any case, Nathaniel for a change fell silent and there were looks of consternation on the faces of his allies. What had they been persuaded to favor? Surely they had had no notion of enriching themselves at the expense of the Order of St. Athanasius. Dark frowns formed and Nathaniel angrily left the room.

Boniface breathed a prayer that he had been spared the need to make known what John Sullivan had told him.

"Has Father Nathaniel made any comment on my presence here, Father?" the visitor had asked.

"Of course he noticed it."

"He is avoiding me."

"Avoiding you?"

"My name is not John Sullivan, Father. It is Stanley Morgan." The mystery of the initials on the man's briefcase was solved. "I am here under false pretenses. I knew Nathaniel in California where he was known as Nathaniel Richards. He stole a large sum of money from me."

"Good God."

"He siphoned money from people's savings and from my firm and transferred it to an account in a Zurich bank."

If Father Boniface had not been sitting, he would have fallen. "Why are you here?"

"To confront him. To demand that he give back that money. I spent time in prison for what he did, but there is no way he could be successfully prosecuted for it. This is a peaceful place, Father, I almost wish I were here for the reason I gave you. But you have a traitor amongst you. Mr. George showed me the story in the local paper suggesting that Richards favors selling this property. I have no doubt that it was the thought of the fortune it represented that drew him back to you."

Nathaniel's reaction to what Father Boniface had said, at last making use of the ammunition provided him by Father Dowling and Amos Cadbury, seemed to justify Stanley Morgan's interpretation of the prodigal's return. In the course of the evening, two of those who had allied themselves with Nathaniel came to Boniface to assure him that they had been motivated solely by the thought that they were preventing worthy people from having the property they themselves loved so much and where they had lived their long lives. In some of their cases, a life lived under the vow of poverty had made money so odd a substance that he would have had trouble imagining himself with several hundred dollars, let alone a fortune.

"Did Nathaniel intend that each of us should become wealthy?"

"Perhaps he didn't know what he intended."

"You are a good man, Father Boniface."

Meaning he had a good face. Black thoughts stirred in his heart, at the enormity of what Nathaniel had done, misleading those good old men. Perhaps he had a further plan whereby he would come into possession of it all, putting it into his Swiss account. Boniface had known annoyance before, he had responded to the small irritations of community life, but never had he felt a temptation to dark and murderous anger. He was in no condition to speak to Nathaniel now. God knew what he might do if Nathaniel's motive had indeed been exposed. But by waiting he was giving the man time to think of some plausible explanation of what he had done. No, the time was now.

But when he left his room and the mansion, Boniface took the path to the chapel and there in the dark church he knelt and asked that his heart be cleansed. He would tell Nathaniel that he must leave, his probation was up and Boniface would not permit him to rejoin the community permanently. He would stand at the front gate like the angels showing Adam and Eve out of the garden, but he prayed that he would not do it from a vindictive motive. He stayed in the church for an hour, but when he left his heart was still not cleansed of anger and hatred.

Nathaniel did not respond to the knock on his door. Had he already expelled himself, slinking off now that his purpose was known? It seemed too good to be true. He wanted the object of his dark thoughts out of the house, off the grounds, gone.

"Have you seen Nathaniel?"

"He said he was going to the grotto."

Boniface looked at his informant, to see if there was any irony in his expression that had not been in his voice. But he was simply answering a question. Full of disappointment, deflated because his thought that Nathaniel had fled was not true, Boniface returned to his room.

The body of Richard Krause, Father Nathaniel, was found at the grotto the following morning. The weapon that had killed him still jutted horribly from his bloody back, a garden tool from the maintenance shed. The victim was wearing his religious habit.

❧ Part Two ❧

Do not fret because of evildoers.

—Psalm 37

Dr. Pippen, the auburn-haired assistant coroner, watched the officious Lubins take command of the scene at the grotto, alienating all and sundry with his many and conflicting orders. The body had been found on a prie-dieu in front of the grotto by Andrew George, the head of the grounds crew. He had come upon what he thought was one of the fathers at prayer and was going respectfully by when he saw the handle of the pickax and stopped. Captain Phil Keegan and Lieutenant Cy Horvath were listening impassively to the head gardener's excited account.

"What time was that?"

"Seven, maybe a little before. Every morning at seven I go to the maintenance shed."

"Were you surprised to see someone kneeling at the grotto?"

George looked from Horvath to Keegan. "That is what they do there."

Pippen joined them, if only to distance herself from the coroner. She was itching to get at the body, but she was damned if she would risk being pushed aside by Lubins.

"Who was he?" she asked Horvath.

"One of the priests."

"That's weird," she said, and then, "Isn't it?"

"Yes."

"Killed with an ax?"

"You're the coroner."

"Lubins is here."

The coroner was not as stupid as Pippens pretended, but Cy Horvath adopted her point of view. Stolidly and happily married, he had never felt the lures of infidelity prior to the arrival of Dr. Pippen as assistant to Lubins. Her hair was gathered into a ponytail, she wore jeans and a baggy sweatshirt against the morning chill on which Greek letters Cy did not understand were lettered. Her ponytail swished as she turned toward Lubins and then back again to Cy.

The medical examiner's wagon had been backed along the path from the parking lot behind the greenhouse, a lot that separated the greenhouse from the maintenance shed. It was from that shed that the ostensible murder weapon had come. George identified it when he was taken to the body. Lubins did not want the ax removed from the body.

"That's mine," George said, having stooped to look at the handle. "Ours."

By concentrating on the handle he could avoid looking at the body. It was not a pretty sight. Lubins called Pippen over and the two of them stood on either side of the body until by some imperceptible sign Lubins gave her the go-ahead and she finally got things under way. Lubins went around letting people know he was leaving, interrupting Keegan who was talking with one of the priests, and then saying to Cy, "Well, back to the salt mines."

. . .

Pippen had the pickax removed, handed it to Cy as if he were
assisting her at surgery, and had the body transferred to the meat
wagon so she could complete the on-site investigation. Cy took
the pickax in a plastic bag to Keegan, who tried its heft as Cy
had, and then it went with other items thought pertinent to the
inquiry. Although it was private property, the area was taped off
and uniformed cops posted as if they meant to hinder the move-
ments of the old priests. The kneeling bench where the body was
found was off bounds, so any praying would have to be done from
a distance. Keegan's phrase.

"Maybe it always is."

Keegan looked at Cy. "Ever been here before?"

"Maybe when I was a kid."

"You ever want to know what the Church used to be, this is
the place."

"I remember."

"But it was still going on here."

"Who were you talking to?"

"Father Watchamacallit. Boniface, the man in charge, is in the
chapel, taking this pretty hard."

What Phil regarded as an island of preconciliar tranquillity
had been shaken by the articles Tetzel wrote in the *Tribune*, but
things were bound to get a lot worse now. Cy spotted Tetzel skulk-
ing around the edges of the little gathering. The dead man was
the one who had spilled his guts to Tetzel, sounding anxious to
sell the property before Leo Corbett could get his hands on it.
Coming up the drive from the county road, Cy had been reminded
of the practice field at Champaign, his freshman and only year in

college. An injury had ended his promising athletic career, but he had joined the force and Phil Keegan, recognizing the name of the local high school star, had moved him swiftly up the ranks in order to have him at his side.

Cy went around the wagon in which Pippen was at work and followed the path back to the greenhouse. It was the old-fashioned kind of greenhouse, hundreds of puttied windows, green frames, the low-angled roof reflecting everything in sight—sky, clouds, trees, the swift flight of a bird. Some of the windows looked white-washed, to cut the sun. The door was open and Cy looked in, expecting to find Andrew George, who had identified the ax. But this was a young kid.

"I'm Horvath," he said, still in the doorway. The kid had an egg-shaped head, large eyes, and needed a shave. Cy went inside. "Lieutenant Horvath."

"Police?"

Well, people say stupid things at a murder scene. He nodded. "Who are you?"

"Michael. I live here."

"In the greenhouse?"

"My father is in charge of the grounds."

"Andrew George."

"That's right. Is he really dead?"

"Didn't your father tell you?"

"My father."

"He found the body. Didn't he tell you?" George's story was that he ran back to the lodge and called the mansion to summon Boniface. Then, on Boniface's orders, he had called the police.

"I haven't seen him yet." The grotto was on the path that came from the lodge to the greenhouse. Of course, there were other ways Michael George could have come.

"You live in the lodge with your family."

"That's right. Is it Father Nathaniel?"

"I suppose you knew them all."

"I grew up here. I went to school here."

"Tell me about Father Nathaniel."

"He was a sonofabitch."

The older George did not want to comment on community affairs, what did he know, but everyone knew that the one who got killed was a troublemaker.

"Maybe you read the articles in the paper?" he said to Phil Keegan.

"Tell me about them."

Phil had read the articles, of course. George's version of them was very personal. His family's tenure as groundskeepers was threatened by all this talk about selling Marygrove.

"A couple months ago, last year, any time, no one's talking about leaving here, selling the property. Things may not be good, talk to Boniface, but leave here? No way. This is where they have been since . . . My father worked here before me. And I have a son."

"He here now?"

"I haven't seen him this morning."

"Is this him?"

A man had looked into the kitchen where Keegan was talking with George, and then withdrawn. "Hey," Keegan called. "Come back."

But this was not the son. This was a man on retreat who was living in the lodge. John Sullivan. "What's going on?"

"You just getting up?" It was now after nine-thirty.

"This fresh air! Windows wide open, I could have slept till

noon. The sun woke me up, shining right in my face."

"Something awful has happened," George said, putting a stop to his guest's cheerful patter.

"I'm Captain Keegan, chief of detectives, Fox River." There was no special reaction. "We've got a murder here."

This got his attention. Phil let George tell him the story. How he found the body.

"But who was it that was murdered?"

"Nathaniel."

"No kidding!"

The man pulled out a chair and joined them at the kitchen table. Cy arrived with the son, who was allowed to go on to his room after an exchange with his father.

"Where you been?"

"In the greenhouse."

"At a time like this?"

Keegan said, "Your son work with you?"

"Thank God his mother's away."

Mrs. George had taken the bus to Peoria to be with her daughter who was about to deliver the Georges' first grandchild.

Cy had gotten the guest away from the table and was talking to him in a corner.

"How come you're staying here?" Cy asked, when Sullivan told him he was on retreat.

"This is where they put me."

"They?"

"Father Boniface."

"How long have you been here?"

Sullivan thought. "It's going on five days."

"How long is a retreat?"

"That depends. You Catholic?"

Cy nodded. "Five days seems a pretty long one."

"To tell you the truth, it's open-ended. I was kind of at the end of my tether when I drove up the driveway. I had a long talk with Father Boniface."

"The head man."

"Yes."

"How many priests here, do you know?"

"Eight."

"A big place for that small a number."

"I think there used to be a lot more of them."

"How did you hear of them?"

"What do you mean?"

"Why did you come here to make a retreat?"

"Pure chance."

"So how's it going?"

Sullivan smiled, man to man. "It's not like riding a bicycle. But I'm getting the hang of it."

"Did you know Father Nathaniel?"

"I can't believe he's dead."

"When did you last see him?"

"Yesterday."

Father Boniface was seated in his choir stall, hands up his sleeves, staring straight ahead. He was startled when Phil Keegan whispered in his ear. Could they talk outside? Boniface nodded, got up slowly, and stepped out of the stall. He genuflected slowly, and Phil realized he had forgotten to, so he bent his knee and bowed toward the tabernacle.

"Have they taken the body away?"

"They're about to, Father."

"I gave him conditional absolution when Mr. George called me. He was already dead."

"You take his pulse or what?"

In his office, Boniface directed Phil to a chair and pulled another out from behind the desk. They sat facing one another. "He had stopped bleeding."

Boniface might have been remembering coming on the body, slumped over the kneeler with the ax handle sticking out the back. That was the blood he meant had stopped.

"This has to be a terrible shock, Father."

"We've been getting a lot of shocks lately."

"The newspaper stories?"

"Recent years have not been good ones for us." He shook his head. "Now this."

"How old was Nathaniel?"

"His early sixties, I think. He was young among us."

"Tell me about him."

"He had been away. He left the Order and lived in California for some years. He came back to us only a few months ago."

"Certainly no one in the community could have killed him?"

"God forbid."

"Any idea who might have? Did he ever mention being under threat?"

"He was killed with an ax."

"That's right."

"The ax belonged to us, Mr. George tells me."

In his oblique way, Father Boniface seemed to be telling Phil not to discount too quickly a local murderer.

. . .

Pippen summed up her preliminary exam for Cy. Death had occurred perhaps six to eight hours ago. It was now ten in the morning.

"Between two and four?"

"You work that out right in your head?" But she smiled prettily. Cy had been sure his attraction for her would diminish when she married four months ago, but she seemed to have passed into another and riper phase.

"Weapon, pickax."

"What is a pickax?"

"You know what a toothpick is?"

"Yes."

"They have nothing to do with one another."

She showed the tip of her tongue. "Ostensible weapon, pickax."

"Ostensible."

"Apparent, seeming."

"Why not just murder weapon?"

"Because I want to do an autopsy before I say that."

"Any other marks on the body?"

"I haven't undressed him yet."

"Be careful, he's a priest."

"Now I'll know for sure."

"What?"

"Whether they make them all sopranos."

"Let me know."

"You should already know. You're Catholic."

"I promised not to tell," Cy said in a falsetto voice. She punched him, tossed her ponytail, and went off to her car.

. . .

"That guy Sullivan who's staying in the lodge?" Phil said. "What do you make of him?"

"He says he's on retreat," Horvath said.

"He seems familiar."

"His face. You saw it on the printouts Edna Hospers's son gave you."

Eureka. The light bulb went on over Phil's head. "Was his name Sullivan?"

"I don't think so. Hogan, Horan . . ."

"Morgan."

"He's making a retreat as Mr. Sullivan."

"Go get him, Cy. I want to talk to him again."

But Sullivan/Morgan/whoever was not in the lodge. Cy went upstairs to the third floor and found the room the man must have been staying in. The bed had been slept in, but there were no articles in the bathroom and no luggage anywhere. He seemed to have gone on another retreat.

Lord, how they have increased who trouble me.

—*Psalm 3*

Father Dowling breathed a prayer for the murdered priest and then his thoughts turned to Father Boniface. What a blow to suffer after recent events. The community had been presented as moribund but tenaciously clinging to its ill-gotten property, and now a murder on the grounds, the victim one of the priests! The man who had spoken in such derogatory tones of young Corbett's claim to the land on which his grandfather's mansion and lodge house still stood. Nathaniel had undercut the reporter's dog-in-the-manger theme by suggesting that the community was thinking of discussing the future use of the land with Lars Anderson, a possibility portrayed as vaguely philanthropic.

Father Boniface had lived into the time when he became the superior almost by default. He was not the youngest but at least the healthiest of the dwindling band. What initially seemed a small ray of hope, Nathaniel's petition for return to the community, had developed into something unexpected. One would have thought that a man who was drawn back to the community he had deserted for the fleshpots of California would be a fanatic defender of the status quo, wanting everything as it had been when he left. But it had not been so with Nathaniel.

Roger Dowling recalled his few encounters with the prodigal returned when he was making his retreat at Marygrove. How he wished now that he had spoken with him more. There had been a book called *Shepherds in the Mist* that had been passed around the seminary when Roger Dowling was a student, the account of a man who had left the priesthood and married and whose wife had died. Now repentant, he told his story as a cautionary tale. Seminarians had read it with a kind of dread. In those days, departures from the priesthood were as rare as Jesuit cardinals. The account E. Boyd Barrett gave of his life was far from the prospect of liberation and insouciance that had led to the flood of laicizations after the Council. The stigma attached to one who defected from Holy Orders was far more indelible than that of an unfaithful spouse. Before his deacon year, the last before ordination to the priesthood, Roger Dowling had stopped at the Trappist abbey New Mount Mellary in Iowa. In those days, only the guest master, Father Louis, could speak. Outside of choir, the monks communicated by means of their own Trappist sign language developed over the centuries. There was another guest at the time, a moody man in black but wearing brown loafers seen from time to time on the paths but who otherwise kept to himself. Young Roger Dowling assumed he was a priest on retreat. At the suggestion, Father Joachim's mouth widened and great teeth appeared as he smiled. He shook his head. "He was naughty. His bishop sent him here to do penance."

"For how long?"

"His bishop will tell him when it has been long enough."

If the past was too harsh, the present seemed to waive all responsibility for what one had done. Roger Dowling had felt this on the marriage tribunal, a man or woman absolving themselves of the past with the suggestion that their real self had not been involved in their deeds. What would Augustine have done with this variation on Manichaeanism?

He shook off these thoughts. If he wasn't careful, he would become a theologian. If such a fate ever overtook him, he would need both the vivid portraits of Dante and the chaste arguments of Aquinas, the one inadequate without the other.

The voice of Captain Keegan was heard in the kitchen, but it was ten minutes before he could get past Marie who wanted to hear all about the murder. She came on with Phil to the study, her eyes popping out of her head.

"Boniface called," he said in answer to Phil's question whether he had heard.

"And you didn't tell me?" Marie looked utterly betrayed.

"I have been sitting here being moody."

"Remember the Bible college?" Phil said irrelevantly.

"Tell us," Marie urged. "Tell us everything."

"Let me have some of that coffee."

"Have you had breakfast?" Marie asked.

"What have you got?"

"Some glazed doughnuts?" She avoided the pastor's eyes. Marie had no willpower when it came to glazed doughnuts and had made a solemn promise never to bring them into the rectory again, adding untruth to intemperance.

"Two," Phil said.

"Don't speak until I'm back." And Marie flew down the hall to the kitchen.

The two men looked at one another and silently agreed that everything must wait on Marie's return. And then she was back with a plateful of doughnuts. She took one for herself. This was an emergency.

Phil put the scene vividly before their eyes, the grotto, the kneeling figure, the pickax plunged into his back.

"Was he kneeling when he was struck?"

"That's the assumption." But Phil acknowledged that he might have fallen onto his knees as the result of the blow.

"Fallen onto a prie-dieu? Bosh." Marie licked her fingers. "He was praying."

"Like Hamlet's uncle? Let's hope his words flew up."

The other two ignored the pastor's enigmatic remark.

"The fellow in charge of the grounds, Andrew George, found the body when he was on the way to the greenhouse about seven and sounded the alarm. Meaning he called Father Boniface."

"The poor man!" Marie said, her words encompassing the victim and the superior of the Athanasians.

"Pippen puts the time of death at about two in the morning."

"And the pickax as the cause of death?"

Marie looked at Father Dowling impatiently. "Who would have done such a thing?"

"Any number of people," Phil said with his mouth full. "A funny thing. Remember that guy Stanley Morgan? He's out there making a retreat."

Marie did not find this surprising. It fitted her picture of the man perfectly. "He was looking for a priest."

"Yes. For Father Nathaniel."

Marie stayed another ten minutes and then went off to pass on what she had heard to Edna, to various friends, to all the ships at sea.

"You said lots of people might have done it, Phil."

"The guy has been making himself universally troublesome since he came back. And then what he said to the reporter . . . Lord, these things are sticky."

"Better wash your hands."

While he was gone, Father Dowling filled and lit his pipe. Smoke rose wraithlike from the bowl and he sent a ring of uninhaled smoke sailing across his desk. In the doorway, Phil stopped and watched the smoke ring rise and slowly disintegrate. "I could never do that."

"You talked to Father Boniface, I'm sure."

"As Marie said, the poor man. I found him in the chapel, just sitting there, stunned."

Mystified silence is a form of prayer. Father Dowling found himself dreading and anticipating his meeting with Boniface. Just in the short time since he had been there on retreat, poor Boniface had been put through a series of agonizing events. The disruptive activities of Nathaniel, the series of articles in the *Tribune*, and now a murder on the grounds. It might seem the dramatic climax to the long years of attrition when the life Boniface had lived, the setting in which he had done so, had imperceptibly altered until only faith could underwrite the hope that better days were ahead and the downward spiral could be arrested. Would the Athanasians ever recover from the murder of Nathaniel?

"A funny thing about Morgan. He was there under the name Sullivan."

"His meeting with Nathaniel must have been a dramatic confrontation."

"Boniface wasn't sure they had met or talked."

"How would that be possible?"

"Morgan wasn't staying with the community. Boniface put him up in the lodge, on the third floor, with the Georges. Mrs. George is out of town."

"You talked to Morgan?"

"He'd been there. But apparently he took a powder."

The search for the mysterious Californian had begun at once. Phil seemed inclined to think that Morgan was the killer.

"Think of it, Roger. He spends time in prison for something he thinks Nathaniel was responsible for. Time during which he nurses the grudge, vows to get even. As soon as he's out, he heads to the place the man he knew as Richards had mentioned. He shows up here, somehow he connects Nathaniel and the Athanasians . . ."

"And decides to make a retreat at Marygrove under an assumed name."

Phil nodded as if this bore out his theory.

3

In the Lord I put my trust.

　　　—Psalm 11

There was a police barrier at the entrance of the grounds, and on the country road long lines of cars went slowly by in each direction, curious passengers staring at the barricade. The cop put up a hand when Father Dowling pulled in, then saw his collar and came around to the driver's side.

"Father Dowling of St. Hilary's. Father Boniface is expecting me."

"Righto, Father," he said, giving a salute and then moving the sawhorse aside so Father Dowling could drive past.

"Thanks, Officer. You're drawing quite a crowd."

The cop nodded. "It's been like that ever since I was posted here. They'd see more watching television."

"It wouldn't be the same."

"I guess you're right, Father."

Father Dowling did not share the cop's attitude toward the curious. It was human, all too human, to draw near to the tragedy that does not wound, other people's troubles. But how easily they could be our own.

The media had indeed been admitted, and now, hours afterward, teams of cameramen and reporters were beaming accounts back to their studios. Not just the local channels; the major Chicago stations were represented, as well as those of surrounding communities. Here were the surrogates of the curious who were driving slowly past the entrance of Marygove. The dimensions of the scandal were impossible to ignore. What strange notions of Catholicism and the Church would be fed by the news of a priest found axed to death while at prayer. Doubtless Nathaniel's colorful history away from his community would come to light.

Boniface was not in his office where they had agreed to meet, and no wonder. Cameras were filming everywhere and watchful men and women with notebooks hovered. When they saw Father Dowling, they rushed toward him, cameras pointing, pencils poised.

"Tetzel, Father Dowling. From the *Tribune*. I recognize you."

Questions were shouted. Who was he? Tetzel turned and gave them his name. Why was he here? Who had sent him, the cardinal? Ye gods. How had Boniface managed to escape? He tried to answer without saying anything, words that would be played back again and again on news reports in the region. He was asked who he thought had killed the priest, he was asked what his connection with the Athanasians was, he felt caught in a net from which there was no escape when a burly figure pushed his way through the mob.

"Cy," Father Dowling said with relief.

Cy took his arm. "I'll get you out of here. He's in the chapel."

And Cy waded through the chattering media as once he had gone through opposing defensive teams. He might not even have heard the questions shouted at him, the protests, reminders of the people's right to know. And then they were through a door, Cy closing it decisively.

"They're not supposed to be in the building. They're everywhere else, like locusts."

In the chapel, Boniface sat in his choir stall as Phil had described him earlier. Father Dowling sat down beside him and put a hand on the old priest's arm. Boniface turned.

"I should have warned you not to come."

"Nonsense."

Boniface was clearly glad to see him. The other Athanasians were safe in their rooms in the mansion. Boniface stood, then knelt, and Father Dowling followed suit. After a moment, they rose and went through the chapel and onto a path blessedly free from the representatives of the media. The rustle of leaves in the trees over their heads, the swoop and songs of birds, a general buzz of insects in the hot summer air made the place seem as peaceful as it had when Father Dowling had been making his retreat some weeks before.

"I hold myself responsible, Father," Boniface said. "Last night in the common room, I exposed Nathaniel's plan, or at least what seemed a relevant part of it."

"What did he say?"

"I told them what you said about the alienation of Church property. Of course, none of them had dreamt for a minute of profiting personally from what Nathaniel was advocating."

"Did Nathaniel admit his aim?"

"In a sense. He went away when it was clear he had lost his following."

"So why do you feel responsible for what happened?"

Boniface looked at him with a bottomless dread in his clear eyes. Did the old man think one of his conferes had killed Nathaniel?

"The police think it was the man who called himself Sullivan," Boniface answered.

"Morgan. Nathaniel had been responsible for his spending time in a California prison."

"A strong motive."

"Perhaps."

"You doubt it, Father?"

But all Boniface's certainties and doubts were scrambled now. Or perhaps the certainties about the range of human weakness he had learned as a priest overcame any doubt that an Athanasian had murdered Nathaniel.

"I could have done it myself, Father Dowling. How I had come to hate that man and his return and what he was doing here. Hate. It was a new experience for me, as if God were showing me that any one of us is capable of any sin."

The old man had to talk, to say things he could not have said to the other priests. The roles that had been theirs when Father Dowling was on retreat seemed reversed. They came to the grotto and the fluttering yellow tapes that marked off the site where Nathaniel had been killed.

"When George called me, I came immediately. I gave him conditional absolution."

"And felt no hatred."

"I was acting as a priest."

"And when have you not, Father Boniface?"

Tears stood in the old priest's eyes. "I know I want you to give me absolution."

Father Dowling did so, with the statue of the Blessed Virgin looking down on them, the Mother of Mercy. Whatever dark thoughts Boniface might have had toward Nathaniel, they were the extent of the burden on his soul. He would not have asked for absolution on the basis of what he had already told Father Dowling if that were not so.

"I told you that the police suspect Morgan. Who has now disappeared."

"I did not believe him when he told me why he was here. The first time. Later he came to me and told me the truth."

"About Nathaniel?"

"Yes."

"He was bitter?"

"Of course. He was driven by the desire for revenge. But he said he did not know how he would exact it."

"Perhaps he found the way."

"Perhaps."

"The police will want to know what he told you."

"And I will tell them."

They walked on to the lodge where they came upon Michael George. He stopped and started to turn away, but Father Dowling called to him. "I want to speak to this young man, Father Boniface."

"Then I will leave you."

"Boniface, if you would like to come stay at St. Hilary's . . ."

"And leave my brothers? Thank you, Father, but there is no place where I can hide."

And Father Boniface went off in the direction of the mansion. Father Dowling turned to Michael George.

"When did you learn that your houseguest had left?"

"My father told me."

"Michael, if his room was on the third floor, you must have heard if he went out during the night."

"But I didn't."

Father Dowling told Michael something about the man who had been staying in the lodge with his father and himself. "His name wasn't Sullivan. He is a man named Stanley Morgan who was in some kind of business with Nathaniel in California. Morgan came here looking for Nathaniel."

"Well, he found him."

"You didn't like Sullivan."

"He was too smooth. And he flirted with Rita. In Spanish."

"I talked to your father. He came to see me."

"Yes."

"You are in a dilemma, Michael. And I don't know what the solution is."

"Wouldn't you want me to become a Catholic?"

"It is not something you can pretend."

"I want us to be married, as soon as possible."

It seemed odd, with death in the air, to hear this confession of desperate love. "Bring her to me, Michael. What you say of her, what her father says of her, makes me want to meet her."

"She is an angel."

He was about to say that would be an impediment to marriage, but he sensed that on this matter, and perhaps all others, Michael had no sense of humor. The first ardor of love, like all first ardors, cools with time, and if Michael abandoned his family faith to marry Rita, with the passage of the years this could become a barrier between them.

"Bring her to St. Hilary's. Call before, if you like, but I am usually there."

Michael put out his hand and Father Dowling shook it. "I have to help my father."

Watching him go, Father Dowling thought again of Romeo and Juliet. Not a very happy outcome to that romantic dilemma. This place was suddenly Shakespearean, with Nathaniel killed at his prayers, perhaps, and with all his sins still on his soul. *My words fly up, my thoughts remain below. Words without thought never to heaven go.*

He ran into Cy Horvath again as he was going to his car. Dr. Pippen the assistant coroner was with him. She was the kind of self-assured, successful woman who is often uneasy in the presence of priests. But Cy's easy manner made her more comfortable.

"Interesting wrinkle, Father. You know the body was found at the grotto."

"Kneeling."

"With an ax buried in his back. The question becomes, when was it buried there."

Dr. Pippen did not wince at this manner of speaking of the deceased, but then she was a coroner.

"When I examined the body, I noticed that the area around that . . . kneeler, do you call it? Well, it looked swept. But farther along the path to the maintenance shed, there were traces of blood. And in the maintenance shed, things looked all scrubbed up, and even repainted."

Cy listened to Pippen talk as if to a prize student reciting.

"She's in the wrong line, Father. She should be a detective."

"You couldn't afford me."

"You're suggesting that he was not killed where he was found?"

Pippen nodded and her ponytail bounced.

"Do you want me to run interference for you again, Father?"

"Are you going that way?"

"We'll drive you around," Dr. Pippen said when she learned where his car was parked.

The reporters were still swarming as Pippen drove past them. Eager faces peered at them, as if wondering whether a shouted question might get a printable answer. But when they saw the impassive face of Lieutenant Horvath in the passenger seat, such wild hopes died.

Delivered safely to his own car, and heading down the drive to the barricaded entrance to the grounds, Father Dowling thought that Dr. Pippen had come up with an interesting wrinkle indeed. If Nathaniel had been attacked in the maintenance shed, and then somehow managed to drag himself to the grotto and die upon his knees, the fact that the body was found there had far deeper significance. If he had been struck with all his sins upon his soul, he would have arrived penitent and, one hoped, forgiven at the grotto.

And, of course, this possibility had significance for discovering who had killed Father Nathaniel.

I am a stranger in the earth.

—Psalm 119

Edna Hospers first heard the amazing news from Marie Murkin, who telephoned all excited and became more excited when it was clear that she was the first to tell Edna. A priest murdered! What a dreadful thing, sacrilege added to murder.

"Who on earth?"

"Phil Keegan has some silly notion it was Stanley Morgan."

"Hadn't he left town?"

"Apparently he was making a retreat at the Athanasians. He was there when it happened, so of course the police point the finger at the stranger."

Marie could not go on, she had other calls to make. Abruptly she hung up and Edna sat pondering what she had just heard. Since talking to Father Dowling about Stanley Morgan, and with more reflection, Edna was less ready to see what she had done as folly. She had had dinner with the man, true, an all-but-perfect stranger, but it had seemed quite natural to accept when he asked her. And the trip to Wrigley Field had been less than a success because the kids hadn't cared for Stanley Morgan, except Eric, of course, and then he had come up with all that information on the Internet. Edna was not inclined to condemn someone just because he had spent some time in prison. Her own husband was in prison for a far more serious crime and she had remained faithful and true to him over the years. She told herself that Earl would understand her having dinner with Stanley Morgan. Not that she intended to put that to the test and tell him. On the whole, she found that she no longer regretted responding to Stanley Morgan. Of course, now all that was in the past, so it was safe to think differently about it.

There was a tap on the door and she called, "Come in." When she turned in her chair there was Stanley Morgan standing in the doorway, a winning smile on his face.

"Surprise."

"Stanley!" He closed the door behind him but remained where he was.

"Have you heard?"

She wanted to shake her head, say no, lie, but her reaction had already given him the answer to his question.

"I didn't do it. They're going to think I did. It will look as if I did. But, Edna, you have to believe me."

He came and took a chair, facing her across the desk. His pleading look was that of a little boy wanting his mother's trust.

"Stanley, if you didn't do it, then . . ."

"It doesn't work like that, Edna. I found that out once the hard way. It's why I wanted to know you, and your family."

"What do you mean?"

"Marie Murkin told me."

"Told you what?"

"About your husband."

"She just told you that?"

"It came out as we were talking."

"I'll bet it did."

"Thank God it did. Edna, I didn't have anyone waiting for me when I got out. No visitors, either, not that I wanted any. But I saw what it was like for the wives and relatives who visited. They were being punished, too, in their own way, but they hadn't done anything."

"So you pitied me?"

"Would that be so awful?"

Despite herself, she felt a wave of tenderness toward him. His manner was not that of the man who had taken her to dinner or taken them all to the ball game. Again she had the sense of him as a boy, allowing her to think of her own feelings as maternal.

"Tell me what happened out there."

He realized that the conversation had taken a decisive turn in his favor. "Don't you wonder what I was doing there?"

"You were on retreat."

"How did you know that?"

"Where did you get all your information about me?"

"Mrs. Murkin?"

Edna nodded. "Father Dowling is very close to two men in the detective division and what he learns, Marie learns."

"I told Father Boniface that I wanted to make a retreat. What I really wanted was to confront Richards and scare him into compensating me for what I had been through."

"What did he say?"

"I never got to talk with him. They put me up in the lodge, with the groundskeeper and his family. Richards was dodging me, of course, but I was there and I could be patient. Too patient. I waited too long."

"But why would anyone suspect you unless Richards—that's Father Nathaniel, isn't it?"

"Yes. Richard Krause, Nathaniel Richards, Father Nathaniel."

"Unless he told someone why you were there, who would know?"

"Father Boniface. I went back and told him why I was there."

"To have it out with one of the priests?"

"Edna, do I look like a violent man? I wanted him to squirm, I wanted him to fear I would blow the whistle on him. The fact is, I think he was planning to plunder the Order. You've heard of all the the pressure for them to sell?"

She believed him. But at the same time she doubted that the police would. Or maybe anyone else. He had come to Fox River in search of the man who had been killed. He had asked about him hither and yon, at the rectory, for example. Marie had said something that turned his mind to the Athanasians—Father Dowling was then on retreat there, a wild hunch, and it had been inspired. He presented himself there as a retreatant. That put him on the ground with what the police would think of as his prey. As he described the estate, the maintenance shed was between the lodge and the mansion. It would be assumed that he had arranged a meeting with Nathaniel and been waiting for him with an ax.

"To kill the golden goose? Edna, I was there to get back money he had stolen so I could rebuild my life."

There was no way the police would believe him. But if he hadn't killed Nathaniel, someone else had, and when the police found the murderer, Stanley Morgan would be safe. The problem with that was, if they couldn't find Stanley, they wouldn't be looking for anyone else. It was a dilemma.

"Stanley, if you run, they will find you."

"But if I don't run?"

"What do you mean?"

He sat back, looked around, extended his arms. "Isn't there somewhere in this building I could stay?"

"You want me to hide you?"

"I want to hide myself."

"It comes to the same thing."

"Look, I've been in this building before. I didn't have to talk to you. I would have found somewhere in the building . . ."

There were several places in the old school he could hide without any fear of being found. Edna thought of the nurse's office on the third floor, a suite of rooms, and no one ever went up to the third floor, it was too much of a climb for the seniors who spent the day here. She realized that she was beginning to conspire with him, doing just what he had hoped she would do. She tried to shake away the compassion she felt. It was a doomed hope that he could just stay out of sight long enough for the murderer to be found. But what if he was the murderer? She was too susceptible to him, she knew that. She wanted to believe him. He had appealed to her at her weakest point, the long trial she had undergone because Earl was in Joliet. But all she had to do was imagine what Marie Murkin would make of her agreeing to let Stanley Morgan hide in the school. She tried not to think of Father Dowling's reaction, but it would certainly be more understanding than Marie Murkin's. She was at a crossroads and she knew it. Reasons for refusing piled up in her mind, her kids, the seniors downstairs. She could lose this job. She could be arrested herself, for harboring a fugitive. The whole project was insane. But he had come to her as to his only hope.

"Where are your things?"

"Outside your door."

"Good Lord. Come on."

She got up and hurried to the door, but he was there first to open it for her. There was a garment bag and briefcase in the hall. He picked them up and she headed for the stairs with Stanley close behind her. On the third floor, in a corner farthest from the rectory, was what had been the office of the school nurse. The door was unlocked. When he had gone past her into the office, Edna pulled the door shut and sighed. He dropped his garment bag and put the briefcase on the desk, looking around. In the inner room was a cot where ailing students once had lain. There was a small bathroom.

"It's a little apartment," he said.

She nodded. They were now partners in this completely foolish enterprise. She was acting against reason, overriding every argument, behaving like a woman. Like a mother, she amended. This was an entirely maternal move. He took her hand.

"I'll never forget this."

"It's not going to work."

"Just let me give it a chance."

She had already done that. She took her hand from his. "Where is your car?"

"It was a rental. I left it at Marygrove."

"How did you get here?"

"The bus."

Her heart sank. If he had abandoned his car, they would assume he had not gone far. With the car, he could have gone to O'Hare and got a flight out of town, if he could have done it before they alerted security at the airport. He looked almost carefree, now that he had a refuge, and her heart went out to him. He was doomed to be found. There was no way he could hide here for the time necessary for the attention of the police to turn elsewhere. His absence would shout his guilt.

"Stanley, you have to think of another way. You can stay here for now, but you have to think of something else."

"Edna, if there had been something else, I wouldn't have come to you."

"We'll both think about it."

He reached for her hand again, but she turned and opened the door, put a finger to her lips, slipped out, and closed the door on his vulnerable little-boy smile.

The enemy shall not outwit him, nor the son of wickedness afflict him.

—*Psalm 89*

It had taken a murder to do it, but Tuttle and Peanuts Pianone the improbable cop were buddies again. On the day of the murder, as soon as the mornings news infiltrated his groggy mind, Tuttle picked up the phone and called Peanuts. No answer. He called downtown. After five minutes, Peanuts came to the phone.

"Pick me up right away, Peanuts. We've got work to do."

"She going to let you out?"

"Forget about Hazel. Get over here. I'll explain over breakfast at McDonald's."

An army might move on its stomach, but Peanuts preferred to be immobile while he attended to his. Food delivered to a location was one thing, but eating in a moving vehicle was against something deep in Peanuts's character. Fast food eaten slowly was not a sacrilege. But fast food eaten fast while moving at a fast clip— here was sin indeed. So it was that Tuttle and his old friend took their trays to a corner booth where the little plainclothes cop fell to. He was a cop because of the Pianone connection and he was plainclothes lest the public realize he was a cop. The demands on Peanuts were minimal, something he would have welcomed if it had not finally dawned on him that he had remained on the bottom rung while newcomers had climbed the ladder of success. He was particularly rankled by the esteem in which Agnes Lamb was held—black and a woman, she activated both his racist and chauvinist glands.

"We got to go out to the Athanasians, Peanuts."

Small, uncomprehending eyes lifted to Tuttle.

"The murder of the priest."

It was clear that Peanuts knew nothing about it. "I'll explain on the way."

Peanuts was driving an unmarked car, but the cop at the barricaded gate knew a police car when he saw it. He broke into a big grin at the sight of Peanuts.

"Gonna solve the crime, Peanuts?"

"Shove it."

The sawhorse was moved aside, and they drove in, through the trees, past the vast expanse of lawn, toward chaos. Tuttle could see the television trucks, with their aerials raised, he saw the milling crowd of reporters, his pulse stirred at the promise of involvement. Somehow his client's interests were at issue here and he meant to represent Leo Corbett beyond the call of duty. He hoped Tetzel was here, hangover or not. The series of articles had been a stroke of genius and Tuttle had another stroke when he heard the morning news. Scandal at the Athanasians. A priest found dead at the grotto. All this was good news for Leo Corbett, Tuttle was sure of it, though he could not have explained why. Fortunately Peanuts was not motivated by explanations. All he knew was that Tuttle was defying Hazel Barnes and they were a team again. Peanuts nearly ran down a televison crew, the cameraman being pulled out of danger before being added to the casualty list. Curses floated after them.

"Keep on this road," Tuttle said.

The scattering media people had revealed a road running through the divided Red Sea Peanuts made of them. They rounded the building and saw the squad cars, the coroner's vehicle, cops everywhere. Peanuts pulled onto the lawn and parked. Tuttle was out of the car before the engine stopped. He had spotted Cy Horvath.

"What the hell are you doing here, Tuttle?" the lieutenant asked.

"Peanuts brought me."

Horvath turned and saw the squat, bloated figure of Peanuts approaching. He shook his head. "The first team has arrived."

"What's going on, Horvath?"

"Ask Peanuts."

Horvath muscled his way through a band of reporters who had been admitted to represent their fellows out front. Tetzel was among them, looking like the wrath of God. He grunted when Tuttle greeted him, glanced at Peanuts, and then took a deep breath, but nothing short of Alka-Selzter would help. Fortunately, Tuttle had some. He shook out two tablets into the reporter's hand.

"I need water."

"Let's find some."

They circled the taped-off area in front of the grotto, Tuttle lifting his tweed hat in deference to the Virgin, Peanuts tracing a cross over his breast.

"What's that building?"

"Where we're going. The lodge. It's where the groundskeeper lives."

Tetzel just opened the door and went into the kitchen. He headed for the sink, picked up a glass, filled it with water, and dropped in the tablets. Fizzing began. Relief was just a swallow away. He upended the glass, swallowing the contents in two gulps, then stood with closed eyes, waiting for the pain to stop. A man came down the stairs and stopped when he saw them, then passed quickly through the kitchen and outside. Tuttle was trying to place the man. His face had been familiar, but he couldn't remember why.

Restored, Tetzel filled Tuttle in on what had happened. They left the kitchen and wandered around, Peanuts ever at Tuttle's side, picking up information here and there. They listened to Pippen talk to the reporters but she didn't have many details. The priest had died about two in the morning, death was caused by an ax.

"You through here, Doctor?"

"Not yet."

The body was taken off downtown in the 911 ambulance. Tuttle broke away from Tetzel and the other news hawks and started up the path that led to the chapel.

"Where we going?"

"To make a visit."

He pulled open the great doors and they stepped into the cool almost darkness. Peanuts dunked his hand up to the knuckles in the holy water and made another cross on himself. Tuttle imitated him. When in Rome. As his eyes became accustomed to the dimness, he saw two figures seated side by side in a stall on the raised level where the altar stood. He made out the distinctive profile of Father Dowling. Why should he be surprised to see a priest in church? Because Dowling belonged at St. Hilary's. What was he doing here? After a time, Dowling and the other man rose, knelt, and then got to their feet. The other man was a priest, too, wearing a robe. They came down from the sanctuary, turned and genuflected, and then left by a side door.

"Father Dowling," Tuttle said.

"Who's the other guy?"

"Must be a local."

Outside again, they found a bench under a great oak and sat there, leaves murmuring above them, birds twittering. Peanuts looked warily upward. But finally the attraction of immobility exerted itself and he relaxed. Tuttle wanted to think.

His thoughts were on his client, Leo Corbett. His first reaction was that what had happened here was good news for Leo, and now he was sure of it. Tetzel's last article had done a real job on the Athanasians who were down to a handful and counting. This murder would put a nail in their coffin. Tuttle saw smooth sailing for Leo's claim on the property. The Athanasians were pretty discredited now. No wonder the priest with Father Dowling had walked as if he were carrying a great burden.

Tuttle thought of Hazel, too, and found himself wondering how he would tell her about all this. Here was proof that his friendship with Peanuts was indispensable. He could never have gotten on the grounds if Peanuts hadn't driven them past those barricades. Oh, there were probably ways to get in apart from the main gate, but if the main entrance was barricaded chances were other entries were, too. Tuttle imagined himself trying to climb the fence. No way. Peanuts had been his open sesame, no doubt of that. And Hazel would have to be impressed by all the inside dope he had gotten.

He hung around Marygrove most of the morning. When he learned that the police were looking for a man who had been staying in the lodge, Stanley Morgan, Tuttle knew that had to be the guy who had hurried through the lodge kitchen when Tetzel was taking his Alka-Seltzer.

You have set our iniquities before You, our secret sins.

—Psalm 90

Charlotte Priebe had fulfilled her mission and brought Leo Corbett to Lars Anderson. The three of them had sat in the great man's office and Leo's prospects had been explained to him.

"What if I don't want to sell?"

"Because you want to live in the house your grandfather built?" Anderson said understandingly. "Don't worry. That will be preserved. You will have the house, the lodge, lots of land. And a ton of money from selling the rest."

Leo tried to look skeptical, but Charlotte knew he was hooked. Because he was hooked on her. Suddenly the axioms of the market economy dawned on her and she wondered why she was delivering this sacrificial lamb over to Lars Anderson with only the prospect of an avuncular nod of gratitude and a bonus to boot. But what bonus could compete with what Leo stood to make if his claim against his grandfather's estate was recognized?

"It's in your self-interest," she explained to Leo, crossing her legs and watching his eyes cross in response. She looked significantly at Lars Anderson. "Maybe I should explain it to Leo, without pressure, setting out the advantages."

Lars, the old devil, took the bait and she led Leo off to the officers' dining room.

"What an interesting life you've led," she said later, when they were settled in a little bar on State, hors d'oeuvres and a bottle of Peruvian red ordered.

He had led an interesting life, one reversal after another. She commiserated with him as he told of his geological father and autistic mother. Her own parents had been consigned to the dustbin of history, as someone had once called it. Leo was delightfully literate, his academic failures not having interfered with his education. They were on Proust when their salmon came, with new asparagus and a white wine suitable for the main course. The Peruvian red remained on the table. Leo had swilled that as if its purpose was to slake one's thirst rather than excite the palate. Sitting across from her, calf-eyed, responsive, Charlotte saw him as a huge mound of clay for her to mold.

"I myself come from a humble family."

"Better than a humbling one."

"And now you have been awarded your grandfather's charter membership at the country club."

"Do you golf?"

"You could teach me."

Midafternoon found them at the practice range, Leo full of theory and hands-on instruction. She backed into him as he positioned her hands on the club. His breath was hot and eager in her ear. Would he believe that she was a vestal virgin? Doubtless he was equally inexperienced. Mrs. Leo Corbett. She tried it out in her mind, but what she saw was the map in Lars's office, with the huge unbuilt-upon expanse that had been Maurice Corbett's seigneurial domain. They would keep the original estate and sell off the rest to Lars and live as high on the hog as one could get.

"Why don't we go to my place?"

"I certainly wouldn't want you to see mine."

Of course, she knew where he lived. On the drive to her condo on the North Shore he vented his resentment against fate and she gave ear as only a designing woman can.

"I blame my father as much as my grandfather," he said.

"There is plenty of blame to go around. Why did you choose Tuttle as your lawyer?"

"What does 'choose' mean when you have only one possibility?"

"Leo, we could have our pick of lawyers."

The significance of the third-person plural did not escape him. She bumped against him as they crossed the parking garage to the elevator. She almost felt sorry for him.

The rites of initiation are seldom unique. In her apartment, she plied Leo with more drink, later she went into her bedroom and disencumbered herself of her street clothes. She was wearing a black peignoir when she called to him.

"Leo, could you come in here?"

She had pulled the blinds but only to a point where a sufficiency of light came through. He stood in the doorway, unable to see clearly at first. When he could, she undid her peignoir and let it slip to the floor. There was an agonizing moment when she feared he would bolt for the door. Then he lunged for her. Like an operation under sedation, it seemed over before it began.

Post coitum, business. She explained to him, keeping any touch of treachery from her voice, that she did not want to see

Lars Anderson take advantage of him. She ran her fingers over his hairless chest. "Leo, you are in the driver's seat."

And barely awake. She slid down in the bed, and brought his sleepy head to her bosom and rocked him gently. She was confident now that she could carry her point with Leo Corbett.

He slept for three hours. When he awoke, the blinds were opened, she was dressed and had coffee on. In the interval, she had thought of herself in bed with Leo and tried to discern some fundamental attitude toward what she had done. She had acted out of blatant self-interest, but Leo was so naive she felt the need to look after him. The carnal solace she had given him, the first gift of herself, in retrospect no longer seemed a mere investment. Charlotte was now of a mind that she could truly like Leo. But the first order of business was legal representation.

"Tuttle is a clown, Leo. We are up against Amos Cadbury, the best there is in Fox River. And as the lawyer who drew up the deed of transfer of the estate, and wrote your grandfather's will, he is deeply involved in the outcome. He will fight to the death to sustain your grandfather's will."

Leo followed this docilely. She was the teacher, he was the student. Her few years with Lars Anderson had taught her much about the way things were done in the real world.

"So what do we do?"

She could have hugged him for that "we," and she did. "I could talk to Amos Cadbury."

"Are you a lawyer?"

"As your friend and advisor."

"What about Anderson?"

"What about him?"

In the ensuing silence, she could almost hear the gears of his mind turn.

"It's just you and me?"

"If that's what you want."

She turned into his arms and lifted her face. Anderson was ruthless, but there were weapons he did not possess.

"So what would you say to Cadbury?"

"No lawyer wants to go to court. What we want is a compromise."

Leo bristled. "He won't. Tuttle said . . ."

"Forget Tuttle." She ran a finger along his pouting lower lip. "I don't say that Cadbury would be immediately forthcoming. The idea has to be put into his mind first. Men like to decide for themselves." A mistake, that, but he seemed not to notice. She outlined for him the approach she would take with Cadbury. If that didn't work, they would see about lawyers.

"I'll have to tell Tuttle."

"Would it be easier if I did?"

"Would you?"

"If you want."

So that was settled. She liked his loyalty to Tuttle. Maybe she should have been less ruthless about dumping the clownish lawyer. She did not want Leo's sense of loyalty to be attenuated.

"Maybe we can keep Tuttle on, in some capacity."

Leo liked that.

"After all, he took you on when others might not have."

"I met him in the courthouse."

"I'll call at his office."

He squeezed her. She squeezed back. She was beginning to like Leo. And it didn't hurt to imagine Lars Anderson's reaction when he realized he would have to deal with his former administrative assistant in the matter of the Corbett estate.

"I should get home."

"Leo, I wanted to cook for you."

"I live on pasta and microwave dinners."

"Not anymore."

He saw the wisdom of staying the night with her. The following day, she suggested he move in. Why should they keep two places? It was all so easy that again she felt pity for Leo, but what ground was there for pity if they were going to be a team?

"I'm so glad I never married," she whispered later that night, snuggled up with Leo in her no longer virginal bed.

"Me, too."

In the morning, she left him there and in her car called Lars on her cell phone.

"Everything's going according to plan," she said.

"What's the plan?"

She giggled for an answer, hung up, and continued on her way to Tuttle's office. Leo had said the little lawyer had met with Cadbury, and Charlotte wanted to be briefed on that. But second thoughts arrived. Tuttle was already out of the picture, even if neither he nor Leo realized it. Coolness is all, as Shakespeare did not say. She drove instead to the office where she administratively assisted the great Lars Anderson.

"I'd like to see the Corbett boy again, Charlotte."

The boy had become a man since Lars had last seen him and she had become a woman. It was surprising how little difference it seemed to make, one more move in a game that was slowly revealing itself. An hour later, she called Amos Cadbury's office and asked to see him the following day.

"And who should I say wishes to see him."

She repeated her name, then added, "I am Lars Anderson's administrative assistant."

A pause while this registered. "Would two this afternoon be convenient?"

"Perfectly. Thank you."

She would jettison Tuttle only after she talked with Cadbury.

The Lord knows the thoughts of man, that they are futile.

—Psalm 94

Cy Horvath went out to St. Hilary's to talk with Edna Hospers about the flown Stanley Morgan when he remembered that Morgan had taken Edna and her kids to a Cubs game. But he was intercepted on the walk by Marie Murkin when he was on his way from his car to the school.

"Lieutenant Horvath, is it true that you suspect Stanley Morgan of this dreadful murder of Father Nathaniel?"

"Have you seen him?"

"What a question."

"He seems to have run away."

"Who can blame him? Innocence didn't save him before."

"He made quite an impression on you."

"I pride myself on being a judge of character, Cyril Horvath."

"You seem to have a bad judgment of mine."

"Only as a policeman."

"Have you any idea where he might have gone? As a judge of character?"

She adopted a tragic look and shook her head. "I wish you would forget about him and start looking for the real murderer."

"Any ideas?"

"I could recite several plausible names. Father Nathaniel had a knack for antagonizing everyone."

"But as you know, Morgan says he went to jail because of Nathaniel."

She let him go then. Surely Father Dowling would not question the reasonableness of wanting to find Stanley Morgan and ask him a few questions. But as he continued to the school, he wondered if Edna Hospers would also have taken the part of the skedaddled Californian.

Every time he entered the Senior Center and saw the old gents and ladies whiling away their day, he wondered if he and his wife would end up there in their old age. But he doubted that any of the people there now had imagined this future for themselves. He had to admit they seemed happy enough. Maybe they didn't think of these as their twilight years, just today, to be followed by tomorrow, the way it had always been. A cry went up from a bridge table, triumph in the afternoon. He headed for the stairs and went up to Edna's office.

"Got a minute?" he asked, looking in the door.

She actually jumped. "Lieutenant Horvath!"

"That's me. I was just wondering if I might end up downstairs after I'm pensioned off."

"That will be a long time from now."

"Care if I sit?"

She waved grandly at the chair and pushed herself backward in her own chair.

"Have you heard about the murder of Father Nathaniel?"

"Yes."

"Remember the guy who came here looking for some priest he said he'd known in California, some ex-priest?"

"You mean Stanley Morgan."

"That's right."

"He took me and the kids to a ball game."

"Here's the funny thing, Edna. It looks like the priest he was looking for was one of the Athanasians. Actually, Father Nathaniel, as they're now calling him again. Stanley Morgan went over there and under another name said he wanted to make a retreat. He was staying there in the lodge when all this happened."

"You think he killed that priest?"

"I don't know. I want to talk to him. But I can't. He's disappeared."

Edna had her hands flat on her desktop and looked at him with an expectant expression.

"You probably got to know the guy better than anyone else did, going to the ball game and everything. Is there anything you can tell me that would be of any help?"

Her chin angled up, her head cocked left, she gave it some thought. She shook her head. "I don't know what it would be. You don't spend a lot of time at the ball game talking."

Cy stood. "Well, this is just a long shot, of course. But we don't have much to go on. I wonder if he might try to get in touch with Marie Murkin."

"What on earth for?"

"He's on the run, Edna. I don't think he just stepped out to go to the drugstore. He packed and left. He's gone. So where might he go? I understand he hit it off with Marie Murkin."

"Then you should be having this conversation with her."

"I tried to. She thinks we're persecuting this nice man who had tea with her in the kitchen. With his record, he's going to know we'll be looking for him . . ."

"His record?"

"He did some soft time in California for some kind of financial fraud. Didn't you know that?"

Edna had stood, too, and seemed to have bristled at what Cy said. "I guess I did."

"Anyway, he could come here. Stupid, sure, but if he's our man he's running scared. I didn't want to alarm Marie—I don't think she would have listened to me anyway. What I'm asking is, keep an eye out, will you? He's got to be somewhere."

Edna nodded and then said, "Just call you at police headquarters?"

Cy fished out a card. "My cell phone number is on there. Try that first."

Down the stairs, another pause at the door of the former gym, looking in at the old people, making sure they were all old people, and then out to his car where he sat thinking for several minutes and then pulled away.

"Was that a cop?"

Edna had waited for Lieutenant Horvath to pull away, counted to ten, and then went up to the third floor. She nodded to Morgan's question.

"He expects you to come here."

"What did you tell him?"

"He thinks you'll go to the rectory, to Marie Murkin."

He shook his head. "Too risky. So is being here. I shouldn't have come."

"Now that you're here, you'd better stay. You wouldn't get far if you tried to leave town."

He seemed to sink into himself. "You're right. And now they'll be watching this place."

She stayed with him, he seemed so forlorn, even if she was worried about being away from her office. If someone called, they would assume she had gone downstairs.

"You have a car, don't you?"

"Stanley, I can't let you take my car."

"You could say it was stolen."

Suddenly he scrambled to his feet, his eyes looking wildly past her. Cy Horvath stood in the doorway.

"Stanley Morgan?" He showed his identification. "My car is downstairs. Why don't you and I just walk down together and go out to the car. No need to alarm anyone. All right?"

Edna's heart nearly broke as she saw the dejected resignation on Stanley's face. But then, he suddenly brightened.

"Good idea. Let's go."

Edna stood at the head of the stairs, watching the two men go down, the cop and the criminal, the man she had offered asylum to. Cy Horvath hadn't said a word to her.

I will make your name to be remembered in all generations.

—*Psalm 45*

The arrest of Stanley Morgan was good news, of course, but it did not set Amos Cadbury's mind at rest. In the narrow perspective of his present professional interest—the defense of the will of Maurice Corbett, as well as the deed of transferal of his estate to the Athanasians—the tragic death of Father Nathaniel was merely an incident. An aggravating incident, to be sure, since it put a bloody exclamation point to the scurrilous newspaper account of the recent history of the Order. How pathetic a band the community had seemed, a mere remnant of what had once been a thriving Order and an important factor within the local community. Now those vast grounds and buildings accommodated seven old men while the grandson of the man who had turned his estate over to them was all but destitute. "Is this justice? Is this fairness? Or, to put it in a more appropriate key, is this Christian charity?" Thus wrote Tetzel in the *Fox River Tribune* in his culminating story on the plight of poor Leo Corbett. And Amos Cadbury detected the hand of the ineffable Tuttle behind this campaign.

How differently a lawyer concerned for the good of his client would have proceeded. Approached properly, Amos might have joined in a petition to make some suitable provision for the grandson. If that had been done, if a favorable judgment had been given, Leo Corbett would accept it and render himself harmless in the future. That is the kind of solution a lawyer looks for, with everyone getting something, no big winner, no big loser, equity. But Tuttle had engineered a scorched-earth policy indicating his client was going for all or nothing. And, of course, what he would receive was nothing.

It was in this mood that Amos was told that a Miss Charlotte Priebe would be gratified to have a few minutes of his time.

"She is the administrative assistant of Lars Anderson," Miss Nitti, his secretary, reminded him.

With this little exchange as overture, Amos was not prepared for the very young lady who was shown in at two o'clock. He rose from his chair, as he would have done for any client, particularly a woman, and for a moment found himself without words. Miss Nitti, as if sensing his surprise, chirped, "Miss Charlotte Priebe. Mr. Cadbury."

She came right to the desk and extended her hand. "I am the administrative assistant of Lars Anderson."

"Please, sit down."

She sat. "As you know, Mr. Anderson very much wants, for purposes of development, property which is covered by the will and recorded wishes of a client of yours."

"A departed client."

"But his will and wishes are very much present. In order for Mr. Anderson to do what he wants to do, he would have to break that will." She paused. "I don't think that would be possible, given your reputation."

"It is not a matter of reputation, Miss Priebe, but of the law."

"Of course. But you will agree that a case can be made for the other side."

"Mr. Anderson's side?" A small smile was Amos Cadbury's comment on that.

"Not quite."

She let a short silence develop. Very effective. Amos was not insensible to the attractiveness of his visitor, although the assaults of concupiscence had long since lost their sting. She was quite pretty, somewhat severely dressed in a suit under which there seemed to be no blouse. But it was her intelligence that was most apparent in her manner and in her way of speaking.

"I subscribe to the belief that half a loaf is better than none. Or even a slice or two of the bread."

"Go on."

"Since Mr. Anderson would surely lose everything if he sought to obtain everything, the question arises as to whether some compromise might be reached."

"As a matter of conjecture?"

"As a matter of conjecture."

"Are you a lawyer, Miss Priebe?"

"No, sir."

"You would make a very good one."

"It's kind of you to say so. But not all lawyers are like yourself."

"And I daresay not all administrative assistants are like yourself."

"I would not like to be a lawyer like Mr. Tuttle."

"Indeed not. One Tuttle is more than the profession can abide. It is because of Tuttle and the slanderous publicity campaign he has engineered through the press, that your visit comes too late.

Total war has been declared, it matters little by whom."

"By Leo Corbett."

"Manipulated by Tuttle."

"Tuttle does seem to be the sand in the machinery, doesn't he? I have undertaken to speak to Leo Corbett directly. I made some of the same comments about Tuttle that you have. I told him how very likely it would be that he would end up with nothing if he persisted in the course Tuttle had laid out."

"Did Mr. Anderson ask you to do this?"

"I acted on my own."

"Is that the prerogative of an administrative assistant?" Why was he so fascinated by this young creature?

"If administrative assistants had to be told what to do they would be useless to their employer."

"So you talked to Leo Corbett. What did he say?"

"He came to adopt my point of view on the matter entirely."

"And Tuttle?"

"Tuttle will no longer serve Leo as lawyer. I hope you will agree that there is now an entirely new setting in which matters can be discussed."

"I wish you had gotten to Leo Corbett before Tuttle did."

"I have tried to undo the damage."

Amos Cadbury spoke with supreme confidence that the law was on his side in this matter, but he knew how much the law was now influenced by what was called public opinion—the manipulation of the many by the few who controlled the media. Murderers were acquitted in the face of overwhelming and damning evidence because the mob was aroused. There were circus lawyers who argued not to the judge or jury but to the television cameras, who massaged newsmen outside the courtroom, campaigned with the public for pressure to be put on judge and jury to give the people what they demanded. And if a murderer was convicted, immediately a campaign was begun to prevent punishment being exacted. People kept vigil outside prisons, holding lighted candles like pilgrims to a shrine, members of a new cult against capital punishment. Of course, it was punishment itself that was the target, the notions of responsibility and guilt. Agents were separated from their deeds, deeds from their consequences, crime from punishment. There were days when Amos was certain he would not willingly be an hour younger than he was. God only knew what lay ahead for the law, and for society. Now the pope and bishops were seemingly aligned with this antinomian crusade, albeit for different reasons, but did they not see the company they were keeping?

No court was untouched by such developments. Tuttle and that dreadful journalist understood this too well. Those articles had been aimed at whatever magistrate might have to decide if a case were brought against Maurice Corbett's will, and Amos no longer believed there was anyone on the bench with the courage to stand against such an onslaught. And so it was that he gave Miss Priebe to understand, with much circumlocution and committing himself to nothing, that the old maxim about half a loaf might still be considered to be in effect. She rose, again she offered her hand. Only then did she give him the benefit of her radiant smile and the daring decolletage. These, he reflected after she had gone, were far older weapons in influencing the course of justice than the manufacture of public opinion. But with Miss Priebe, feminine charms had followed rather than preceded their conversation. A most impressive young woman.

9

Rise up, O judge of the earth; render punishment
to the proud.

—Psalm 94

Tuttle had returned from the scene of the crime with his tweed
hat on the back of his head and the chest of a pouter pigeon.
Hazel rose from her desk like the angel of judgment.

"Where have you been till this hour?" She put the wrist on
which she wore her watch beneath her chin, but her eyes did not
leave Tuttle.

"Any calls?"

"Do you have any idea what's been going on all morning?"

"Tell me about it." He sauntered into his office, swept off his
tweed hat, and sailed it toward the coat rack in the corner. It
dropped on the pole, rotated several times, and was hung. Tuttle
stared. He had never done that before. Clearly a new epoch had
arrived. He dropped into his chair, pulled open the bottom drawer
of his desk, and propped his shoes on it. Hands behind his head,
he looked insolently at Hazel. Her expression changed. Something
like doubt came into her eyes.

"You know about the murder of the priest?"

"Father Nathaniel? I've spent the morning there, as the guest of the police."

"You mean that Pianone?"

"Officer Pianone and I were admitted at the barricaded entrance and then were briefed by police, coroner, and reporters. I came away satisfied that an already tight case had now become a walk in the park."

Hazel sat. Was that an admiring smile? Did this harridan who had acquired squatters' rights in his office realize the caliber of the man to whom she had presumed to attach herself?

"Tell me everything."

There are triumphant moments in every life, a time when everything has suddenly fallen into place in one's favor, enemies vanquished, all hopes realized, legitimate enjoyment in victory permitted. Such moments were rare to the point of nonexistence in Tuttle's life. All the more reason for him to wring from this one every ounce of satisfaction. He recounted his activities of the day in minute detail and he had in Hazel Barnes a listener transfixed by his narrative. Even without embellishment, it would have been an interesting story. Nor did Tuttle fail to underscore the role that his friendship with Peanuts had played.

"You should take him to lunch," she said.

"Peanuts and I frequently have lunch together."

"You should ask him here, order something in."

"He wouldn't come."

"I'll ask him myself."

Oh, how sweet is the taste of victory. Tuttle might be slouched behind his desk, feet in a drawer, hands behind his head, but metaphorically he stood tall with his foot pressing on the neck of his humbled oppressor. She would call Peanuts! He could imagine her wheedling voice, the honeyed words, the begging.

"We'll see."

"Leo Corbett should hear this. Have you talked to him yet?" The question was asked with a trembling voice, as if she feared the extent of his declaration of independence.

"Get hold of him, would you? I'd like to see him."

But Hazel's efforts to locate Leo were in vain. At his apartment, she got only the message on his answering machine, a droning, psychotic request that she say something after the beep. The voice descended into the depths at the end of the message. Nor was he at the country club.

"Keep trying."

Hazel kept trying with similar results and gradually the atmosphere in the office altered. Leo's mysterious absence was interpreted as points against the hitherto triumphant Tuttle.

"You should have gone to get him and brought him here."

"But he isn't at home."

"Not now. You should have had that Pianone pick him up before you went to the scene of the crime."

Sensing the turn of the tide, Tuttle scrambled to his feet. "I'm going to track him down."

"He's not a fugitive, Tuttle."

He remembered the scene in the kitchen of the lodge, when he had seen a man who could only have been Stanley Morgan slip out of the house. Should he tell this now, to regain the ascendancy? But he feared that the results would be negative. He slapped on his tweed hat, circled Hazel, and took the stairs, not wanting to wait for the elevator and feel her malevolent eye on him.

. . .

Hazel said Leo wasn't a fugitive, but Tuttle was experiencing the all-too-familiar feeling that a client thought safely in the bag had made his escape. That the grandson's prospects had been brightened by the murder of Father Nathaniel and the further lowering of public esteem for the Athanasians would have occurred to others and Leo's susceptibility to professional advice made it all too plausible that some vulture had gotten to him. But what lawyer would welcome the thought of going mano a mano with Amos Cadbury in any Fox River courtroom? And then the darkest thought of all occurred. Cadbury had alienated his client from him! Oh, he could do this in the most ethical way, manage to have Leo banging on his door and demanding admission, all too willing to repudiate the lawyer who had stood by him when no one else would have given a plugged nickel for his chances. Tuttle jerked open the door of his car and Farniente, the private investigator, nearly fell onto the sidewalk, sputtering with indignation as he came awake.

"For crying out loud, Tuttle, you trying to kill me?"

"Just the man I want to see."

"What do you think I'm waiting here for?"

"Waiting?"

"I know something you want to know."

"Leo Corbett?"

Farniente's sly smile faded. "You know."

"Move over."

Farniente eased himself with considerable concern for his manhood over the shift which separated the two front seats. Tuttle got behind the wheel.

"What about Leo Corbett?"

"He's thick as thieves with Lars Anderson's Girl Friday."

"Leo? Don't be nuts. He's more likely to join the Athanasians."

"Tuttle, think about it. You want to lose your client?"

"How am I going to do that?" Tuttle turned the key and listened to the engine emit a series of complaints before it finally turned over.

"It suits you fine that Corbett is in bed with Anderson?"

"I thought you said his administrative assistant."

"A figure of speech, a figure of speech. She is Anderson's indentured servant, anything she does, she is doing for Anderson. When your client moves in with her, I smell a deal. Admit it, you didn't know anything about it."

Tuttle felt desolated. An hour ago he had been on an emotional high, king of the mountain. Now he was shagged out his office by Hazel on a comeback and confronted by Farniente with the confirmation of his worst fears. Anderson, of course. The wily builder would want his hooks in Leo now that the young man might be the way of getting hold of that property.

"How do you know this?"

"I never reveal my sources."

"Neither does the Mississippi. Who told you?"

Farniente was silent. Tuttle turned and saw that the private detective was jabbing himself in the chest. "Me. I saw her lead him into corporate headquarters like a lamb to the slaughter."

"When was this?"

"Two days ago."

"And you rushed right over to tell me?"

"Tuttle, it could have meant anything. You're a busy man. Then, when that priest gets killed and the stock of those other priests is bound to plummet and your client looks to be in a much better position, I put two and two together."

"So why didn't you come upstairs?"

"Hazel would have wormed it out of me and then what good is my information?"

"The question is, what do I do with it?"

"You go see Leo."

"He doesn't answer his phone."

"Does that mean he isn't there?"

The apartment house in which Leo lived had been built during the 1920s, the last word at the time, but many architectural words had been spoken since. He was on the third floor, back, and there wasn't an elevator. In the entryway, unlocked, was a wall of mailboxes, arranged according to the floors of the building. There was no name in the box for Leo's apartment.

"You sure this is the building, Farn?"

"You want to call Hazel and have her check the address he gave you?"

"Let's go up."

Three flights, and the huffing and puffing he heard was Farniente's as well as his own. Tuttle felt like a process server. He beat on the door of 3D the way he would like to beat on Leo if he was pulling a rat on him. Farniente reached forward and turned the knob. The door opened. They walked into a minimally furnished apartment, a sofa and an easy chair, another chair with a padded seat, a lamp from whose shade dangled the kind of chain Tuttle hadn't seen in years.

"He rented it furnished," Farniente concluded.

But Tuttle had gone down the hallway and pushed open the bedroom door. A queen-size mattress on a frame, no headboard, a chair in the corner, an empty closet.

"He's moved," Farniente said.

"I didn't need a detective to tell me that."

Downstairs in the lobby, they opened the door to stairs leading down. The basement apartment was occupied by an old guy, sitting before a blaring television with a headset clamped over his ears, looking bug-eyed at the screen. Farniente removed the headset.

"Hey, what the hell?"

"Police," he lied, then covered it with a truth. "I'm Detective Farniente. Where is 3D?"

The old man studied the remote control he grasped as if 3D might be there. "This is a black-and-white."

"Leo Corbett," Tuttle explained. "The young man who lived on the third floor back. He's wanted for questioning."

The old man's milky eyes lit up like Newton's when he got hit with the apple.

"He moved! He's gone." And then, in a semblance of indignation, "What do you mean, busting in like this? That's the White Sox."

"Where'd he go?"

"How should I know? He was paid up and he waived his deposit. He can go wherever he wants."

"Was he alone?"

"Let me see your identification."

"I was about to ask you for yours," Farniente said. "How do we know you are who you say you are?"

"But I didn't say."

"That's what I mean."

Tuttle turned and dragged himself up the stairs. Farniente followed a few minutes later. They went back to Tuttle's car and sat in silence for five minutes. Then Tuttle spoke.

"You're hired."

"You want me to find Leo Corbett."

"That's right. Where can I drop you?"

"My car is parked near your office."

"Take a cab. I'm not going back."

"It'll be on your bill."

Tuttle nodded. Farniente opened the passenger door. "I'll find him." The door slammed. Tuttle adjusted his tweed hat. He took it off and looked at it. He remembered sailing it at the coatrack and making a ringer, the first in his life. When he looked up, he turned on the windshield wipers. It's wasn't raining. There were tears in Tuttle's eyes.

The Lord is gracious and full of compassion.

—Psalm 145

At the grotto, yellow plastic ribbons fluttered in the evening breeze, and a uniformed officer was on duty. Boniface had seen them at work and heard from others how they had gone over the scene, gathering evidence for what now seemed the obvious explanation. Stanley Morgan had been arrested and was being held under suspicion of murdering Father Nathaniel. Father Dowling had come with that news. The unspoken message was that Boniface no longer had to fear that someone in the community had done the awful deed. But he had thought no one capable of it other than himself. No need to say that again. Father Dowling seemed to think that he was dramatizing his role.

"It's quite by accident that it happened here. People will realize that eventually. Morgan might have taken his vengeance in California and we would never have heard of it."

"Does he admit it?"

"Criminals almost never do. I quote Captain Keegan."

"What must the life of a policeman be like?"

"Phil Keegan sees life in terms of justice, you and I in terms of mercy."

But the mercy Boniface craved was for himself. He had confessed his murderous thoughts, he had been absolved, but the stain remained on his soul. We are not so easily rid of what we think and do and even the certainty of having been forgiven does not undo the past. Throughout his long life as a religious, Boniface had regarded the violent deeds of men as the actions of almost another species. The sins and faults of the religious must look to worldly men as mere peccadilloes, but it was the work of a lifetime to root them out—not to be annoyed by the foibles and weaknesses of others, but to be patient, to try to fill the heart with charity, forgiving others as one had been forgiven. Pride was a constant threat, particularly when one began to think he was making great progress in holiness, but the capital sins became almost unimaginable. And now, in his twilight years, he had had in his soul the hatred Cain had felt for Abel. Even now, when Nathaniel was dead, carried off in a bag to be transferred to the icy fastness of the coroner's lair, to be opened and examined, all observations recorded, he could not forgive him for the trouble he had brought upon the Order. But he knew he must forgive him and pray for his soul.

How different an ending to this life than Nathaniel would have imagined when he was a novice and a young priest. Long years doing the work to which he had dedicated himself, eventually wearing out and dying with all the consolations of the Church. His body would have been lying in state in the chapel now, and the rest of them would have kept vigil through the night.

"He must be buried from here, Father Dowling."

The pastor of St. Hilary's frowned. "I was going to suggest a quiet funeral at my parish."

"No. He had returned. He wanted reinstatement. It will be granted to him posthumously."

Yes. That was the way. They would wake him in the chapel and he would be buried in the community cemetery out beyond the orchards, the simple cross over his grave identical to all the others. His birth date, his profession, the date of his death. No need to mention the long gap when he had lived in the world.

"I should never have permitted Stanley Morgan to stay here. From the beginning I distrusted him. When he told me who he really was and why he had come, I should have made him leave immediately."

"How were you to know?"

But in retrospect, it seemed that he'd had an intimation, that letting Morgan remain had been an unconscious acquiescence in the solution of their difficulties. Wasn't it a matter of pride to want to take such responsibility? He must rid himself of these self-indulgent thoughts. It seemed to him that he was wallowing in self-pity and, worse, enjoying it.

He looked beyond the fluttering ribbons to the statue of Mary. Had Nathaniel dragged himself here, mortally wounded, wanting to pray again that prayer that is repeated minute by minute all over the world. *Pray for us sinners, now and at the hour of our death.* To say those words as one was dying, *in ictu mortis*, must give them an irresistible power. He would have liked to kneel and say that prayer for the repose of Nathaniel's soul now, but the grotto had become the scene of a crime and he could not disturb it. So he whispered the prayer where he stood and then walked on in the direction of the lodge.

Attend to my cry, for I am brought very low.
—*Psalm 142*

Leo was not in her apartment when Charlotte returned from her meeting with Amos Cadbury. She called out his name when she shut the door and waited, expecting him to appear. "Ta-da," she would say, allowing herself that little gesture of victory. Now she could move toward the next phase of the plan that seemed to have formed as if this were her moment of destiny. But where was Leo? She ran through the apartment, but she already knew that he was not there.

She made herself a cup of tea and sat at the kitchen counter. Coolness is all. She could not believe that her beautiful plan could go awry so easily. She had been so sure of Leo. She *was* sure of him. She called his apartment and listened to the funereal message, then hung up. No. She dialed the number again, took the phone from her ear when the message was repeated and at the sound of the beep said, "Leo, if you're there, it's Charlotte. Call."

She hung up and an hour went by and there was no call from Leo.

An omelet and a glass of white wine for dinner, then more waiting. She must begin to consider alternatives. Tuttle. She had to cut any ties Leo had with the lawyer lest he try to return to *status quo ante*. She left a message on Tuttle's office phone.

"This is Charlotte Priebe. Mr. Leo Corbett wishes you to know that he has chosen other arrangements. Please send your bill to me, care of Anderson, Ltd. Thank you."

She went to bed, where she had never felt so alone before. If Leo were here . . . She turned on her side, and crushed her cheek into the pillow, eyes wide open. Sleep came without warning, and dreams, strange dreams. She was walking on the campus of the University of Chicago, dressed as she dressed before she wearied of undergraduate imposture. She felt again the intensely sexual atmosphere of the alleged intellectual life, young people thirsty for adventure, some of them perhaps indulging, but for the most part it was a cerebral matter. Casual talk, knowing asides, virginal hearts. At least in her case. All that could wait. It was better to think of it as a great mystery just over the horizon for which she was not yet ready. Clarity of mind and a new direction of her studies intervened, and then she was too busy for adolescent chatter. On the campus walks then she might have been in disguise as she passed the clinging couples, bumping hips as they moved along, expressions of sedulous abandon on their faces. She was in a skirt, a young woman now, no longer a coed, and then she saw Leo Corbett coming toward her on the sidewalk, an unsure but pleading expression on his face. She woke to the sound of a buzzer. She sat up. The digital clock beside the bed said 3:00.

She scrambled from her bed and ran into the living room where she pressed the button on the intercom.

"Charlotte?"

"Leo."

She pressed the door release and then waited as she was, her heart in her throat. She calmed herself. Of course he was back. Had she ever doubted it? A tapping on the door and she removed the chain, turned the lock, opened it. Leo stood there with clothing over one arm and a suitcase in his hand.

"I left my books in the trunk of the car."

She pulled him inside and closed the door. "It's three in the morning!"

"I told myself it was all a dream."

She took the clothes from his arm and threw them on the couch and waited for him to take her in his arms.

"I need a shower."

She smiled up at him. "So do I."

But she gave him time to himself before she joined him. The clothes he had worn were rolled into a ball, the bathroom was full of steam. She could see him impressionistically through the glass door of the shower, his face lifted to the water. She opened the door and stepped in.

Later in bed, in his arms, she listened to his rambling account. He had moved out of his apartment, gotten everything into his car, and then . . . She waited.

"Charlotte, you are the first woman I ever . . ."

She put a finger to his lips. "I know. Was it worth waiting for?"

What a tiger he was. He gave the impression of being awkward, uncoordinated, weak, but she felt almost fear as he gathered her to him and crushed her against his chest. She felt a great tenderness for him, her ten-ton gorilla, her odd and fascinating man, with a head filled with lore in geological strata that had to be gone through layer by layer until she reached the level where he was the true grandson and heir of Maurice Corbett. He fell away and into a deep sleep and she lay beside him, thinking of his account of how he had driven aimlessly, unsure whether he should come to her, fearful that she would laugh away their time together and mock him for thinking it meant anything beyond itself. Now he was reassured.

In the morning, she prepared a gargantuan breakfast for him then sat to watch him eat. His eye was on the muted television, bringing in the news of the day. "Turn that up."

It was the news of the murder of Father Nathaniel at the grotto of the Athanasian Order. The full significance of it did not strike her at first. She had sat there, waiting for the right moment to tell him of her visit to Amos Cadbury, wanting him to appreciate what she had done to advance his cause. Now, the scandal of the murdered priest was an unexpected boost.

"This will completely discredit them, Leo. That estate is yours."

And then she told him that Amos Cadbury was in the mood to compromise. Leo could have the original estate and make a deal with Anderson as well. The media would be in full cry again. Tetzel and the others would get a second wind from the murder. On the screen, the activities at the Athanasians' Marygrove were shown as background for the constant chatter of the reporter superimposed on it. A shot of the grotto, taped off, officials moving about, the camera zooming in on the prie-dieu where the body had been found by the groundskeeper. That the priest had been murdered at his prayers threatened to divert the accounts into a sympathetic vein, but then from the studio came a review of recent events, supporting the stories Tetzel had written for the *Tribune*. And then came still photographs. One of Maurice Corbett. While the long-dead gentleman looked out at Fox River viewers, the reporter spoke of the grandson, Leo, and how he had been cut off from his father's wealth.

"I have to go to the office," she told him.

"I'm still dead tired."

"You can go back to bed. You deserve it." She smiled. But first he wanted a blow by blow account of her meeting with Amos Cadbury. In retrospect the meeting seemed even more triumphal. Well, it had been a genuine coup, and Leo realized it. He sat on the couch, among the clothing she had flung there when he arrived, hands hanging between his knees, listening intently.

"If Tuttle had the sense to do this, you would not have needed me, Leo."

"Did you talk to him?"

"I told him you had made other arrangements."

"What did he say?"

"Does it matter?"

Only after she left Leo did the events of the day sink into Charlotte's mind. Her first reaction had been right, but it seemed an inadequate appreciation of what a favorable turn the death of that priest was for Leo's chances of coming into his inheritance. Of course, Lars was cognizant of what the murder of Father Nathaniel did to advance his own ambition to develop that choice property. Charlotte gave him a laundered version of her appointment with Amos Cadbury.

"You didn't tell me you were going to see him."

"It might have been a disaster."

"But it wasn't?"

"Anything but."

"Charlotte, I will be very generous if this finally goes through."

"It will."

He liked it when she exhibited confidence because she never did unless it was justified. She might have felt duplicitous with Lars if she had not learned her skills from him. The promised bonus was his recognition that she had not acted simply for his benefit. The assumption was that everyone had his own interests primarily at heart. As in fact she did. But it seemed clear that there could be many winners here. There was no need for him to know that Leo was now her live-in lover. Even less need to let him know of the terrible hours she had spent not knowing where he was or if he had slipped from her hook. She rejected the image. Leo was more than a momentary instrument of her own designs. Allied with him, she would gain doubly from the success of Anderson's project. If there was an apparent conflict of interest here, it did not jeopardize what each party wanted.

"You don't think these events will change Cadbury's attitude?"

"Why should they?"

"He is a prominent Catholic layman."

"So?"

"Catholics are different from you and me, Charlotte. He could be affected in unexpected ways by the death of that priest. Have you ever heard of Father Roger Dowling?"

"Tell me about him."

He was not, as she imagined, another Athanasian, but pastor of a local parish, a dear friend and advisor of Amos Cadbury. And close to the detective division of the local police.

"Do you think I should visit him?"

"I will leave that to you."

Meaning he wasn't sure that such a visit would be successful. Charlotte could not understand why Lars had mentioned Dowling, until he added, "He is, I understand, also very close to Father Boniface, the superior of the Athanasians."

Charlotte nodded. Maybe talking with Father Dowling would serve some purpose.

Have mercy on us, O Lord, have mercy on us.
—Psalm 123

The sunglasses that Nathaniel had affected since returning to the community from California were found on the floor of the maintenance shed, beneath a fertilizer spreader where they had come to rest. This was taken to strengthen the likelihood that it had been in the shed that Nathaniel was attacked and that he had indeed stumbled in a grotesque final walk, an ax buried in his back, to the grotto where he fell on his knees and eventually died. There was a note of awe, even of reverence, in Phil Keegan's voice as he told Father Dowling.

"Plus the fact that an effort had been made to clean up the shed. There had even been some hasty painting, but the lab found blood beneath it. Nathaniel's blood."

"Good Lord."

"So it looks as if he wasn't attacked when he was already at prayer."

"The maintenance shed."

"Andrew George sounded the alarm."

Silence. Few people had a greater complaint against Nathaniel, given the prodigal priest's campaign that the Athanasians give up their property.

"Sell all they have and give to the poor?" Phil said.

"If only it had been that simple. Nathaniel seems to have had something else in mind. Unless the members of the Order are to be counted among the poor."

"Divide it among them?"

"It was when the others realized he had that in mind that the tide turned against him."

"Imagine what each of them would have got!"

"They are all under the vow of poverty, Phil."

"Then what are they doing living on that choice property?"

"You sound like Tetzel. When it was given to them it was almost as beautiful as it is now, but people weren't clamoring to get hold of it then."

The moment had arrived for Father Dowling to tell Phil what Father Boniface had confided in him. He had just returned from Marygrove when Phil arrived at the rectory.

Marygrove was yesterday's news so far as the media were concerned and there was no sign of a police investigation under way. But it was clear that Father Boniface did not think his troubles were beginning to recede. He said what he had to say in a single passionate burst.

Andrew George had come to Boniface with what he himself

realized was a damning revelation. "When I found the body, I ran to the maintenance shed to use the phone there."

"And called me from there."

"Yes."

His next words were spoken with a sob. "Father, Michael was coming out of the shed when I got there."

What more could the poor man have said? Boniface saw the implications of this immediately, of course, as George had known he would. Neither man had the heart to put into words the thought they shared.

"Have you told anyone?"

"I swore I would never tell even you, yet here I am. If anyone else has to know, you must tell them."

And so Boniface had shouldered another cross. He embraced the groundskeeper and the two old men wept. The two of them seemed to have lived into old age only to see their world collapse around them. After George left, Boniface sat in silent agony, as Father Dowling could imagine.

"Could anyone else know this?"

"He commissioned me to do with it what I thought I should." Boniface moved the tips of his fingers down the sides of his face. "Now I commission you, Father Dowling. You are close to Phil Keegan, the man investigating this murder."

Now the moment had come for Father Dowling to tell Phil who listened with lifted brows.

"Sounds suspicious."

"It does indeed."

"I'll have to talk to the son again, Roger."

"You can imagine how hard it was for the father to tell Boniface this, and for Boniface to hear it."

"I'm almost surprised he didn't keep quiet about it."

"And go on living with his son?"

"I'll have Cy talk to him," Phil said after a moment. "He can have the kid show him around the maintenance shed, ask about the cleaning up there. Maybe it won't be necessary to let him know how we found out."

Phil was a father himself, so perhaps this magnanimous suggestion was not surprising. If young George had a guilty secret, no one was more likely to induce him to blurt it out than the stolid Cy Horvath. No need to bring his father into it all, if things went right.

"You're a good man, Phil Keegan."

Phil was embarrassed. "Right now I'm a confused one. I thought we had our man in Stanley Morgan."

"What has he said?"

"Just that he's innocent. He is resisting getting a lawyer. He says he knows all about lawyers. The court will have to appoint one."

"Maybe he is innocent."

"Maybe the moon is made of green cheese."

"What about young George?"

"We'll see. If there's really anything there, Cy will get it."

Out of the depths, I have cried to You, O Lord.
—*Psalm 130*

Together and one at a time, taking turns, Phil Keegan and Cy Horvath, had talked with Stanley Morgan. Everything the man said contributed to the case against him. He had been shafted by Nathaniel, whom he knew as Richards, in California and had been left holding the bag when the financial consulting firm they jointly owned came under suspicion. Morgan could provide no proof of Richards's involvement and himself became the object of an investigation for diverting investor's money. The books showed that a significant sum had been transferred to a Zurich account, which Morgan explained as his partner Richards's share of the profits. It was impossible to gain access to the Swiss bank account. Richards, according to Morgan kept the books, but again he had no proof of this. The secretary of the firm gave ambiguous testimony that hurt Morgan more than it helped him. He was persuaded to plead guilty to an innocuous charge, but the publicity had labeled him a defrauder of the elderly. So he spent a year in a minimum-security, white-collar crime institution near Fresno, easy duty as prison time goes, but more than enough solitude for him to reflect on what Richards had done to him.

"You wanted revenge?" Cy asked.

"Of course. Though not in the sense you probably mean," replied Morgan.

"What do I probably mean?"

"I didn't kill him. I intended to do him no physical harm. I wanted simply to confront him, to let him know that I had survived and that I was in the world."

"You thought that would trouble him?"

"He was a funny guy. After he told me he'd been a priest, I thought I understood him."

"How so?"

"Whatever he did, he wanted to retain his reputation. The way he explained leaving the priesthood was a good example. It wasn't that he had abandoned it, but that it had failed to live up to his expectations. Everything was like that. His wife was different."

"You knew her, too?"

"The three of us were very close. And then she died."

The wife had been a nun, and she like Richards thought that the religious life had let her down, taken her best years under a false assumption. It got murky then, and neither Phil nor Cy could follow Morgan.

"So you served your time, got out, and tracked him down in Fox River. You showed up at Marygrove under a false name and asked to make a retreat."

"It was my chance to confront him."

"And how did that go?"

"What?"

"When you confronted him."

"I never did. That was the irony. Once I settled in—they put me in the lodge with the Georges—I was in no rush. I had the luxury of being able to move slowly. He was there, I was there, it would happen."

"Cat and mouse?"

"Cat and mouse."

"And then you confronted him."

"But I didn't."

"And then he was killed."

"I was astounded. But before that happened I went back to Father Boniface and told him my name really wasn't Sullivan, and that I had known the man he called Father Nathaniel in California. That way I felt certain that he would know I was there. And he would know others knew."

"You expected him to seek you out?"

"Whatever. One way or the other, it seemed inevitable that we would meet, living there at Marygrove."

"Look, if you went to all this trouble to find him, it stands to reason that you went ahead and did what you had come to do."

"But I didn't. I waited. Do you think I'm not sorry I did?"

"Are you?"

"Now it is something that can never be resolved. For the rest of my life . . ."

"Morgan, you are going to be indicted for the murder of Father Nathaniel. Everything points to you."

"I didn't do it."

"So who did? Murders are seldom complicated, you know. It's usually pretty obvious who did it. In this case, the obvious one is you."

"I'm innocent."

"You better get a lawyer."

Morgan laughed. He was a pleasant enough guy, but unreal.

He said what he said with apparent sincerity yet at the same time did not expect to be believed.

"You'll get a lawyer whether you want one or not."

"It won't be my responsibility. So I go back inside. I almost miss it. Staying there with those priests was like being back. Maybe that's why I was in no rush. I felt at ease again."

"He's a goner," Phil said to Cy after they let Morgan return to his cell where maybe he could feel at ease.

"Funny guy. California must be a strange place."

It helped not to feel vindictive toward the person you were investigating for murder. The newspaper accounts of the slaying of Nathaniel treated it as particularly horrible because the victim was a priest. The way Judas was a priest, Phil thought. He got nowhere with Roger Dowling when he vented his anger at priests like Nathaniel who went on leave, got married, then wanted to come back as if they could shuck the intervening years like skin. It wasn't that he thought Morgan had the right to kill Nathaniel because he'd been a renegade priest, but it didn't have the same shock value as it might have if Nathaniel had spent his life where he belonged, living the life of a priest. Of course, none of this would have happened then.

And now came the twist that young George had been seen by his father coming out of the maintenance shed when he went there to report finding Nathaniel at the grotto with an ax in his back. The ax was from the maintenance shed. There were oddities about the shed that Pippen had turned up. Someone had cleaned it up, someone had hurriedly painted the corner of the work bench. When Nathaniel's sunglasses were found in the shed, the paint was removed and found to cover some of Nathaniel's blood. All this pointed to the attack having been made in the maintenance shed. Young George popping out of there at the crack of dawn when his father came running to use the phone, sounded like good news for Morgan. So why didn't Cy Horvath think so?

"There's more physical evidence pointing toward the boy than in the case of Morgan, isn't there, Cy?"

"We don't have any physical evidence against Morgan."

"So why don't these facts shake your convictions?"

"I want to talk to the kid."

Roger had interpreted his reaction to the news as some kind of heroic virtue. Well, Phil didn't want the kid to know that his father had brought suspicion on him, if he could help it. But part of that was the unlikelihood that, in the crunch, a father would be a witness against his son. And so far at least it was only the father's testimony that put young George in the maintenance shed at a suspicious time.

You have shown your people hard things.
                                        —*Psalm 60*

Edna waited anxiously to be confronted with the fact that she had provided Stanley Morgan with a hiding place in the old nurse's office on the third floor of the school, but nothing happened. When Cy Horvath discovered Stanley Morgan, he had said nothing to Edna and she had found this ominous, as if he did not want to dilute the arrest of Morgan with taking her to task for what she had done. When Stanley was taken away it came home to her that what she had done could be construed as a crime, even if at the time Stanley was accused of nothing. How then could she be said to have harbored a criminal? Or a suspected criminal?

But all the excuses she thought of made her dread having to state them aloud in self-defense. And she was sure that it was Father Dowling who would ask for an explanation. And then, with the passage of time, it became inescapable that Cy Horvath had not said anything to anyone. Edna did not know quite how to react to this. But, of course, it was Marie Murkin who fussed about the circumstances of Stanley Morgan's arrest.

"On the third floor of the school!" she cried, in a simulated state of shock.

"In the nurse's office."

"How on earth did he think of hiding there?"

"You must have made him feel at home here."

Marie looked at Edna sharply, then saw it as a compliment. "That's true. But, Edna, imagine him knocking at the rectory door when I knew they were looking for him."

Marie was soon caught up in this possible drama and wanted to explore the many and various reactions she might have had.

"I don't think I could have turned him away," she said.

"But where could you have hidden him?"

Marie fell silent, perhaps thinking of various hiding places in the rectory. "If I did hide him, I could never have turned him in."

"I suppose the question is, why did he want to hide any-where?"

"Oh, that's obvious. And I don't mean he's guilty. But if you'd been through what he has, no matter how innocent you were, you'd run, too."

236   Ralph McInerny

"I suppose."

Later, it was Marie who relayed to Edna the news about the groundskeeper finding his son in the maintenance shed when he had gone to sound the alarm after finding the body.

"Now, Edna, this is absolutely confidential. The boy mustn't dream that his father made this known."

Edna crossed her heart and hoped to die.

"But how can one feel relief? This lets Stanley Morgan off the hook, but only because Michael George now looks like the one."

"But why on earth would he have killed that priest?"

There was no doubt that Marie got more information at the rectory than Edna could ever get at the school, thanks largely to the frequent visits of Captain Phil Keegan. Edna had always felt ambiguous toward Keegan and Horvath because of her experience with the police when Earl fell afoul of the law. All the more reason for her surprise and gratitude that Cy Horvath did not press her on how Stanley Morgan happened to be hiding in the nurse's office on the third floor of the school. He must have sensed, when he appeared in the doorway, that Edna was talking with Stanley in a conspiratorial way. Now with her fears lifted and with Marie Murkin accepting the suggestion that she herself was the target of Stanley Morgan's seeking refuge at St. Hilary's, she realized how she had been governed by her feelings rather than by her head when Stanley Morgan appeared in her office and put himself in her hands. How foolish that had been. How long could Stanley expect to elude the police. And why had Cy Horvath shown up at the nurse's office?

It was inescapable that the fact that she had had dinner with Stanley Morgan, that she had allowed him to take her and the kids to a ball game, was anything but a secret. Had that been enough for Lieutenant Horvath to decide to check out the school?

But now when she thought of the son of the groundskeeper she was certain she would act equally foolishly to help him, and she did not even know the boy. Instinctively, she found herself sympathizing with anyone in trouble with the law. Well, not anyone.

The newspaper reports omitted any mention that Stanley Morgan had been arrested at St. Hilary's. Marie reacted to this strangely.

"I suppose it's just as well," she said, and sighed.

"How so?"

Marie looked at Edna, then let her eyes drift away. For heaven's sake. Edna felt a girlish impulse to tell Marie which of them Stanley Morgan had really been interested in. Instead, she hurried back to the school. If she didn't watch out, she would become another Marie Murkin.

The lines have fallen to me in pleasant places.
                                    —*Psalm 16*

Amos Cadbury was having lunch at the Cliffdwellers Club near the Chicago Art Institute. His primary loyalty was to Fox River, but he was perforce a Chicagoan and held memberships in both the University Club and the Cliffdwellers, which were often more convenient places to meet with certain clients and colleagues than his office in Fox River. He and Lars Anderson had finished dining, they were sipping Mirto, a Sardinian liqueur Anderson insisted he try. Amos found the liqueur everything Anderson had said it was.

"How did you come upon it?"

"On vacation in Alghero, a lovely town on the west coast of Sardinia. Have you ever been there?"

"To Sardinia? No."

Amos had grown up in a time when a trip to Europe meant taking a train to the East Coast and then sailing from Manhattan or Newark, a six-day voyage to Southampton, then a Channel boat to France, long train journeys to Italy and Rome. This he had done with his wife on their honeymoon trip, and like the honeymoon itself it had not seemed a repeatable performance. Now people were driven to O'Hare and seven or eight hours later dropped any place on the globe, and many did it. It surprised Amos that Anderson, a man his own age, should talk so casually of visiting Sardinia!

"Do you ever go to Rome?" Amos asked.

"I didn't like it."

Amos said nothing. He and Mrs. Cadbury had put up at the Hassler in Rome and seen everything, ancient, medieval, Renaissance. As part of a sizable group they had an audience with Pope Pius XII. Those memories, vivid after the passage of years, had served for a lifetime. But Rome had been the high point of their European experience. Amos sipped his Mirto, finding it very good indeed.

"Charlotte Priebe has been to see you," Anderson said.

"A remarkable young woman."

"I wish I had a son like her. Or a daughter. Sometimes I feel

I am just building castles in the sand." Anderson's hair had grayed, but it still looked blond and his weathered complexion told of hours on building sites. Or was that the Sardinian sun? "I seem to have gotten to old age instead without someone I can pass things on to."

"The way Maurice Corbett did?"

Anderson frowned. "I used to think a man like that was nuts. Handing over huge sums of money as well as his estate to strangers."

"I don't suppose he thought of the Athanasians as strangers exactly."

"It's not because they're priests. I make charitable contributions, who doesn't, but it seems part of making out my taxes. I have been asked to endow a museum. They say they would name it after me. It would be filled with pictures I couldn't understand, if there is anything in such paintings to be understood. What I want is to leave something that is mine, things I've built. I suppose that's what Corbett had in mind, give it to those priests and it would be kept up, the house he built, the grounds."

"They have certainly done that, and more."

"I bid on some of their buildings but didn't get the contract." But the slight frown was fleeting. "Some time I'll show you the model of what I would like to do with that property if I can get hold of it. It would be my monument."

Perhaps Mirto made one philosophical. Lars Anderson had come to the time of life when he wondered about the significance of what he had done. An Anderson home was a byword west of Chicago. But gaudy and expensive as many of them were, Anderson dreamt of something lasting. Perhaps Father Dowling would think of this desire as a surrogate of eternity.

"Maybe you will get your chance."

"I hope so." Anderson hunched over the table.

"Miss Priebe put your case very well. The Athanasians are a dwindling Order. I think that even they must wonder if they are destined to survive. There are vast acres of their property that they would not have done much with even in their years of flourishing."

"They would never regret selling to me."

"But what of the grandson?"

Anderson smiled slyly. "I wouldn't worry about him."

"Oh?"

"He put himself in the hands of fools."

"Tuttle."

"Tuttle. The boy, too, might have gotten something if he hadn't wanted everything."

"Have you spoken with him?"

"Charlotte has."

"And?"

"He won't know what hit him."

Amos had no love for Leo Corbett, but Anderson's rough business sense seemed hard on the grandson of Maurice Corbett. Perhaps the Athanasians might be more amenable to seeing that the young man got something. But Anderson wanted to get down to cases on the Corbett property and Amos reined him in.

"I have not yet put the matter in this new light before Father Boniface, the superior. Recent events have made that unseemly for the moment. But I will make the strongest case I can for some such compromise as Miss Priebe brought."

Anderson thrust forward a great hand, and Amos took it, wondering how many witnesses in the dining room noticed it.

"So far as my own inclination goes, we are of one mind," Amos said.

"I'm sure the priests always take your advice."

Amos smiled. "I try to give such advice that its refusal is not attractive. In this case, I think what you are proposing is the happiest of compromises."

"Good." Anderson sat back. "Let me tell you a little secret. Charlotte Priebe talked to you before she told me anything about it."

"What a singular young woman."

"One of the shrewdest associates I have ever had."

"She would have made a great lawyer."

"It would have been a waste. No offense. I expect that some day she will offer to buy me out."

"She seems a mere girl."

Anderson shook his head. "She's tough as nails."

"And would you sell?"

"After what I want to do with the Corbett property? Perhaps. It would be interesting to negotiate with her."

"You could settle in Sardinia and drink this."

And the two men touched glasses and finished off their Mirto.

16

The Lord tests the righteous.

—*Psalm 11*

Rita Martinez was devastated when Michael George was questioned about the murder of Father Nathaniel. Lieutenant Horvath had talked with him at the lodge first and then asked him to come downtown and go through it all again with Captain Keegan. Afterward, they had let him go home, but it seemed only a matter of time before something worse happened. And then he had come to her.

The boy she had loved because he had such a stable family, such a wonderful prospect in life, carrying on after his father, was a fading memory now. Despite the obstacles there had been before, neither she nor Michael had believed anything could stand in the way of their marriage and their life together. Rita was confident that theirs would be a Catholic wedding, whether or not Michael came into the Church. It was not simply that all that had changed now. While Rita listened to Michael, she found herself doubting what he said.

"Rita, I saw the body first." He paused. "I got up early and before breakfast I went over to the shed. That place is so wonderful at the beginning of the day, large, quiet, dark, the smell of oil and gas, all the machinery and tools in perfect order. When the large doors are opened from inside, you look out as if from a cave to the grounds, the trees, the plants, the lawn, as the sun strikes them for the first time that day."

This was the Michael she loved, but all this was prelude to his great revelation.

"That's why I liked to go over to the shed even before breakfast. Passing the grotto, I saw one of the priests kneeling there, but I didn't really look at him. I kept on to the maintenance shed. What a shock when I went inside. It was a mess. It looked like some drunk had been in there, crashing around. My first thought was vandals." He looked at her. She knew what he meant. There were boys who resented her going with this gringo. "I started to straighten things up. I didn't want my father to see the shed like that. And then I saw blood."

He couldn't say it. He stared at her, wanting her to know his thought but not express it either. It was too horrible.

"I cleaned up as best as I could and then I heard something. I opened the door . . ."

His father had come running toward him. "The telephone. Something awful has happened."

"Rita, I listened to him when he talked with Father Boniface. I went back to the grotto and saw that Nathaniel was dead. An ax in his back."

Rita shuddered but would not let him take her in his arms.

"That's it. My father was running around. He didn't even seem to notice the mess the shed was in. When he left, I finished the cleaning up I had started."

"Cleaning up?"

"Yes. But the blood left stains. I decided to paint over it."

"But why?" He had to put it into words for her. Michael looked past her, then met her eyes.

"I didn't want my father to see it."

"Oh, Michael."

What would the police make of a story like that. Michael had developed a deep dislike for Father Nathaniel. "I'd like to drug him or get him drunk and ship him back to California," he had said once. "Buy him a ticket, pour him onto the plane. Maybe he wouldn't dare come back a second time. He's ruining everything."

She wanted to tell him that their happiness did not depend on his living as his father had lived. He could find another job. She did say that, but her heart sank when she did. Her dreams of the future involved herself and Michael settled in the lodge, living with his parents until . . .

"What did the police say?"

"They don't believe me."

"But your father?"

"What about him?" he said sharply.

"Does he believe you?"

"What difference does that make?"

"Michael, what is going to happen?"

"I don't know." He puffed out his chest, lifted an eyebrow, and said, "And frankly, Scarlett, I don't give a damn." But the old tricks would not do now. Michael had a gift for mimicking movies. His "Bond. James Bond" was one of his best, the exact intonation of Sean Connery's voice. Now she tried to take him in her arms, but it was he who twisted away.

"Rita, I don't want you mixed up in this. Nothing is going to be the way we hoped. Maybe we should just cool it for a while."

It would have been kinder if he had struck her. Then he left hurriedly and before she could go to her room, her father came in from the kitchen. "What did he say?"

All she could do was cry, like a kid. She did go to her room then and lay on the bed sobbing. Her father looked in at her, but thank God he said nothing. What was there to say? He knew and she knew that Michael was in very deep trouble. She tried to imagine herself asking him if he had killed that priest, but she could scarcely form the question in her own mind. To say it would be to acknowledge that it was all over between Michael and herself.

After half an hour, she washed and got herself looking presentable, then went to St. Hilary's. As she approached the rectory, she thought of how she had dreamed of Michael and herself coming like this to make arrangements for their wedding. She stopped, fearful that she was going to start bawling again. And then a voice called her name and she turned to see Mrs. Murkin the housekeeper coming from the school. It was written all over her face that she knew about Michael. Mrs. Murkin came right to her and took her in her arms, and then Rita did start crying again and they went together to the rectory door.

"Is Father Dowling in?"

"What you need first of all is a cup of tea."

Rita never drank tea, not even iced tea, but she sat at the kitchen table, almost glad of the delay before she talked to Father Dowling. It helped that she seemed not to have to explain to Mrs. Murkin why she was here or why she was crying. The housekeeper fussed about the kitchen, putting on water, getting out some cookies, putting a napkin at Rita's elbow. Then she sat across from her while they waited for the water to boil.

"Father Dowling isn't here just now, but I know you need someone to talk to."

"Oh, it's so awful."

"What does the boy say?" The boy was Michael.

She tried to tell her what Michael had said, but she couldn't look at her because Mrs. Murkin obviously thought this was only part of the story. If this was the reaction from a sympathetic person, what must the police think?

"Just think," Mrs. Murkin said, "if his father had said nothing."

"What do you mean?"

"That he had seen his son in that shed when he ran there to call the police."

"His father?"

Marie Murkin put a hand over her mouth and looked at Rita with rounded eyes. "Of course, the police would have found out anyway."

Why should such a revelation have been welcome? Suddenly Rita thought she understood what Michael was doing. But she didn't want to talk about it anymore.

"What a nice kitchen you have here."

"You should have seen it when I first came."

"How long have you been here?"

Tea was poured, cookies were eaten, Marie Murkin told war stories about life as a rectory housekeeper. Rita listened with an expression of rapt attention, but her thoughts were elsewhere. She left as soon as she could do so without abusing Marie Murkin's hospitality. From the rectory she drove to the lodge.

Michael could not conceal how glad he was to see her.

"I thought you would never come here again."

"Let's walk."

They walked to the north, through the orchards, the blossoms long gone and the fruit now beginning to form among the rich green leaves.

"Telling you was the hardest thing of all."

"You're protecting your father, aren't you?"

"What?"

"Michael, you didn't kill that priest."

He had never said he had, just painted himself in the blackest colors he could and let others draw their own conclusions. But why, if he hadn't done it? Even now, he couldn't bring himself to say that he had killed Father Nathaniel.

"You cleaned up because you didn't want anyone to know that it had happened in the shed."

"I told you that."

"But who were you cleaning up after?"

He didn't have to say. She knew. He had thought his father had done it, in the shed, but cleaning up, painting, turned suspicion on him. The police would never learn the truth from him. He would never point the finger at his father although, if Marie Murkin knew what she was talking about, Mr. George had turned attention to Michael. Things were as black for Michael as they had been before, but Rita no longer felt toward him as she had. She took him in her arms and they stood in silent embrace among the apple trees for a long time, and then they walked slowly back to their fate.

Behold, how good and pleasant it is for brethren to dwell
together in unity!

—*Psalm 133*

"You have been suffering terrible things of late, Father Boniface."

"Yes, Your Eminence. That is why I asked to see you."

"You are an older man than I, by a great margin, I should
say."

"It is a matter of office, not of age."

The cardinal smiled. His zucchetto was not worn at the back,
a covering for the tonsure when tonsures set the clergy off from
the laity, but perched on the top of his egg-shaped head. But that
head was hairless, tonsured all over, so to speak. The cardinal
lifted it, looked inside it, then put it back where it was. "I was a
bishop and an archbishop before being given Chicago, but I have
never become used to the zucchetto. Worn on top like this, it is
less likely to be pulled away when the miter is removed."

"We wear one with our habits."

"Ah. Then you are senior to me in that as well. And father
superior of your Order."

"A very deflated honor, Your Eminence."

The cardinal nodded and thoughts came and went in his large

philosophical eyes. "I am a member of an order, too."

"Yes, I know."

"When I professed, I never dreamed that I would end up here."

It occurred to Father Boniface that the archbishop, as a young cardinal, would be an elector at the next papal conclave. That, too, must have eluded his youthful imaginings. Old men dream dreams as do the young, but neither has prophetic dreams.

"The last time we spoke I mentioned one of our priests who wished to return."

"And now he is dead."

"Murdered, Your Eminence."

"God rest his soul. I understand he was attacked while praying at your grotto."

"He may have made his way there after he was attacked."

"To die before Our Lady?"

Father Boniface bowed his head at the pious thought. He wished that he could share it.

"And what would you have recommended, Father? Would he have become a member of your community once more?"

"No. I would have refused."

Pale brows rose above the round eyes. "Indeed."

"I came to think that he was not sincere. I fear he came back because we are few and yet a wealthy community."

"Covetous eyes are turned on what you have?"

"He wanted us to sell. He had formed a faction."

"Sell."

"I think he believed that each of us would come into a share of the purchase money."

The cardinal smiled. "But I would have opposed any sale that had such an end in view."

"I was told that in canon law that would amount to alienation of Church property."

"Ah, canon law. No doubt other opinions could have been found. But I would have done everything in my power to prevent its happening."

"I wish now that I had asked you earlier."

"The advice you were given is what I would have accepted. Now selling some or all of that very valuable property in order to further the goals of the Order of St. Athanasius, that, of course, would be a very different thing."

"The fact is, Your Eminence, there may be none of us left in a few years. I intend to ask my fellow Athanasians to deed everything to the archdiocese if that should happen."

The cardinal frowned. "Are you so resigned to the death of your Order?"

"I would give anything to prevent it. I have been there boy and man my whole life. It is my whole life. But realistically . . ."

"Realistically, you are in a position to do something about it. What I will ask you to do is draw up a plan for the revitalizing of the Athanasians. If you should sell some of your property, you would be able to finance a sustained campaign to attract new vocations. There are priests who feel abandoned by their orders and societies although they remain within them because that is what they vowed to do. I have talked to some . . ." He stopped himself. "What if you had a handful of younger priests—I mean younger than yourself—who would join you and help in attracting vocations. You have all the facilities, Father. And I would begin at the beginning. I believe you told me that you were thirteen when you began your studies."

"I was just out of grade school."

"Is that true of others there?"

Boniface thought. "They are all products of our minor seminary."

"Minor seminaries were one of the casualties of the postconciliar enthusiasm. It was thought that a boy cannot make a lifetime decision. But, of course, one does not make it fully until many years have passed. I think a grievous mistake was made in this matter." The cardinal smiled. "I had some research done. On the theory used to close down minor seminaries, you would expect that defections from the priesthood came from those who had started their studies at too tender an age. Not at all. Such men remained proportionately more faithful than those who began later."

This was not at all what Boniface had expected to hear. He had asked for an appointment in order to discuss the demise of the Athanasians and his own resignation. But he found himself stirred by the cardinal's words.

"Delayed vocations are very much part of the picture now, men in their late twenties, in their thirties, older, discovering in themselves a vocation to the priesthood. If you complemented the reopening of your minor seminary with a program for delayed vocations, well, who knows what might come of it? I have read about your founder and about the origins of the Order in Italy. The spirituality and charism of the Athanasians would be attractive to many. Perhaps there could be a reunion with the Italian branch."

"You have given this a great deal of thought, Your Eminence."

"I have. And I have outlined for you some possibilities for restoring your Order. Would you put your mind to this, Father? Would you consult with your fellow Athanasians and get their thinking on the matter?"

"Yes!" The word flew from his mouth. He was at once stirred

by the prospect of a renewed Order and ashamed of himself for not having adopted on his own the optimistic attitude expressed by the cardinal. "Yes, I will."

"Good."

"I had come here expecting a severe judgment on myself and the Athanasians."

"I will leave the examination of your conscience to yourself. And I will be looking forward to our next talk."

Boniface rose and then dropped to his knees, asking the cardinal's blessing. It was not given hurriedly, but with deliberation, each Latin word pronounced distinctively. Then the cardinal helped Father Boniface to his feet. "And now, Father Boniface, I will ask for yours."

And the cardinal dropped on his knees before him, taking off his zucchetto. Boniface laid his hands on the hairless head and felt as he had when he gave his first priestly blessing after his ordination, to his parents. *Benedictio Dei omnipotentis, Patris, et Filii et Spiritus Sancti descendat super te, et maneat semper.* Afterward, the cardinal allowed Boniface to help him to his feet.

"Our Lord began with twelve, Father. And he had one defector. But all the others deserted him temporarily when trouble came. Vessels of clay, that's all we are. But fired clay endures."

On the drive back to Fox River, Boniface's elation began to fade, but then on the long contemplative drive on the interstate, it returned. He felt that he was emerging from nostalgia and self-indulgence. Herman Melville had in his writing box a motto that sustained him during the composition of his last novel after years of obscurity and failure. *"Be true to the dreams of your youth."* That was not a call to nostalgia. One might even call it *aggior-*

namento. And as he drove through the gates of Marygrove Boniface thought how ironic it would be if Nathaniel's return, whatever his motives had been, should prove to be the beginning of the resurrection of the Athanasians.

This is my resting place forever.
                    —*Psalm 132*

Sometimes, despite herself, Charlotte Priebe remembered the enthusiasm of her first years as a student at the University of Chicago, the authors she had read, the questions discussed, all the intractable matters of literature and philosophy. Was unconscious art possible? Is the unexamined life worth living? But she found in those memories a justification of the turn she had taken in her studies and in her life. Thales, the first philosopher, was said to have cornered the olive presses so that after harvesting he became wealthy. The point was not to prove that wealth was desirable, but that a philosopher could excel at the things that he disdained. And so she told herself that, once she had achieved her financial goals, she would walk away from it all and, like Thales, devote herself to philosophy once more. But there was another tale about Thales. Once, walking at night, contemplating the starry heavens, the philosopher had fallen into a well. Proving that philosophy could tell jokes on itself as well. Leo half understood.

"I detest disinterested knowledge. My father devoted himself to geology and ended up with rocks in his head."

"Were they real or imaginary?"

Leo let it go. He, too, knew how to play that game. First he wanted the good things of the earth, then he would think of heaven. Would he turn to the priests? And what did he think of the priest who was murdered?

"He deserved it."

"How so?"

"He wanted to sell out to Anderson."

"Leo, that might not be all bad."

"If he had had his way, it would have been bad for me."

"Maybe if you had talked with him." She meant, of course, if she had talked with him.

"I did. It didn't do any good. He called me a greedy parasite. He told me to get a job." Leo made a vulgar wet noise with his lips.

"Well, anyway, he's out of the picture. So the present question is how do we get you what you want?"

She had gone over the compromise with him, and he seemed to welcome it, but after so many years of distrust and despite their intimacy he did not thoroughly trust even her. Intimacy has its limitations, she was beginning to learn. They were living together now, in the phrase, but it was their little secret. No need for Anderson to know. He had talked with Amos Cadbury over lunch and then called her in so she could give him another summary of her meeting with Cadbury. Lars Anderson had developed a smile that meant nothing. He could even smile while he threatened a competitor. He smiled throughout her repetition of what had passed between Cadbury and herself.

"He is a wily old gent, Charlotte. He could lawyer me out of my shoes."

She nodded. "He is as good as they get."

"He had nothing but praise for you."

She shook her head. "It has nothing to do with me. He saw the advantages of your suggestion."

Above the unrelenting smile his ancient glittering eyes told nothing of what he was thinking. "Did I ever tell you about Beamish?"

She sat back and put on her own meaningless smile. "Tell me again. Sometimes I think I want to write your biography."

"It couldn't be done. Most of it's up here." He tapped his weathered forehead.

"You can tell me."

He told her about Beamish, the long-ago partner who had taken Anderson for a dumb Swede and plotted to take over the business they had started.

"He sought his allies with the wrong people. He is part of the concrete foundation of the Wackham Building."

"You're kidding."

His smile might have suggested this. But he moved his head slowly back and forth. "They shoved him into a cement truck and in the morning he was poured into the frames of the foundation of the Wackham. Our first really big job."

"Was he ever found?"

"Nope."

This time through she wondered how Anderson could know these things if "they" had done them. Who were they?

"You ever hear of the Pianones?"

"Of course."

That seemed to be the answer. But that meant the Pianones

would have had to tell Anderson. So how could they have been the allies of Beamish, the man who had tried to unseat him? Charlotte looked it up in the microfilm of past issues of the *Fox River Tribune*. CONTRACTOR MISSING. *Willard Beamish, of Beamish and Anderson, has been reported missing by his wife. . . .* Lars Anderson would say only that accountants were at work on the problem. What accountants? "Arthur Anderson." All in the family. She could imagine him smiling when he said it. Later issues recounted the fruitless search for the missing Beamish. A final story concerned the lavish memorial service his partner put on for him when Mrs. Beamish saw the advantages of being a widow. Beamish was eventually declared legally dead. Mrs. Beamish moved to Sarasota on the settlement Anderson gave her. In that story he had been Lars Anderson of Anderson Ltd.

There were several possible interpretations. It was an invented cautionary tale Lars gave to those in whom he placed trust. Or it was true and that meant he knew what he could not know if he were merely an innocent bystander.

"What exactly did Beamish try to do?" she asked after her research at the library.

He held up a hand. "Always speak well of the dead."

You wouldn't have to tear down the Wackham to see if the story was true, just use a high-tech sensor on the basement walls to see if it detected anything other than concrete. Charlotte decided to accept the story as a cautionary tale, whether true or false. And she wondered what notions Anderson had picked up from his lunch with Amos Cadbury.

"What's your real interest?" Leo said.

"I assume I am going to be Mrs. Leo Corbett."

Once that prospect would have made him drool. It no longer did. He had seen the promised land, he had enjoyed the fleshpots of Egypt. Charlotte had learned another truism. If a man can get what he wants on the cheap, he will not buy it dear. She had made a tactical mistake. She had assumed that Leo was as overwhelmed by their bedtime intimacy as she was.

"And we live happily ever after?"

"Anything wrong with that?"

"Yes. It never happens."

He was thinking of his parents. When she thought of hers it was as people she intended never to be like. Her father had freaked out, tried everything from peyote to LSD, and died at forty without having had a clear thought in twelve years. Her mother immediately latched on to another loser. Charlotte studied to keep her mind off her parents, her teachers recognized her talent, she got a scholarship to Chicago. By then her father was so far gone he wouldn't have understood if she had told him. Her mother said, "That's nice," recognizing the scholarship as the end of any responsibility she had for Charlotte.

"Why did you name me Charlotte?"

"Charlotte Bronte." The memory came out of a druggy fog.

"Did you ever see a height wuther?"

"Lots of times." Followed by hysterical laughter. At the University of Chicago Charlotte said she was an orphan.

"You having second thoughts on the idea of a compromise?"

"What were my first thoughts?"

"You liked it."

"Did I? I'd like to put all those priests out of commission."

Had she pulled a Beamish? If Lars Anderson's confidence in her was shaken and if Leo's ardor was cooling . . .

"How's our boy Leo?" Lars asked.

"You want to talk to him? I'll bring him here."

"That might be hard."

"Why?"

"He moved without leaving a forwarding address."

He knew. He knew she had a personal plan as well as the one she had worked out for him and presented to Amos Cadbury. It was time for fresh and ruthless thinking; she did not intend to end up in the *Fox River Tribune*'s morgue—or any other.

Consider my affliction and deliver me.
            —Psalm 119

"Of *course* he can't find him," Hazel sneered. "The man is an idiot."

"He is a licensed private detective."

"Dogs have licenses." And she looked at Tuttle as if she were going to make an invidious comparison with his credentials as a lawyer.

Farniente had been keeping vigil outside Leo Corbett's deserted apartment on the chance that he might return.

"But he moved out," Tuttle said, glad that Hazel wasn't there at the Great Wall where he was receiving the detective's report, which was heavy on what Farniente had been doing, or not doing, and empty so far as the object of his search, Leo Corbett, went.

"What if he is a homing pigeon?"

Farniente was a turkey, in Hazel's judgment. She had completely reversed her estimate of the detective, whom she had regarded at first as an upwardly social move from Peanuts Pianone. ("At least he can speak.") So can dogs, Tuttle thought, remembering it now. But Farniente had plunged in Hazel's judgment when he hadn't delivered Leo to the office within hours of taking the assignment.

"What's he doing?"

"A man has to eat and sleep."

"We're talking of men?"

Hazel in a bad mood was only a tick of the clock away from Hazel in a good mood, but she hadn't been in a good mood since Leo, the "golden calf," had disappeared from sight. Behind the closed door of his office, among the neatness and order, Tuttle brooded. He reviewed his meeting with Leo in the courthouse, he remembered the pivotal scene when, with Leo at his elbow, he had outlined for Tetzel the series that was to put Leo definitively into the picture as the grandson who had been jobbed out of his heritage by a senile grandfather scattering his wealth to the winds. Had he expressed admiration for the success of the series? The only article of Tetzel's he had commented on was the last which all but featured the unfortunate Father Nathaniel.

"How'm I going to get anything if they sell?"

"Talk, Leo, talk. That's all it is."

But in truth, Tuttle was made nervous by signs that the Athanasians were open to a deal with Lars Anderson. It was easy to enter into Leo's discontent. The poor lad had been in the habit of haunting the one-time estate of his grandfather. Tuttle had been surprised by how well Leo knew the grounds: He seemed to carry a map of the place around in his too-large head.

"My father would have started digging there if he had gotten the place."

Leo was a man of many discontents. Why should it surprise him that a man who spoke with such contempt of his father should be deficient in every loyalty? Tuttle himself was oriental in his reverence for his father, the parent who had never lost faith in his son.

"Farniente, listen," he said in the Great Wall where his supposed employee was gobbling down half a dozen dishes at the same time. "Forget the apartment."

He directed Farniente to camp outside Anderson Ltd.

"You think old Lars will lead me to him?"

Tuttle sighed. A man like Anderson left his fingerprints nowhere. He had flunkies to do his work for him. He told the detective about the young woman who was Anderson's right hand, of whose activities his left hand was supposedly unaware.

"Tail Charlotte Priebe," Tuttle ordered.

Within hours, Farniente, to his own surprise, had struck oil. He had followed Charlotte to where she lived and ingratiated himself with a woman who spent several morning hours mopping the lobby floor. They discussed the businesslike young woman who lived in an apartment on the third floor.

"Alone?"

Matilda's eyes slid back and forth and she showed her irregular teeth in a smile. "Not anymore."

Matilda's description of the man who had moved in with Charlotte was close enough to Leo Corbett to make Farniente bring out his cell phone. He hesitated, thinking of Hazel, then rang the number.

"Tuttle & Tuttle," Hazel said with sweet efficiency.

"I've found him."

"Farniente?"

"Yes. Give me Tuttle."

An excited Tuttle came on in a minute, with Hazel chattering advice in the background as Farniente reported.

"Don't move. I'll be there in twenty minutes."

It was a half hour before he got there, and Farniente was nowhere to be found. Tuttle went into the lobby and sidestepped a mop wielded by a woman who seemed to be memorizing the floor. Tuttle got out a twenty-dollar bill and began to fold it lengthwise, keeping the denomination prominent. This distracted the cleaning lady from the floor. Her eyes fixed on the twenty.

"He left," she said, when he described Farniente.

"Did he say where he was going?" He asked it in despair.

"He was following the man."

"Ah." In his elation, Tuttle gave her the bill which had been intended only as a prop to gain her attention. He went back to his car, got behind the wheel, pulled his tweed hat over his face, and waited. Thus did Napoleon wait on Elba, thus had Patton stewed in England before being given the Third Army. Unlike these lofty analogues, he fell asleep, sweet sleep coming as it will when the clouds lift, and the sun once more puts in an appearance.

When he awoke, he called Hazel. "Have you heard from him?"

"Aren't you with him?"

"That answers my question."

"Lose him again and you lose a secretary."

A tempting offer, but Tuttle let it go. He called Farniente's cell phone, risking distracting the detective from his task. There was no answer.

Clouds gathered, the sun went into eclipse, darkness fell on the soul of Tuttle. In such a slough of despond, he was shaken when someone bumped into the back of his car. He pushed back his tweed hat and looked angrily into the rearview mirror. It was Farniente who had pulled in behind him. And then Tuttle saw Leo going into the building. When Leo was inside, Tuttle got out of his car and went back to Farniente, ignoring the angry horns of motorists who swerved to avoid him. Farniente had his window rolled down and a smile of triumph on his narrow face.

"Where did he go?"

"In and out of several buildings, then back here."

Tuttle relieved Farniente. He would take up the vigil himself. An hour passed and then Leo appeared, loaded with luggage, clothes draped over his arm. He carried them to his car and tossed them inside. When he pulled away, Tuttle was hard behind him. Leo drove with abandon but with an end in view. The hotel was two blocks from the building Leo had moved out of a few days before. He parked, gathered up his belongings, and went inside. Five minutes later, Tuttle went in to see about renting a room.

"Full," said a voice from behind a newspaper. Tuttle, throwing all habits of parsimony to the winds, displayed a twenty-dollar bill over the newspaper. The *Sun-Times* set and a wizened man wearing an Irish tweed hat looked up at Tuttle. He saw Tuttle's hat. A camaraderie was established. The young man who had just moved in? Leo Corbett. He took the room for a week. Tuttle pushed the twenty across the counter. The twin of his tweed hat swayed negatively.

"Keep it."

Tuttle felt that he had been readmitted to human society, where people trusted one another, where favors were done without the prospect of gain, where he was not the only one who wore a tweed hat throughout the year.

Teach me good judgment and knowledge.

—*Psalm 119*

Stanley Morgan might have been freed on bail, or gone free without it, if he had followed advice and hired a lawyer. But he remained in a cell while the judge sought someone available to come to Morgan's defense at the county's expense. The questions raised by young George's story about cleaning up the maintenance shed would have provided a reasonable basis for letting Morgan go free. But, to Phil Keegan's relief, Morgan remained in custody.

"He wants to see a priest," Phil said on the phone to Father Dowling.

"Is he Catholic?"

"I didn't ask. Why else would he want to see a priest? The man has something on his mind. It would be crazy to let him out."

"I'll be down, Phil."

Phil would, of course, be thinking what he himself was. A priest was sought to make a confession and it could be that what Morgan would not admit to the police he would tell a priest under the seal of the confessional. But before Father Dowling left the rectory, Marie announced that Michael George had come to see him. When she brought the young man to the study, she had a protective arm around his shoulders.

"Here he is, Father." She might have been producing a long-sought friend.

He thanked Marie. Michael seemed glad to get out from under that maternal embrace.

"Rita came to see you," he said, when the door was shut.

"You were with her."

"She came yesterday, alone."

Father Dowling fell silent as he thought about the day before. He had been away from the rectory for several hours. He would have liked to summon Marie Murkin and ask her in front of this young man if she had been practicing without a license. But such pusillanimous thoughts did not seem fitting given the anguish on his visitor's face.

"If she did, I didn't see her. I was out part of the day."

Michael almost relaxed. "We came to talk to you about getting married. Now I think she is changing her mind. Because of Father Nathaniel's death."

"From what I've heard, you've all but admitted to killing him."

"I told them what I did. That's all. If they want to make me a murderer, okay."

"Okay?"

"I cleaned up the maintenance shed."

"Why?"

"Because my father liked everything in its place, tools, machines, everything."

"So you did it for your father?"

"Did Rita say that?"

"I told you I haven't spoken with her since the two of you were here together. Is that what she thinks?"

Michael was silent, working his mouth, searching Father Dowling's face.

"Is that what you're doing, Michael? Do you think your father killed Nathaniel?"

"No!" The word emerged like a primal scream.

"Then why did you feel you had to clean up the shed? Whoever attacked the priest must have done it there. You were making it difficult for the police to find any clues or indications of who it might have been."

Father Dowling was certain the story would come out, and eventually it did. Michael had come here because Rita had, and he thought she had told him that her fiancé was willing to risk being charged with murder in order to protect his father. His account of that morning made clear why he had acted as he had.

The night before the murder, at the lodge, his father and Stanley Morgan had talked about Nathaniel, Morgan telling Mr. George of his experiences with the former priest in California. They were drinking retsina wine and his father was affected by it as he always was when he drank too deep. The two men agreed that Nathaniel was a devil.

"I'm here to let him know I'm here. Maybe I can stop the trouble he is causing."

"I'd like to go after him with a hedge trimmer," George cried.

That was the drunken threat Michael remembered the following morning. He had not expected his father to rise as early as was his custom. But he was not in his bed. Michael, before having breakfast, went to see if he was already at work, making up for the previous night's excess by getting to work at the crack of dawn. When he came to the grotto, Michael saw Nathaniel on the kneeler, the ax buried in his back. He had never seen a dead man, but he was sure the priest was dead. He hurried on to the maintenance shed where chaos had replaced order. What would his father say? And then he thought, My God, he did it. And then he set to work cleaning up, removing hurriedly the traces of a struggle, splashing paint over the blood on the workbench that would not wipe away. When he was done, he heard someone running toward the shed and he stepped out to meet his father.

"Someone killed him," his father cried. "I have to phone Father Boniface."

Michael returned to the house and waited and soon the 911 ambulance roared up the drive and backed down the path to the grotto, being directed by his father.

"That doesn't sound like a guilty man."

Yet both father and son had feared that the other was a murderer. But two men had sat over retsina the night before, two men had talked of avenging themselves on Nathaniel.

"And your guest disappeared. Now he has been arrested."

"He was just taking up my father's anger."

"Was he? He had a real past grievance against Nathaniel. Your father's fear was for what Nathaniel would do."

"Father, I don't know."

"Do you want my advice? Go talk to your father. Tell him what you thought and why you did what you did."

"How could I tell him that?"

"How can you not tell him now? Believe me, it will come to him as a tremendous relief."

"If he didn't do it."

"Won't he tell you if he did?"

Michael did not know. But his agony had deepened because he avoided his father, afraid to speak to him. He decided that he would rather hear his father's response, no matter what it was.

"And the two of you should then tell the police everything."

Father Dowling thus went downtown to speak with Stanley Morgan, wondering if he was not on his way to speak to the murderer of Father Nathaniel.

I said in my haste, "All men are liars."
—*Psalm 117*

Jails are like hospitals in the sense that every day, all day, they are passed by people who do not dwell on what others like themselves are undergoing within. Illness, when it comes, is not accompanied by guilt, whereas the jailed are doubly the outcasts of society. Yet how many innocent people might they contain? Starting with St. Paul. But guilty or innocent, Stanley Morgan would want to see a priest to speak of more than just crime and punishment.

Phil went upstairs to the cells with him, smoothing his way, and left him waiting in a visitor's room for Morgan to be brought to him. Morgan came in, stopped, and stared at Father Dowling.

"You wanted to see a priest?"

"I thought they would send an Athanasian, given what I'm being held for."

"A priest is a priest."

Morgan laughed an unhappy laugh and sat down. "I hope Richards—Nathaniel—was not a typical priest."

"Tell me how you knew him."

The story as told by Morgan was substantially what Father Dowling had already heard from Phil Keegan and Boniface, but with understandable differences of emphasis.

"I was a naive fool from the beginning. I see that now so clearly. How could it have seemed perfectly natural to me that a man who had been a complete stranger days before should offer to set me up in business, finance the whole thing, and himself play only a background role? I knew nothing of the man, but then he knew very little more about me. As with most things that seem too good to be true, our partnership turned out to be just that."

"When did you learn that he was a priest?"

"Do you know, that's when any doubts I might have had were laid to rest. The way he described his leaving left him with all the idealism he'd had when he became a priest."

"How did he describe his leaving?"

"Vatican II." Morgan looked at Father Dowling. "I say that and I realize I don't know what it means. When I was a kid, reference was made to it all the time."

"So you are a Catholic."

"The way Nathaniel was a priest," Morgan said wryly. "I had convinced myself that the Church had failed me, don't ask me how. It was a relief to get away from all the restrictions and rules."

"Is that all it was?"

"That was my story."

"And now?"

"When I asked Father Boniface if I could make a retreat with him, I felt that I had already been on a retreat. Being locked up, even in as easy a place as I was, gets you thinking. The main thing was that I was not free, and for a while at least I welcomed that. Now it no longer depended on me what I did tomorrow or the next day or for months. You ask yourself what use you had made of all that lost freedom. My life didn't make a pretty picture. I tried to do well by my clients, it was easy to think that I was doing them an essential service. I thought I was. But what kind of service is that, helping people to increase their wealth when they already have more than enough? It's a game, finally, trying to take advantage of the market, watching your investments increase in value. But it's addictive. There's no natural limit to it. There is always the desire for more. I was as bad as my greediest clients."

"So what did you conclude?"

"Oh, it wasn't a matter of any definite conclusion. More of a negative one. I knew the kind of person I no longer wanted to be."

"And the Church?"

Morgan smiled. "We had a part-time chaplain, a priest who said Mass on Sunday and came by once in a while. His sermons seemed part of the punishment."

"He let you down?"

"Touché. I suppose I wanted him to. I didn't want ready-made answers, not that he had any. He spent most of his time wondering what Christianity was, and why we should think ourselves better than others. My experience as a Catholic was that I had thought myself worse."

"You met Nathaniel's wife?"

"Yes. Marilyn. I liked her. She was thoroughly California, but still a nun in a way, a woman with a message. Only now it had to do with sex. Getting rid of inhibitions was the purpose of life.

My faith may have gone, but I knew that was a pretty limited notion. She worried about me. She had a video she insisted I watch. We watched it together. She and Richards snuggled on the couch while we watched."

"You never married?"

"I have been unlucky in love as well."

He seemed to insist on the banality of his life, and yet it does not require utter tragedy to bring a person low, to the realization that the world is not one's own artifact. Or that where moth and rust consume and thieves break in and steal cannot be our ultimate treasure. Morgan remembered the passage.

"It's a cliché, of course. Some prisoners read up on the law, others read the Bible. There must have been a dozen new translations of the Bible in the prison library. I settled for the King James version."

"No Douay-Rheims?"

"What's that?"

"We used to call it the Catholic Bible. A translation of the Latin vulgate less elegant than Cramner's."

"You seem to think I know things I don't."

"Well, I don't know why you asked to see a priest."

"Are you happy in your parish?"

"Yes."

"Never thought of getting out of the priesthood?"

"My worry is that the priesthood would get out of me."

"I took Edna Hospers and her kids to a ball game. For a moment there, I was seeing myself as having a wife, kids like hers. And then her boy looked me up on the Web."

"And you went on retreat."

"I decided to do what I had come here to do. Confront Richards and see how he would react to seeing me."

"How did he react?"

"I never found out. For a while I thought I would just let him worry, knowing I was there. We could talk face to face after he'd had plenty of time to wonder why I had come."

"So you didn't kill him?"

"It doesn't seem to matter if you're innocent once the police get hold of you."

"You fled the lodge. Where did you go?"

Morgan looked surprised. "Don't you know?"

"I know that you were discovered in my school."

After a moment, Morgan said, "It was the only haven I knew."

"You didn't count on Cy Horvath remembering that you had taken Edna Hospers to dinner and had treated her and her kids to a ball game?"

"I didn't even think that I might get Edna into trouble. Oh, I thought of it, why deny it? But I had no alternative. She isn't in any trouble, is she?"

"Not that I know of."

"That's one good thing anyway."

"So what can I do for you?"

"You're doing it. I have longed just to talk like this."

"And that's enough?"

"Did you expect me to ask you to hear my confession?"

"Yes."

A long silence. "I wouldn't know where to begin."

"Would you like to try? You've told me an awful lot already."

Father Dowling took out the miniature stole he had brought. Morgan stared at it.

"You came prepared."

"Should I put it on?"

A series of expressions fluttered across his face. The final one was resigned.

"Yes."

O give thanks to the Lord, for He is good!
                                        —*Psalm 118*

The superior of the Athanasians had come to the rectory, showing up without fanfare and startling Marie Murkin with his almost ebullient manner.

"Ah, Mrs. Murkin, you are a sight for sore eyes."

"I have wanted to talk to you so much," the housekeeper had said, but without any hope of becoming the confidante of Boniface and having him pour out to her the troubles that had visited the Athanasians. Marie had belatedly wondered at the fact that Stanley Morgan had been discovered hiding in the school and developed an explanation of it.

"Had you heard that Edna went to dinner with him?" she had asked the pastor. "Did you know he took the whole family to a ball game?"

"As you always said, Marie, he was a good man."

"Some people dissemble very well."

"Stanley Morgan?"

"And others." And she had expressed her wonder that Edna had been with the man when Cy Horvath made the arrest. "She had the nerve to suggest that he had come here because of me."

"That's hardly impossible, Marie."

"Then why didn't he come to the rectory? There's something fishy, Father Boniface."

"Oh, I doubt that, Marie."

The fact was that Father Dowling had talked with Cy Horvath, but the lieutenant had been unwilling to say whether Edna had anything to do with Morgan's being found in the nurse's office on the third floor of the school.

"Anyone can just walk in and walk around. As I did when I found him."

"What prompted you to look for him there?"

Cy's silence could be as uncommunicative as his speech. "It's where I would have gone if I were him. He was a stranger here. How many places did he know of? No doubt he saw he could slip into the school and find some empty room."

Perhaps Cy thought Father Dowling meant to ask Edna about it, but he did not. Whatever had happened had ended differently and sooner than Morgan had imagined. Nor had Father Dowling pursued that aspect when he spoke to Morgan in the visitor's room of the jail.

When he had heard Father Boniface speaking to Marie, Father Dowling had emerged from his study to greet his unexpected visitor. Marie had watched the two men head back to the study with a forlorn expression.

"I will make tea, Father Boniface."

"Not for me, Marie. I only drink it during Lent."

"Lent?"

"I hate tea."

And so Marie had been shut out and Father Dowling heard the good news of Boniface's meeting with the cardinal.

Boniface was a changed man, no longer despondent and beaten, and Father Dowling understood why when his old friend told him of his meeting with the cardinal.

"Do we never stop being children, Father Dowling? I realized that I had been seeing everything in terms of its effect on me. If my life was coming to a close, then that of the Athanasians, too, would soon be over. Nonsense. It is the destiny of an order to outlast its members. I feel I have been an utter failure as superior. The Order has been in melancholy hands. But no more."

Clearly Boniface was eager to lay out the lines for the renewal of his Order and report to the cardinal. But his next appointment would be a very different one. And his attitude toward the tragic happening at the grotto had also changed.

"They have the murderer in custody. Doubtless the trial will prove a sensation for the press, but it is merely an event. Not that I downplay the death of poor Nathaniel."

"I am sure the murder will be solved and the one responsible prosecuted."

"How I lament the way I treated the return of Nathaniel and the way I reacted when he began his little campaign. I should have stopped it immediately as I did eventually."

"Let us hope that proves to have been the turning point for the Athanasians."

"I think I may have been unjust to Nathaniel."

"How so?"

"Perhaps he was not acting out of the hope of personal gain."

"Was that unclear?"

"Or perhaps he did not see it for what it was."

"May he rest in peace."

"Amen. Amen. I suppose I should show more responsibility for poor Morgan, although I cannot think what I can do for him."

"If he is tried, you will be called to testify."

"Oh, my God." And for a moment the beaten Boniface was back. But not for long. "I will do what I must do. You have visited him?"

"He wanted to see a priest."

The implications of putting it that way were not lost on Boniface and he did not pursue the subject. What would Boniface's reaction have been if he had heard the man's confession? Father Dowling asked him to say more about the plans for renewal. They were indeed exciting and, the more one thought of it, possible of realization. But the attempt alone was worth it and the prospect had transformed Boniface.

An aspect of Boniface's previous downheartedness was that the drama of the Georges had passed him by. His only mention of them was that the new plan would be reassuring to the Georges, father and son.

"I shall also propose to the cardinal that we resume pastoral work for the archdiocese. Not a parish, of course, not yet. But helping out, for example. Would you want someone here, Father?"

"Only if it's you, Boniface."

The superior beamed. "That is what I was going to propose. I want to set the example. I won't be in your way?"

"A Mass on Sundays, perhaps?"

"And Saturday confessions."

And so the bargain was struck. But Boniface was not done.

"Whatever Morgan's motive, the reason he gave for wanting to stay with us, plus the memory of your recent retreat, suggests another avenue to be explored."

A retreat center. For priests, but for laity as well. "Separately, of course. This will acquaint people with our new lease on life."

"If you need a recommendation with priests, I shall be happy to give one."

He himself had found the melancholy Boniface a good retreat master, the task enabling the Athanasian to put aside for the nonce his gloomy forebodings and draw on a lifetime of spiritual development.

"And I look forward to teaching Latin again. Did I ever tell you of the visit I once made to Horace's villa near Tivoli?"

He hadn't and he almost chattered as he recalled the sunny day he had climbed into the hills and seen the remains of the country redoubt where the Roman poet had escaped from the suffocating patronage of Augustus. "Of course he had Lalage there," Boniface said. "His slave girl. You remember the phrase, *Dulce ridentem Lalagen amabo, dulce loquentem* . . . Of course, that is an ode I never dwelt on with my students. Young George was my last great success as a teacher."

"Michael?"

"He was educated with us. There were only a few seminarians then, many of whom left, but I went on with Michael. He is a gifted Latinist."

A delightful surprise. When Boniface left, Father Dowling felt that he had been given a glimpse of the bright future awaiting the Athanasians.

"Well, he was cheerful enough," Marie said.

"Indeed he was."

"Odd."

"Do you prefer melancholy visitors?"

"I mean, after what's happened."

"He is putting his mind to what is going to happen."

"The trial? Oh, I dread being asked to give testimony. I hope nothing I say hurts the man half as much as he has hurt himself, but justice must be done."

"And mercy bestowed."

"Not by a court of law, Father Dowling. That is not its purpose."

"How hard you are becoming."

"I hate to be made a fool of."

Oh, do not let the oppressed return ashamed!
—Psalm 74

Tuttle took up his vigil in the lobby of the hotel where Leo Corbett had rented a room and imagined the scenario when Leo came down and found the lawyer he had been avoiding waiting for him. But it was difficult in imagination to go beyond the startled reaction he expected from Leo. An hour passed and Tuttle's stomach began to rumble. There was no restaurant in this hotel, but there was candy displayed on the counter. Tuttle went over to his tweedy counterpart and bought a bag of M&Ms and a sack of potato chips. And then he had a thought.

"Let me use your phone," he said to the desk clerk.

"There's a booth over there."

"I'd rather not use a public phone." Tuttle had allowed the seedy custodian of the desk to believe that he was with the police. That had inspired the usual reaction.

"Hey, there's nothing going on here."

"We know that. And you know why I'm here."

The man glanced at a form before him. "Corbett?"

"Right."

He lifted the phone and put it before Tuttle. Tuttle dialed police headquarters and said audibly, "Officer Pianone, please."

Peanuts was found napping in the press room and the call was transferred there.

"Tuttle."

"Yeah."

"What are you doing?"

"Working."

"Good. I need you."

He gave the name of the hotel and Peanuts asked if he had been thrown out of the office. Tuttle suffered the nasal chortle that followed on this.

"There's a new day dawning, Peanuts. Look, stop at the Great Wall on the way. You know what I like. Get anything you want. I'll pay you when you get here. But you better hurry."

Peanuts agreed and hung up. Tuttle replaced the phone and stood for a moment as if in thought, then pushed the phone away.

He returned to the shapeless lobby chair and decided it had been wise not to call Hazel. Victory was about to be snatched from the jaws of defeat, at least that was the hope, but the world was a funny place and he did not want to crow before he had his man.

When Peanuts arrived the man behind the desk objected to their turning the lobby into a fast-food place, but Peanuts gave him an egg roll and he subsided behind the counter beneath his tweed hat. It was like Peanuts not to be curious why he had been summoned, since food was in the offing and Tuttle paid him before they set to.

"Ah, for a six-pack," Tuttle sighed, when he was restored.

Peanuts nodded.

"Things are going to be like they were, Peanuts. That's a promise."

"Sure."

An understandable skepticism, the way he had allowed Hazel to take over his life. His professional life. He had fended off her suggestion that she put a little order into where he lived as well. She had driven by the place.

"That's a nice building."

"My parents lived there."

Mention of his parents always quieted her. She could not grasp the piety he felt toward those who had borne and raised him. He discouraged all talk of his personal past. There was a limit. And things were going to go back to the way they had been in his office, too, or he would know the reason why.

The elevator door opened and Leo Corbett emerged. He came up to Tuttle. "They told me you were down here."

A traitor in a tweed hat.

"Long time no see."

"There's something I've been meaning to tell you, Tuttle."

"I was going to say the same thing."

But before he could say more, the revolving door was set in motion and in walked Cy Horvath.

"You're under arrest, Tuttle."

"You should stay out of the heat, Horvath."

"Matilda identified you. Come along."

"Matilda!"

"The cleaning lady where Charlotte Priebe lived."

"What are you talking about?"

"She's dead, Tuttle. Matilda found her and ran into the street to find a cop. She described you to a tee."

Horvath glanced at the desk and at Tuttle's clone and hesitated for a moment. "Peanuts, we're arresting Tuttle."

"Okay."

Et tu, Brute? Meanwhile, Leo had disappeared. They took turns going through the revolving door, Horvath first, then Tuttle, then Peanuts, coming into the summer heat.

"You'll regret this, Horvath."

"Tell it to your lawyer."

"I am a lawyer, dammit."

Tuttle's car was left where he had parked it, to be ticketed and towed some hours later. On the ride downtown, he asked Horvath how he had known where he was.

"We got an anonymous call about a vagrant doing a sit-in in the lobby."

Tuttle fell back. The Judas in the tweed hat? Leo? It gave him something to think about while he was taken to be booked. It wasn't until then that the reason for all this soaked in. Charlotte Priebe was dead.

❧ Part Three ❧

My God, My God, why have You forsaken me?
—*Psalm 22*

Keegan and Cy took turns questioning Tuttle, arresting him having seemed the best way to get his cooperation.

"I was looking for my client."

"Get tired of chasing ambulances?"

"Leo Corbett had been staying with her. I had the place under surveillance and when he moved out and went to that hotel, I followed him. He had just come downstairs when you showed up."

The information that Leo had been living with Charlotte Priebe was news, if true. Matilda hadn't mentioned that. They put Tuttle in a cell while he shouted law at them. Give him a little shaking, that was the idea. But Phil Keegan was almost glad to be diverted from the murder of Father Nathaniel. Tetzel wouldn't let up about the slowness of the investigation. He drew attention to the religious persuasion of Keegan and Horvath, intimating that they had some ulterior reason for letting the pursuit of the priest's murderer wither and die. The reporter even supplied information about the percentage of successful arrests and convictions in murders over the past decade in Fox River. Now the murder of Charlotte Priebe would be front-page stuff.

When the traffic cop called in to say a cleaning lady was reporting a murder, Cy Horvath had gone to check it out. He was taken up to the apartment and let in and found her in the bathtub, submerged. Fortunately Pippen and not Lubins came to check on the body.

"She drowned," Pippen said.

It was something, standing there beside the comely coroner surveying the nude body of the young woman.

"People don't drown in bathtubs."

"There could be any number of explanations."

Photographs were taken, the lab exports went over the apartment with extraordinary care, every once in a while ducking in to look at the corpse.

"Necrophilia is everywhere," Pippen murmured.

"Something wrong with her neck?"

"No, your head."

Cy rummaged around in the desk and discovered that she worked for Anderson Ltd. As he was turning over papers, a lab girl said they were going to take the computer downtown. But Cy was wondering what sort of hell Anderson would raise when he found out that a woman who had obviously been high on the corporate ladder was found dead in her bath. He decided that Anderson should hear the news from him.

Anderson's eyes were cold but he was smiling when Cy went into his office.

"What the hell is this about Charlotte Priebe?"

"Did she work for you?"

"Did she? What do you mean?"

"She's dead."

Anderson sat down and his smile went, but the wrinkles where it had been remained. Cy told him what they knew. Anderson gave an incredulous laugh when told the woman he described as his administrative assistant had drowned in her bath.

"People don't drown in bathtubs."

"Someone else said that. That's why I'm here. I'm in homicide."

Anderson looked at Cy's card for the first time. "Okay, Horvath. You're a lieutenant in homicide. I want you to find the bastard who did this. That girl was like a daughter to me."

"She live alone?"

Anderson exploded. "I won't have you dragging her name through the mud. Just find out who killed her."

Cy decided not to tell him that Leo Corbett had spent some nights in Charlotte Priebe's apartment. Maybe she took in stray cats as well and there was nothing to it. He asked Anderson if anything related to her work might explain what had happened.

For fifteen minutes, Anderson told him what a genius Charlotte Priebe had been. "Came to work for me and within a couple of years, her office was next to mine. I invented the title administrative assistant for her. Vice president of whatever couldn't have covered it."

"What had she been assisting you on lately?"

Anderson looked at him shrewdly. "Why did you ask if she lived alone?"

"Tell me."

Anderson's response was an exercise in circumlocution. He told Cy in great detail about the plans he had developed for the Corbett property, if he could get hold of it. Charlotte worked with him hand in glove. He couldn't pay her enough for all the things she did.

"For example, Corbett's grandson."

"Leo Corbett."

"So you read the papers. Young man couldn't find his rear end with both hands. He had fallen into the hands of a shyster lawyer named Tuttle and it was Charlotte's aim to free him from the association. I just learned that she had hid him in her apartment, so Tuttle couldn't get at him. She came up with an idea to break the logjam with those priests who own the property. Do you know Amos Cadbury?"

"Yes."

"The lawyer?"

"I know him."

"Talk to Cadbury and he'll tell you about it."

"So who would want to kill her?"

"Well, one guy who had a pretty good motive was Tuttle. Do you know him?"

"He's under arrest."

"Already? Good. Good. Lieutenant, anything I can do."

So later, when he was questioning Tuttle, Cy asked him what Lars Anderson had against him.

"Who's Lars Anderson?"

"Funny."

"I don't know the man."

"He knows you. He says you talked Leo Corbett into being your client. Tuttle, we know Tetzel got the idea for that series from you. A real scorched-earth policy. Anderson says the girl you drowned in her bathtub had come up with a compromise and that meant getting Corbett away from you."

"Horvath, I was never inside that apartment. Scout's honor."

Tuttle raised his left hand and tried to touch his little finger with his thumb.

"Just talked to the cleaning lady?"

"That's right. Ask her if I went upstairs."

"You camp in the lobby there, too?"

"I waited in my car." Tuttle flipped off his hat. "Talk to Farniente, he'll back up everything I say."

"Farniente!"

"Ask him. You got to let me out of here."

"Know any good lawyers?"

Tuttle, who never swore because his father never had, swore now. "Let me call my office."

"Did you find him?" Hazel cried.

"I'm in jail. I've been arrested."

Her mocking laughter invaded Tuttle's ear like a gas. "Mentally?"

"If I want jokes, I can listen to the cops."

"What did you do, run a red light?"

"Charlotte Priebe is dead."

"Miss Efficiency?" Like all dominating women Hazel despised other women.

"In her bathtub."

"You're kidding."

"I went there, trailing Leo Corbett, and the cleaning lady fingered me."

"Why don't you start at the beginning?"

Where is the beginning? And what was the point of telling her all this? But he did, in as much detail as he could summon, wanting to use every moment of phone time they would allow him.

The cell gave him the creeps. He had visited clients who had been arrested, he had watched them taken away after the interview and never really given a second thought to the door clanging on them. Hazel had about as much sympathy for him. He would like to lock her up and throw away the key. Tuttle listened to himself telling Hazel what had gone on since last they met. He recognized a boondoggle when he heard it.

"What hurts is, just as I had him, the police barged in and made this ridiculous charge and the next thing I know Leo Corbett has vamoosed."

What did staking out the Priebe woman and tailing Leo have to do with one another?

"He had been staying with her?"

"Leo?" Again that noxious laughter. "She must have been really hard up."

"It really helps to talk to you."

"What do you want me to do?"

"Get hold of Farniente. Tell him to come down here and clear me."

"He should be a big help."

"Do it." He hung up. The silence of the cell was better than talking to Hazel. Who did she like, anyway? She had contempt for Peanuts and thought Farniente was a joke. She wasn't leading any cheers for him, either, so why had he gotten stuck with her?

Farniente, when they brought him in, was the soul of prudence. Cy thought he would deny he even knew Tuttle.

"All right, he hired me."

"What for?"

"This guy Leo Corbett? He was giving Tuttle the dodge. He wanted to locate him. So he called me in."

"And you found him?"

"He was shacking up with this woman who got herself killed."

It was difficult to establish a timeline on the basis of either Tuttle's or Farniente's stories. And then Pippen came through with her preliminary report.

"Overdose."

"Of what?"

"Sleeping pills."

"Suicide?"

"Looks like it."

Cy went over to the lab to see what they had. They had dusted the whole apartment but come up empty.

"Nothing anywhere. The place had been wiped. There were only a couple fingerprints of the woman."

Consider my enemies, for they are many.
—*Psalm 25*

When Amos Cadbury came to St. Hilary's rectory to go over recent events, the venerable lawyer was visibly unhappy. He had met and admired Charlotte Priebe and found the story of her suicide incredible.

"No container for sleeping pills was found in the apartment I am told," Father Dowling said.

"It is as likely that it walked out of there as it is that Charlotte Priebe committed suicide."

"Was she religious?"

"I wouldn't go that far."

Amos felt somewhat foolish giving this testimonial for Charlotte Priebe on the basis of their one encounter, but that had been an occasion when so many of the difficulties facing the Athanasians seemed to lift. And then came the murder of Father Nathaniel and now that of Charlotte Priebe. Who would not think that there was a connection between these deaths and the compromise Charlotte had broached? But a surprising call from Lars Anderson addressed that very issue.

"We owe it to Charlotte to carry it through, Cadbury."

Business as usual seemed a strange memorial, but doubtless Anderson was right. Amos assured him that nothing was changed so far as he was concerned and that he would be speaking to Father Boniface that day. But he had allotted time for this visit to St. Hilary's first.

"I cannot regret old Corbett's prodigality, Father, but it has created circumstances he could hardly have foretold."

"The incidental effects of our intended actions."

On any other occasion, Amos would have welcomed this opening to philosophical reflection, but he had come for more pragmatic reasons. Before he talked with Boniface, he wanted to know the latest results of the police investigation, and Father Dowling was almost sure to know them. Amos was reluctant to go hat in hand to the police asking for information. That was to run the risk of getting some condensed version. And he wanted to supplement what he could learn from the ineffable *Fox River Tribune*.

"Does Dante have a place in hell for yellow journalists, Father?"

"I am afraid he has a place for all of us if we misuse our freedom. That is what, in his letter to Can Grande della Scala, he gave as the allegorical meaning of the Comedy."

Another tempting tangent, but Amos was due to see Boniface in an hour. Tetzel had written a saccharine story of the suicide of a young woman, broken under the stresses of ruthless capitalism. He had found that she had once been a student of the liberal arts at the University of Chicago and conjured up an image of corporate recruiters descending like roaring lions on such lambs, seeking whom they might devour. The suggestion was that Anderson Ltd. had diverted Charlotte Priebe from the life of the mind, exploited her talents, burned her out in a few years until she bade good-bye to all that in the manner of a Roman Stoic by slipping out of life in her bath.

"That would have been written before doubt had been cast on its being a suicide," Father Dowling said.

"Don't be too sure. That man and the truth are strangers. At least it has gotten him off the subject of Father Nathaniel."

"Stanley Morgan cannot be blamed for the death of Charlotte Priebe."

"And there is a connection between those deaths, Father. I am sure of it. They should release the man."

"Morgan still doesn't have a lawyer."

"Have you seen him?"

"He asked for a priest."

Father Dowling's tone of voice suggested that was an avenue they could not pursue. "Why doesn't he have a lawyer?"

"He refused to get one. He has suffered much because of lawyers."

"Who is the judge in the case?" He was putting the question to himself, and he gave himself the answer. "Holmes. Christina Holmes."

"Apparently she has been having trouble assigning a lawyer to Morgan."

"I will talk to her. There are young people in the firm . . ." The firm of Amos Cadbury was not one any judge would regard as a pool of publicly appointed defenders, but Amos could alter that with a word. And suggest names.

"Phil Keegan dismisses the notion that the two deaths are connected, which is why he sees no reason to reconsider holding Stanley Morgan."

"It is logically possible that they are not connected. But life is not that logical."

"And the link would be the Corbett estate?"

"Exactly."

Amos went off to meet with Boniface, leaving Father Dowling to puff meditatively on his pipe and reflect on recent events. A unified theory attracts the logical mind, and Amos Cadbury was a man of reason. But the theory faced imposing obstacles. Stanley Morgan had to be seen by the police as a plausible murderer of Father Nathaniel, and Phil showed great reluctance to give weight to the strange behavior of the Georges, father and son. The father had revealed that Michael had come out of the maintenance shed as he ran to it to report the body of Nathaniel at the grotto. When it was discovered that the shed had been hurriedly cleaned up, the son admitted that he had done this. An attempt to destroy clues as to what he had done to Father Nathaniel there? That was the implication. But another and more poignant possibility had arisen. Michael had seen the body at the grotto when he arose early and was on the way to the shed, to see if his father had already gone there. He was surprised the old man was not still in his bed at the lodge, sleeping over the long session with retsina wine he had enjoyed the previous evening with Stanley Morgan. He came upon a shed that indicated to him that a great struggle had taken place there. When he came out and met his father the dread that had prompted him to clean up the shed seemed verified.

Phil Keegan had listened to Cy Horvath recall the actions of the Georges and drew another conclusion.

"Morgan sits up drinking with the old man, the old man goes to bed. Morgan lures Nathaniel to the shed, buries an ax in his back, and then returns to the lodge. That would have been around two in the morning. The scene for the Georges to suspect one another is set. When we arrive, Morgan disappears. Why? Cy picks him up right here, Roger, in the school. He has been in jail ever since, which is where he belongs."

"So who killed Charlotte Priebe?"

"That is a whole 'nother matter."

Father Boniface tried unsuccessfully to take an interest in the murdered young woman that Amos Cadbury told him of. Obviously this meant a good deal to the venerable lawyer, but Boniface could summon little more than generic sympathy several times removed. Until the relevance of Charlotte Priebe's death to the affairs of the Athanasians became clear. She had worked for Lars Anderson, she had presented Amos with a proposal that seemed the solution to all recent troubles.

"I would ask the Order to surrender very little in return for a great deal. As a not-negligible bonus, it would get you off the front pages of newspapers."

"Of course we would be guided by you, Mr. Cadbury."

"One of the lamentable effects of this young woman's death is that it prompts the police to release the man they have had in custody, under suspicion of murdering Father Nathaniel."

"Stanley Morgan."

Amos nodded. "While it would be absurd to suggest that an imprisoned man could commit another murder, it is equally absurd to think this exonerates him of the murder of which he is already suspected."

Of course, Amos Cadbury was right in rejecting any connection between the dreadful thing that had happened to Nathaniel and the death of this unfortunate young woman.

"Now I suppose the police will take a different attitude toward the Georges, father and son."

"The Georges."

"Would it occur to anyone that either of them could have done harm to Nathaniel?"

Amos Cadbury was not being ironic. Perhaps he didn't realize how threatening to the Georges all the talk of selling Marygrove must have seemed. However, that did not mean that . . .

"Why would the police think such things?" Boniface erased the question with an impatient gesture. "What do they think?"

"Only what they were invited to think."

How odd that Amos Cadbury should bring to him news of such matters on the grounds of Marygrove. The venerable lawyer adopted elegiac tones to tell the story of the son who suspected his father and the father who suspected his son. The strange condition in which the police had found the maintenance shed was now explained. Insofar as he had thought of it before, Boniface assumed that Andrew George would have taken the first opportunity to clean up the shed. Nothing sinister about that. The man had a passion for order and neatness. But to learn that Michael had hurriedly cleaned the place up, even slapped paint around to cover bloodstains, put a new face on events Boniface had almost succeeded in consigning to a locked compartment of memory. His heart was wrenched with agony thinking of the reactions of father and son. But surely their doubts had been lifted when Stanley Morgan had been arrested. And just as surely the release of Morgan would bring back their doubts—as well as the curiosity of the police.

"Father Dowling visited him," Amos Cadbury said.

"Morgan?"

"Yes. He had asked for a priest. I suppose he meant you."

Boniface had the sense that one, if not the main, purpose of Amos Cadbury's visit had been reached. The lawyer was of the opinion that Father Boniface owed it to himself, to his Order, to the Georges, and to the prisoner himself to pay a visit to Stanley Morgan before he became a free man once more.

To You, O Lord, I lift up my soul.
                    —*Psalm 25*

Fingerhut from the lab stood in Phil Keegan's doorway, chin on chest, looking over his glasses, combing his beard with fat fingers until he was noticed. Phil jumped.

"How long have you been there?"

"What day is it?"

"Come on."

Chortling, Fingerhut crossed to Phil's desk. "Boy, have I got something for you. Where's your computer?"

"Computer? I don't use one."

"Ye gods, a Luddite. You're going to have to come to the lab, then."

Phil went with him to the lab. Fingerhut never exaggerated the importance of what he found, quite the opposite; he was wary of creating false hopes in detectives. He waved a disk. "I took this from Charlotte Priebe's laptop."

"Laptop."

Fingerhut smiled wistfully behind his russet beard. "She could have been my laptop any day. A laptop is a portable computer, Keegan. Let's look at the file on the computer since you're here."

Most of the files had to do with Charlotte's work at Anderson Ltd. and would have to be gone through for whatever light they cast on things. An operation Fingerhut now regarded as superfluous.

"I was just running down the contents of her hard drive when I saw this." He highlighted an item on the screen: IN CASE I DIE. Fingerhut waited for Keegan's reaction as he had waited in his doorway.

"Is that it?"

"It's the name of a file."

Fingerhut clicked the mouse and there on the screen was a statement bearing the title *In Case I Die*. Again he waited in vain for a response.

"You want to read it on the screen or should I print it out?"

"I can't read anything but the title."

"That's because of where you're standing. I'll print it out."

He connected the laptop to a printer, clicked on an icon, clicked again, and the lights on the printer lit up. There was a whirring sound and then a page began to emerge from the printer. The first was followed by another.

"I made one for myself as well." He handed the first one to Phil.

In Case I Die

I have never felt afraid before, but I am afraid now. To explain why, I will set down a story that Lars Anderson told me on two separate occasions. The second time was today, and I am sure it was meant as a warning.

Many years ago, when the enterprise that is now Anderson Ltd. was just beginning, Lars had a partner named Beamish. His story is that Beamish tried to squeeze him out of the business by enlisting the help of a local family whose reputation is well known, the Pianones. Lars got wind of it and went to the Pianones, made his own deal, with the result that Beamish ended up in a cement mixer and was poured into the foundation frames of the Wackham Building. I should say that Lars did not in so many words say that he dealt with the Pianones, but that Beamish's supping with the devil had ended in the way just described.

What is wrong with this story? I checked the contemporary issues of the *Tribune* and found that Beamish had indeed been reported missing. A national search was undertaken, without results. Mrs. Beamish was given a sizeable amount of money and moved to Sarasota where eventually she died. How would Lars know the whereabouts of Beamish if he had not been instrumental in doing his partner in?

What is the relevance of this to me? I suggested a compromise to Amos Cadbury, who represents the owners of a property Lars is determined to get. Leo Corbett, the grandson of the man who gave the property to its present owners, the Order of St. Athanasius, had become the client of a local lawyer, Tuttle, who engineered a series of devastating articles in the *Tribune* aimed at claiming the entire property. The chances of this succeeding were virtually nil, however much harm the articles did to the present owners. I was asked by Lars to contact Leo Corbett, the grandson, and I did, persuading him that a compromise was his best hope of getting some of his grandfather's property. Lars told him he would get the original estate buildings, mainly the mansion and the original gardens and lodge. Whether or not Lars was sincere, Leo Corbett took the bait. It was then that I proposed a compromise to Amos Cadbury, who was open to the possibility. But I did more.

I took Leo into my apartment, to make him inaccessible to Tuttle, and Leo and I fell in love. In all frankness I cannot say whether this happened before or after another idea occurred to me, one beneficial to myself. As Leo's wife, I would gain twice—the bonus Lars promised me if the compromise went through, and co-ownership of what Leo got. Fatally, I did not tell Lars of this. Nor did I tell him that the safe house I had put Leo in was my apartment. Lars found out about that and must have surmised that I was working on behalf of myself as well as Anderson Ltd. That is when he told me the story of Beamish for the second time.

As I write this, Leo has left my apartment. I do not know where he went. But I suspect that Lars persuaded him to go. The scene is set for something to happen to me, the sort of thing that happened to Beamish. Perhaps I am being paranoid. Perhaps not. I think not. Hence this statement which I trust will be discovered and read if I should die mysteriously.

—Charlotte Priebe

"It's not dated," Keegan said, after he read it.

"The computer dates it. She wrote it the night before she was found dead."

Phil took the second copy of the printout from Fingerhut.

"Lock up that laptop. This is going to be kept utterly confidential. The whole statement is a time bomb. You got that? Don't tell anyone about this."

Fingerhut looked sad. "You don't have to tell me that, Keegan."

"I'm sorry. I know I don't. But it's just as well that we both understand that whatever we do with this is going to have to be cleared. And I don't have to tell you the complications of that."

"Robertson?"

"Robertson." Robertson was chief of the Fox River police, a sinecure he held thanks to the Pianone family and others. From the point of view of these patrons, Robertson's principal function was to deflect legal attention away from them.

"And there is Anderson. If we take this statement seriously, we would bring him under suspicion of two murders, Beamish and this girl. And Amos Cadbury is mentioned in a way that might sound compromising to some."

"So you're going to sit on it?"

It was Keegan's turn to look sad. "I didn't say that."

"Sorry. I know you didn't."

Before leaving the lab, Phil folded the two printouts carefully and put them in an inside pocket, patting them as if to prevent any telltale bulge. Then he went back to his office and told his secretary to get hold of Cy Horvath.

It is not a pleasant thing to spend one's career in a police department that is more or less in the hands of the enemy, but such was Phil Keegan's fate. When he had first learned of the influence of the Pianones on the force, his impulse was to resign and then raise public hell about it. His wife was alarmed at the prospect, he had her and his two little daughters to think of. There was no way he could sound the alarm about the inroads the Pianones had made into the department and then settle down peacefully to run a cigar store, say. The certainty he had of what would have happened to him made Charlotte Priebe's fears more than realistic. There had been rumors for years that Anderson's way with the building trades had been smoothed more than once by the intervention of the Pianone family. While he waited for Cy to come he thought of Beamish immured in the foundation walls of the Wackham Building. And he thought of Charlotte Priebe, submerged in her own bathtub with an overdose of sleeping pills in her system.

"Close the door," Keegan said, when Cy arrived. He began to take the folded sheets from his pocket, then stopped. He stood. "Let's go for a ride."

In his present mood, he did not consider even his own office secure. He and Cy went down to the garage and checked out a car. Horvath did not question this. He was one colleague Keegan would trust with his life. When Cy's athletic career at Illinois went aglimmering and he got on the force, Keegan had taken him under his wing. The integrity of the huge Hungarian was untouchable.

Keegan drove. He got on the interstate and headed for the Belevedere Oasis where he parked. Over coffee in the franchise restaurant, he handed Cy a copy of Charlotte Priebe's statement.

"That was on her computer. Fingerhut found it."

Cy read the printout without any change of expression. His eyes lifted to Keegan's.

"What are we going to do?"

"That's what we came here to talk about."

Cy nodded. "There isn't a clue in her apartment. The woman who sounded the alarm saw no one come or go during what would have been the relevant time."

"Was she paid off?"

Cy thought about it. "I don't think so. Her name is Matilda Szabo."

"Hungarian?"

"Only by marriage. I don't think she could keep her mouth shut."

"Maybe we better provide her with some protection."

"And take out an ad in the *Tribune*?"

"Okay, what do you suggest?"

"Checking out the basement walls of the Wackham Bulding."

"And take out an ad in the *Tribune*?"

Cy never laughed, but he wrinkled his nose and that was a seismic event in his facial expressions. "There are pretty simple ways to detect human remains. Pippen was telling me about them."

"Does she know how to do it?"

"I would say yes."

"Do you trust her?"

"I trust her."

"Then do it."

It made sense. If the Beamish story was only something Anderson used to scare young ladies and nothing more, the statement would be half discredited.

"Can I show her this?" Cy tapped the printout.

"You said you trusted her. Make sure she knows how explosive all this is."

Even the sparrow has found a home, and the swallow a
nest for herself.

—Psalm 84

As superior, Boniface was celebrant at the final rites for Richard
Krause, Father Nathaniel in religion. He had wandered in exterior
darkness for years but finally returned. He had died in the habit
he would not have been permitted to wear had he lived and Boniface given him his verdict on his reinstatement. All that was irrelevant now. Death made so many things irrelevant. The mind
concentrated on the grim boundary between life and death and
the great questions surged up within. For the believer, those questions had received their answer. The religious lives out his ac-
ceptance of those answers day after day, year after year. For such
a one, the words of the liturgy seem particularly apt: *Vita mutatur
non tollitur*—life is altered, not taken away. There were ironies
in according Nathaniel all the deference due a deceased priest.
The casket of a layman pointed feet forward toward the altar, that
of a priest was reversed. In the stalls were the four priests whose
loyalty Nathaniel had divided.

The ceremony was swift and simple, as required by the Rule

of the Order. Afterward, the casket was lifted to a flatbed and the diminished community followed Andrew George as he drove slowly toward the cemetery. The undertaker followed in his car. Looking into the grave that had been dug for Nathaniel, Boniface resisted the thoughts that came, thoughts that might seem lugubrious to some, but not to him. But he was here to fulfill a function, not meditate on the last things. Within minutes it was over. The old men turned from the new grave and walked slowly and in silence back to the mansion.

When Mr. Cadbury told him the story of Mr. George and his son Michael, he seemed to think that Boniface had already known it. Hearing that father and son had suspected one another and that the son had made a hurried cleanup of the maintenance shed in order to cover up what he thought his father had done filled the old priest with a tremendous sadness. What has become of us when we can suspect one another of having done so awful a deed? Boniface thought it was obvious who had killed Nathaniel. After Mr. Cadbury left, he drove downtown to police headquarters and asked if he could see Stanley Morgan.

Morgan came into the room with a smile, then stopped. "I thought it was Father Dowling. All they said was a priest."

"Will you talk with me?"

"Of course. Father Boniface, I can't tell you how I regret having tried to deceive you as I did, at least at first."

"What you told me helped change the minds of those who had sided with Father Nathaniel."

"Good."

"Mr. Morgan, why did you run away the morning Nathaniel was found?"

"That was cowardly. But after what happened to me in California, I could not stay."

"Running away was like an admission of guilt."

"They would have thought me guilty anyway."

"The Georges didn't."

"They are good people."

"Yes, they are."

Then Boniface told the story of Michael George and the maintenance shed, of Mr. George's anguished admission that his son had been in the shed when he went there to telephone.

"Michael is putting himself under suspicion in order to protect his father."

"My God."

"You didn't know this?"

"No. Father, neither of them could have done such a thing."

"That is what I think."

Father Boniface sat in silence, certain that he was in the presence of a murderer, but a murderer with a strange conscience. He seemed genuinely moved by what the Georges had done.

"Neither of them ever said he thought it was you."

Morgan asked to hear it all again, as if he wanted to memorize the events recounted. He shook his head sadly. "The short time I spent with them . . ." Again he shook his head. "The father and I stayed up until all hours that night, drinking Greek wine and talking."

"About Nathaniel?"

"About him. About everything. Here was a man who had spent his life on that same plot of ground, gone nowhere, seen nothing, and yet he was wise. Of course he was angry that Michael might not follow in his footsteps because of Nathaniel. Some would call it a small ambition, wanting his son to be the groundskeeper there.

But it was his whole world, and it was threatened with destruction."

"It is difficult to think of our lives without the Georges."

"But you said Nathaniel's supporters had deserted him."

"There are other ways in which that future for Michael can be ruined. It is well on the way to being ruined now. Do you know what I fear? I fear that Michael will take the final step and confess to murdering Nathaniel."

"No."

"Of course, you have been arrested and are being held here. Largely because you refuse to get a lawyer. That does not seem to be the act of a man who is worried about himself."

"I hate lawyers."

"There are good ones and there are bad ones."

"Why do you think that Michael will confess?"

"For the same reason he has done what he has already done. To protect his father."

"But who else thinks George could do such a thing?"

"One is sufficient, if it is Michael."

Whatever Boniface had expected from the conversation failed to happen. And he did not know whether or not he was disappointed. When he left he met Lieutenant Horvath who talked to him of the death of the young woman, but Boniface listened to the story as if it were an event on another planet.

Horvath said that there were those who thought the two murders were connected, but gave no indication he thought the same. It seemed to Boniface a far-fetched idea. His one desire was to have the death of Nathaniel cease being a matter of public discussion. But that wouldn't happen until the murderer was tried and convicted. Complicating the issue by trying to link Nathaniel's death with that of this young woman would only prolong the publicity and postpone the implementation of the plan he would present to the cardinal.

"So what brings you here, Father?"

"I have been speaking with Stanley Morgan."

Cy pulled on his ear. "He still insists he is innocent. Maybe he is."

Father Boniface felt a chill. Was this a warning that the police were now ready to act on what Michael had done? He couldn't bring himself to ask.

It was some hours later, that evening, when Boniface looked into the common room where the old priests were dozing in front of the television. The local news was on. And then it had Father Boniface's full attention. Stanley Morgan had just confessed to the murder of Father Nathaniel.

For they have consulted together with one consent.

—*Psalm 83*

Tuttle had been booked as a material witness and bail was set. Hazel Barnes came down to get him out. Tuttle felt like refusing. There were worse things than jail. Hazel stood with the bail bondsman, an inscrutable smile on her face, looking again like the angel of judgment. It was a moment that might have been covered with glee by his friends in the pressroom, but only Hazel and Crawford the bondsman were present.

"Where is everybody?"

Hazel snorted. "You were expecting a brass band? What a sight you are."

Tuttle still couldn't believe that this was a private event. If Tetzel were in his spot, he would have been here to enjoy the occasion. And then the sergeant told him that Stanley Morgan had confessed.

"To murdering Charlotte Priebe?"

"Don't be an idiot," Hazel said. "The man was locked up when that happened. It's too bad you weren't. Honestly, you need someone to look after you."

"Run away, Tuttle," Crawford said, slapping him on the arm. "I could use the money."

"How much is this costing?"

"She beat me down," Crawford said. "A fraction of a fraction. But she promised me free legal representation besides."

"So go get in trouble," Hazel said, grabbing Tuttle by the arm and leading him out to her SUV. Getting into it used muscles that atrophied in civilized society, but Tuttle was happy to clamber aboard.

"I suppose you want to go to a Chinese restaurant to celebrate."

What could he say? Hazel was his misfortune cookie and she seemed impossible to get rid of.

Farniente was at the Great Wall and he invited them to join him. Hazel pulled on Tuttle's arm, but this was one time he was too strong for her. He slipped into the chair across from Farniente. When Hazel sat, she said, "Take off that stupid hat."

Hazel lectured with her mouth full or empty and the two professionals ignored her, or tried to. Her words came to Tuttle as those of people disgustedly tearing up their tickets after the last race has run, of people wanting a divorce and to whom he had sometimes listened before refusing their custom—he lived by a rigid if eclectic code—of losers everywhere, of Saliari being wheeled through the nuthouse, bestowing a blessing on mediocrity. How long, O Lord, how long?

"I could use a secretary," Farniente mumbled through a mouthful of egg roll.

"What you could use would make up a long list."

For a moment, hope had flared. Even Farniente would look like a better bet than himself. He had had plenty of time in that damnable cell to think of the big one that had gotten away. Where had things gone wrong? He had the client of a lifetime, he had inspired Tetzel to write a series that might win him a prize, unimaginable fees were within his reach, and then, poof! The goose was gone before a golden egg could be laid. Leo Corbett had dropped him without telling him, had gone off with Charlotte Priebe, no doubt to form an alliance with Anderson Ltd. that excluded Tuttle. He had thought of his vigil outside the building in which Charlotte Priebe lived once the perfidious Matilda had described the man living with Charlotte in a way that matched Leo. He remembered following Leo to the hotel where he took a room, and then camping out in the lobby. What was lost had been found. He was sure that he could shame Leo into loyalty. And then without warning the roof had fallen in on him. He had no doubt that it had been his clone in the tweed hat behind the counter who

PRODIGAL FATHER 311

had blown the whistle on him. Leo appeared, his moment had arrived, and the next thing he knew, he was in Horvath's custody, and Leo had slipped away.

That sequence of events, to suspicious eyes, had been sufficient to land him in the cooler. While he was being questioned, he tried to piece together what in the minds of Horvath and Keegan had happened to Charlotte Priebe. She had drowned in her bathtub.

"What did you do with the bottle for the sleeping pills?" he had been asked during the third round of questioning.

So that was what had happened. The young woman had been put into a drugged sleep and then into her bathtub and held beneath the surface of the water. He had not done that. So who had? This was a question he would like to put to Leo Corbett. Tuttle paused in his eating, completely deaf now to Hazel's continuing lamentation. That question gave him the leverage he needed to get Leo back under his thumb. He sat back and rubbed his middle.

"Well, that hit the spot."

"Tasty," Farniente agreed.

Tuttle stood, announcing a call of nature, and catching Farniente's eye tipped his tweed in the direction of the john.

"Look," Tuttle said, when Farniente came into the men's room. "Get rid of her, will you? There's something I have to do."

"Me, too," Farniente said, stepping up to one of the baby shower-style urinals.

Tuttle positioned himself at the adjoining one. "Will you do it?"

"Tuttle, I can't tell you how glad I was to see you walk in that door tonight. It's a travesty that a man with your background should be held in jail." Farniente glanced at him. "You didn't kill her, did you?"

"If I ever kill a woman, it will be Hazel."

Farniente shook his head. "She reminds me of my first wife."

"Are you divorced?"

"No."

Tuttle debated with himself the wisdom of letting Farniente in on the epiphany he had had at the table. He won the debate. Farniente was not a good luck charm.

"Aren't you going to ask me why I was so glad to see you, Tuttle?"

Tuttle stepped away, zipped, and went to the washbasin, trying to be patient. Farniente was getting to be like Hazel, always interrupting. Next to him, Farniente turned a faucet, and then danced away from an errant splash.

"You remember Solomon, the retired cop? He is now doing security at the Wackham Building, nights. He called me on my cell phone just as I sat down to eat. Something's going on over there and he wanted me to know."

"Why?"

"He wishes he had become a PI instead of a cop." Farniente looked shy. "You wouldn't believe what an exciting life he thinks I lead. It's all those paperbacks he reads on duty."

"Why did he call you?"

"Cy Horvath and Pippen the coroner's assistant had just showed up and asked to be taken to the basement."

"So?"

"They were carrying some kind of electronic equipment."

"No kidding."

Tuttle's father had worked on the construction crew when that building went up. And the builder had been Lars Anderson, early in his career. He weighed the possibility of finding Leo Corbett tonight and checking out the Wackham. There was time to do both.

"Solomon said it was all hush-hush."

The basement of the Wackham did not sound like a rendezvous to Tuttle. Horvath was sweet on Pippen like everyone else; but this had to be something important.

"We have to get rid of Hazel," he said.

"There's a back door."

"But the bill?"

Farniente smiled wickedly. "I think you paid for your supper just listening to her."

"My hat is at the table."

"Get it later."

He would feel like Samson shorn, but he made a reluctant decision. A moment later, he and Farniente were stealing through the odorous kitchen and slipping out the back door into the parking lot.

My days are like a shadow that lengthens.
—*Psalm 102*

Horvath carried the little case, slung over his shoulder, when he and Pippen entered the Wackham Building and approached the desk where Bill Solomon was engrossed in a paperback. Solomon hadn't heard them come in so either what he was reading was fascinating or his ears were worse than they had been when he was on the force.

"That elevator go to the basement?"

The watchman levitated and lost his grip on his paperback. "Cy! How are you?" Solomon looked at Pippen, then pushed his glasses to the tip of his nose for a better look.

All over town, former cops were supplementing their pensions with jobs like this—security at the mall, at supermarkets, in schools, in downtown buildings. Soft duty, but what good was retirement if you went on working? He felt a sudden compassion for Solomon, bored to death through the night hours, driven to cheap novels to keep his mind from working, he might have been a symbol of Christmas future. He repeated his question.

"That depends on what you mean by basement."

Pippen said, "What does the word mean to you?"

"There are two basements," Solomon said brightly, happy to acquaint the uninitiated with the lore of the Wackham. "The basement and the subbasement."

"We'll start with the subbasement," Cy said.

"Start what?"

Cy hunched over the desk and fixed Solomon's eye. "Remember when you were sworn in as a police officer, Bill? That oath still stands. We're on a very confidential mission. If anyone hears of this, it will be because you told them. I don't have to tell you what would happen then."

Solomon seemed to want to know, but Cy stood. "Come on," he said to Pippen, and started for the elevator.

"It won't work without this key," Solomon called after them.

Cy returned to the table with his hand out. Solomon reluctantly removed a key from a large ring of keys that swung from his belt when he stood.

"This could mean my head, Horvath."

"That's what I said."

"How long will this take?" he asked Pippen when they were in the elevator and he pushed SB.

"The ride down?" Radiant smile, great green eyes, auburn hair pulled back and gathered in a ponytail. She was wearing a long skirt and an open jacket that hung below her hips. Their presence together in this intimate, enclosed space constituted what the nuns had called a proximate occasion of sin. But all they had ever done is innocently flirt with one another. And that is all they would ever do. Virtue is a habit hard to break.

The subbasement was a great rectangle with rough concrete walls and hooded lamps dangling from the ceiling. In its center, enclosed by a screen fence, was what looked like a generator. Otherwise the space was empty. Cy unslung the case. Pippen opened it and withdrew what looked like a stethoscope. There were dials set in the top of the instrument.

"No headset?"

"The dials do it."

Carrying the case, Cy picked a wall at random and Pippen began to move the detecting device along the concrete, her eye on the dials. The wall was maybe seven feet high.

"Why don't I do that and you watch the dials."

As she could not, he could hold the porous disk that spoke to the dials to the top of the wall. But if what they were looking for was here, chances are it would not be up very high. Probably more in the middle. It was a dull task, made interesting by the presence of Pippen, and the knowledge that they were together on a job.

"Isn't this fun?" she said, when one wall had been traversed without results.

"A barrel of laughs."

They had worked silently up to then, but now she began to talk. Sometimes she wished she were a detective rather than coroner. She was just a year married and Cy would have asked what she planned to do when the children came, but there are questions one does not ask of professional women. Not that he thought of Pippen as one of a type. However efficient she was in her job, she seemed miscast to Cy. He saw her bouncing babies on her knee, a Renaissance Madonna, the essence of womanhood.

She had reviewed her girlhood, college, medical school, her family, the awful men she might have married and how lucky she was to have found the husband she had, and there was one wall left. A wall they might have started with. They had been in the subbasement two hours when the elevator door opened and Tuttle and Farniente emerged.

"Horvath! I heard you were down here."

Horvath thought of what he would do to Solomon. Obviously the security man had gotten on the phone to spread the news. But Farniente and Tuttle? He would have expected the rat to call Tetzel. Too late, he remembered that Solomon had frequently been under a cloud when he was on active duty, leaking to the press everything he knew, which was never much, but it did not endear him to his colleagues. He should have brought Solomon with them.

"Glad you could come," Cy said. "You know Dr. Pippen."

Farniente was ogling the coroner with undisguised admiration. "You remind me of my first wife."

"What are we doing?" Tuttle asked.

Cy ignored him, starting on the remaining wall. Tuttle and Farniente fell silent, moving along with him and Pippen as they sounded the wall.

"Something in there?"

"You ever read Edgar Allan Poe?" Pippen asked him.

"Does he write for the *Sun-Times*?"

"Nevermore."

With the arrival of Tuttle and Farniente, the futile became farcical. Cy no longer expected that Pippen's gizmo would detect the remains of the late and unlamented Beamish. Charlotte Priebe had taken some sick boasting seriously. Lars Anderson had not made a pile because he was dumb enough to confide in a young woman something that could have caused him real trouble. He reached the corner and looked at Pippen.

"Nothing," she said.

"Well, now we know."

He had told her only that they had been given information about a body buried in the concrete.

"Could it be in the basement?"

They headed for the elevator, with Tuttle and Farniente at their heels. The four rose a level to the basement. It was the same dimensions as the subbasement but had a claustrophobically low ceiling. Pippen suggested they switch roles. They did, and she began making great swift arcs with the detector, moving much more quickly than he had. The dials did nothing.

"We going to do all twenty floors?" Tuttle asked.

"As many as we can get to," Cy said.

"What are we looking for?"

"Promise you won't tell?"

Both Tuttle and Farniente raised their lying hands.

"I made the same promise."

It was three in the morning when they packed up the equipment and headed for the elevator. A sullen Tuttle and Farniente grumbled as they rose to the lobby.

"Look at it this way, Tuttle. You might still be in jail."

"They threatened me," Solomon whined when Cy stopped at his desk.

"I thought I did that."

"What are you going to do?"

"Get you reinstated. You'd make a good partner for Peanuts Pianone."

"Sorry," Cy said, when he and Pippen pulled away.

"Sorry that we didn't find a body?"

"Thanks for helping."

"Hey, what are the long night hours for?"

"Where's Mr. Pippen?" he asked. She had retained her name after her marriage.

She laughed. "Dr. Foley is attending a medical convention in Seattle."

They stopped for coffee, they ordered ham and eggs. "You never talk about yourself, Cy."

"Not when I'm on duty."

She might have taken it as a rebuff, but it was his shield against temptation. And it was tempting to think of them as a couple out on the town, ending up here with platters full of bacon and eggs and coffee so hot it would have gotten McDonald's a lawsuit. He took the printout of Charlotte Priebe's file from his pocket and showed it to her. She read it while removing egg from the corner of her mouth with a long-nailed little finger. Her brows rose.

"Wow."

"We just disproved it."

"I'm glad you didn't tell me before. I thought it was the confession of some convict at Joliet or something."

"That's about what it was worth."

"But you had to know."

Even negative information is a gain. One possible explanation of the death of Charlotte Priebe could be dismissed. Cy was almost sad. It would have been something to present Robertson with a question of conscience, not that he had one. Sometimes he dreamed of Keegan being named chief and the department being made over to his image. It would never happen. Okay. If not Anderson, Tuttle? That was ridiculous. They had just been teaching the lawyer a lesson. A process of elimination went on in Horvath's mind.

"You're thinking."

And he was. First thing in the morning he would scare up Leo Corbett.

The fool has said in his heart, "There is no God."

—Psalm 14

Father Dowling awoke at five in the morning, tried to regain sleep first on one side, then the other, then on his back. Perhaps sleep would have come again, if he had not started thinking. He put his hands behind his head and looked at the ceiling in the first dawn and made his morning offering. Then, with great concentration, he said an Our Father. That done, he reviewed the events of the past week. They almost seemed to have begun with his retreat at the Athanasians. Something in Father Boniface's valedictory air had touched his own soul, not altogether bad when on retreat, but it would not do as one's natural attitude, as Boniface himself had come to see. Mortality was a fact, death would come, and a retreat offered the opportunity to think on the life that led to that definitive moment. As he rarely did, he thought of his early life as a priest, a member of the archdiocesan marriage tribunal, widely regarded as a man on his way up the ecclesiastical ladder. And then he had been brought low, suffering a humiliating debility that altered forever his prospects. His assignment to St. Hilary's had seemed to seal his fate. So thought others, so at first thought he. But with time he came to see in this apparent reversal a providential reordering of his life.

He thanked God for this parish, for his pastoral work, for his friends. A bonus had been the renewal of an old acquaintance with Phil Keegan, once a lower-classman at Quigley who had washed out because the intricacies of Latin escaped him. Roger Dowling had the vaguest of memories of Phil as a boy, but to Phil he had been an upperclassman and thus more noticeable. Phil's wife had died, he was a widower who tried to make his work as captain of detectives the whole of his life, and the St. Hilary rectory soon became almost a second home to him. Thus Father Dowling had learned more than he might have wanted to of the seamy side of the city in which he lived.

His retreat had refreshed his memories of Marygrove and the Athanasians so that he had acquaintance with the setting in which bizarre events had then occurred. Boniface had told him of the surprising return of a laicized member, who had lived like a prodigal in a far city but finally asked permission to return to his community. Yet even while on probation, he had become a source of division, something Boniface tolerated because of Nathaniel's role in the restoration of the common office and Gregorian chant. But Nathaniel had started a faction that threatened to bring on more quickly than Boniface feared the end of the Order. The idea of selling off the choice property on which the Athanasians had lived their American existence had appealed to some of the old priests because it appealed to their sense of the demands of their vow of poverty. Their home began to seem a place they unjustly occupied. And not only the Athanasians would be affected by such a sale. The Georges, from time immemorial the groundskeepers at Marygrove, would find themselves unemployed as the land they had so lovingly cultivated was divided into plots and great expensive houses rose. In a short time, Nathaniel had made many enemies.

And then Stanley Morgan had brought Nathaniel's California past to Fox River. When Mr. George had discovered the corpse of Father Nathaniel on a prie dieu at the grotto, Morgan had been staying in the lodge, there to be a grim reminder to his erstwhile silent partner of past injustice. When Morgan disappeared while the medical examiner and police swarmed over the scene of the murder, he became the obvious suspect. He was arrested in St. Hilary's old school, doubtless given sanctuary by Edna Hospers. Morgan had been a danger to Edna, but that was all. If Morgan had made a sincere confession, there had been nothing untoward between him and Edna. And, equally on the assumption of his sincerity in laying his sins before a priest, Stanley Morgan had not killed Father Nathaniel. Father Dowling had waited for Phil Keegan to look beyond the presumed guilt of Morgan, unable to say anything that was based on Morgan's confession.

The murder of Charlotte Priebe had turned up an ominous file on her computer. *If I Should Die.* Phil Keegan had shown him the printout.

"So what will you do?"

"Proceed with caution."

"But proceed?"

And then Phil told him of the planned nocturnal visit to the basement of the Wackham Building to be made by Cy Horvath and Dr. Pippen. By now, they should know whether credence could be put in Charlotte Priebe's account of Lars Anderson's story. Discovery is largely a matter of eliminating possibilities and that was what the pastor of St. Hilary's did, ticking off the suspects as he lay awake. All but one.

At five-thirty, Father Dowling got out of bed. His day had

begun, whether he liked it or not. He shaved and showered and dressed and went downstairs. In the kitchen, he drank a glass of orange juice and left a note for Marie Murkin. WILL BE GONE FOR SOME HOURS. BACK FOR THE NOON MASS. Then he went out to his car and drove downtown.

When he entered the hotel lobby he thought it was Tuttle behind the desk, snoozing under his tipped-forward tweed hat. Father Dowling tapped on the counter with his car keys and the figure lurched into wakefulness. The sight of the Roman collar brought him to his feet.

"What room is Leo Corbett in?"

"You want me to call him?"

"Just give me the number, I'll go up."

Hesitation gave way before the reassurance of a clerical presence. "307."

"Thank you."

"Should I let him know you're coming up?"

"Thank you."

The elevator seemed undecided between upward and sideways movement. There was a strong smell of disinfectant that was lifted with Father Dowling uncertainly to the third floor. The hallway into which he emerged was poorly lit and needed all the disinfectant it could get. Father Dowling started in one direction, then altered course. When he turned, a door opened and Leo Corbett looked out, disheveled and testy.

"What do you want?"

Father Dowling walked to the opened door, laid a hand on Leo's arm and gently moved him inside. "We don't want to discuss this in the hallway."

"What 'this'?"

"Many things, Leo."

"I don't know you. Are you one of them?"

"Them?"

"Athanasians."

"No. I'm Father Dowling. I have a parish here in town."

"Look, I don't want to talk about this or anything else. I'm not a Catholic."

"Your grandfather was."

"Senility," Leo said contemptuously.

It was not a room in which anyone would care to spend much time. The bed looked as if Leo had spent the night wrestling with bad angels. The shade hung crookedly at the cloudy window, the ceiling lamp diffused weak light over the messy scene. A pile of clothing lay in the corner. On the little table beside the bed there was an overflowing ashtray and a small gooseneck lamp with a yellowing shade. Newspapers were scattered on the floor next to the bed.

"Senility? Do you mean his conversion or his transfer of his estate to the Athanasians?"

"They are two ends of the same thought."

"I see in the paper that you consider yourself to have been disinherited."

"Well, what would you think if your grandfather was one of the richest men in town and all he left his son was an annuity that ran out when he died?"

"Your father?"

"My father."

"So you have put yourself in the capable hands of Tuttle?"

"Not anymore."

"No?"

"Look, why are you here? Is this what priests do, call unin-vited on hotel guests?"

"You must be anxious to talk to someone."

"About what?"

"Father Nathaniel, for one thing."

"He's dead."

"Indeed he is. By violence. Why did you do it?"

Leo gave him a look, then smiled sarcastically. "What do I do now, break down and confess?"

"That would be a start. How did you lure Nathaniel to the maintenance shed in the middle of the night?"

Leo looked at him for a long minute, his face registering a sequence of thoughts. Then he got up and locked the door. Loung-ing on the bed, he said, "Why not? What would you like to know?"

Father Dowling rested his back against the dresser. "I already have a question on the floor."

"How did I lure Nathaniel to the maintenance shed? I called him up and said we had to talk. You see, your approach works. I told him there was a way to accomplish what he wanted. He told me it was too late, he had lost support. I told him my support was all he needed. It was he who suggested the maintenance shed. Since I was calling from my car, I was there before him and found what I wanted."

"An ax?"

"A sort-of ax."

"What was the point of killing him if he no longer presented a threat?"

"Do you think I believed that? Do you imagine I really be-lieved that they would do a deal with Anderson and I would get my grandfather's house?"

"So what was your plan?"

"You realize I'm telling you these things because you can be no danger to me."

"Your worst enemy is yourself. And then you killed Charlotte Priebe."

"I don't want to talk about her."

"Why not? As you say, I'm no danger to you."

"Don't you know what I meant by that?"

"Given your recent actions, I have a fairly good idea."

"Aren't you frightened?"

"Not as much as you must be."

"The police? They're stupid. Besides, they have a confession from Stanley Morgan. Don't you watch the news?"

"Now they can concentrate on what happened to Charlotte. I should tell you the police found a very interesting file on the computer in her apartment."

"How would you know that?"

"Believe me, they did. A very incriminating document. She spoke of you. She feared for her life."

"I don't believe it."

"Why did you flee from her apartment?"

"I'm losing interest in this."

"She took you in and you killed her."

"She tried to take me in, you mean. The oldest trick in the world. It was fun while it was lasted, but was I supposed to believe a woman like that had fallen madly in love with me?"

"That was no reason to kill her."

"She knew too much. And now so do you."

"I know enough to know that you have destroyed any chance of getting what you think is owed you."

"I am not working alone."

"Lars Anderson?"

"Why do you say that?"

"I told you of the statement found on Charlotte Priebe's computer."

"I think you're making that up."

"No you don't."

Leo lurched forward and rose awkwardly to his feet. He was a huge young man, pudgy but powerful. "Come on, we're getting out of here."

"Where can you hide, Leo?"

"You should be worrying more of what could happen to you."

"I have a suggestion."

"Yeah?"

"Why don't we visit your grandfather's grave?"

Keep me as the apple of Your eye.
                    —*Psalm 17*

A note that Marie Murkin had called was waiting on Phil Keegan's desk. And a message from Cy: *Nothing*. Phil was relieved as well as disappointed. There was one crisis he didn't have to face. He picked up the phone and called the St. Hilary rectory.

"I suppose I'm just a worrywart," Marie said, after telling him that Father Dowling was gone when she came down to the kitchen. "He left a note."

"What does it say?"

She read it to him.

"Probably out on a sick call."

"But he would have said if that's what it was."

"Marie, he's hardly a missing person."

"I know. But I had to tell someone."

"I'm glad you did. I'll call back in a little while. Maybe eleven. He said he'd be back for the noon Mass?"

"Yes."

"There you are, then."

It was ridiculous, but Marie's worry had transferred itself to him. Roger Dowling was not an impulsive man. But during their last conversation, Phil had the impression that Roger was waiting for him to say something. They had been talking about the deaths of Father Nathaniel and Charlotte Priebe. Roger had frowned when told that Morgan's confession to killing Nathaniel pretty well severed any link between the two killings.

And then the call came from the desk clerk at the Stella Hotel. The officer answering the phone said Phil would probably want to hear this himself.

"Captain Keegan," he said, when the call was transferred.

"This is Brink at the Stella. Something odd is going on. A priest showed up here an hour ago and asked to see one of the guests and just now the two of them left. It looked to me as if the priest was being taken away."

"What did he look like?"

Roger Dowling might not have been flattered by the description of him. Tall, thin, profile like an eagle.

"What's the guest's name?"

"He signed in as Leo Corbett."

Leo's license number was acquired and the make of his car and the search began. It ended at the Stella Hotel, where Leo's car was found parked in the diminutive lot behind the building, backed up against the trash cans. Feeling like a fool, Phil Keegan put out a bulletin on Father Dowling's car, a ten-year-old Oldsmobile Cierra. Meanwhile, Cy had come in.

"He must have come to the same conclusion I did when we came up empty at the Wackham."

"You think Corbett did them both?"

Cy nodded. "It seems inevitable. All the other possibilities have run out."

"We should have thought of Leo right away."

But Cy wouldn't give him that discomfort. Morgan had made himself the obvious suspect and if they didn't like him, the Georges, father and son, seemed to be claiming the role.

"They wouldn't have fouled their own nests."

Cy said nothing. If murders made sense there would be fewer of them. They went off in separate cars, as reachable in them as anywhere else, destinations random. Phil drove to St. Hilary's to find that Marie Murkin had called Father Boniface and the Athanasian had come to say the noon Mass. Phil knelt in back, feeling that Roger was almost posthumous, his place taken by another, as priest can easily be replaced by priest. Marie was in stoic self-control.

"Come have lunch with Father Boniface," she whispered in his ear when he was trying to pretend his anguished thoughts after communion were a form of prayer. He felt empty at the thought that Roger Dowling might already have met the fate of Nathaniel and Charlotte Priebe. Suddenly Phil felt that whatever future was left to him was uninviting. He would retire, he would . . . He got up and followed Marie to the rectory.

Lunch was like a wake, everything reminding Phil of the missing pastor. He had called his office and was given the rectory number. He had no appetite, but he ate everything Marie put before him. Boniface could not substitute for Roger at that table. He wondered what Marie would do.

Boniface began to speak of old Maurice Corbett. "He was a presence around Marygrove when I was a student, a silent, imposing old man. When we prayed for our benefactors I suppose we all thought of him."

"Did you know the son?" Marie asked.

"The prodigal son of a prodigal father, in different senses of the term. He was a geologist."

Their thoughts went on to the grandson. That a highly successful and finally generous man should have had a son whose passion was rocks and the ages of the earth was odd enough, but that the grandson should have developed a deep resentment because of the wealth he felt should have been his seemed a commentary on the ages of man.

"Maybe we are all composed of layers, like the earth," Boniface said.

"Where is he buried?" Marie asked and Boniface stared at her. "I mean the grandfather."

"Ah. In Resurrection Cemetery. He raised a great stone to his wife and he was buried next to her."

When Phil went out to his car, he sat for a while before starting it. He called in to find out if anything had been heard, but of course they would have let him know. When he started off, he drove aimlessly for a time, his ear cocked to his radio, and then he headed for Resurrection Cemetery.

The Lord preserves all who love Him but all the wicked He will destroy.

—Psalm 145

"Good idea," Leo said as he guided him through the lobby of the Stella Hotel. The man behind the desk had his tweed hat on the back of his head and waved at them. "I've visited there often to cuss him out."

"If it weren't for him, you wouldn't be, Leo."

"You can say the same of Adam. And look what he did to all of us."

"We won't be condemned for Original Sin."

Outside, they stood for a moment in front of the hotel. Father Dowling considered raising a fuss. What could Leo do to him there on the sidewalk? No doubt it would have been a futile gesture. The cars would have continued to speed past, hundreds of people hurrying to a hundred different places, unlikely to notice what was going on in front of a sleazy hotel. But then a watery-eyed man with reddish stubble on his face came up with his hand held out.

"Give a fella the price of a meal, Father?"

"Beat it," Leo said.

"Hey, I asked him."

"And I answered you. Get lost."

Indignation made a showing in the watery eyes, but before he shuffled off Father Dowling gave him the change in his pocket.

"Bless you, Father."

"For I have sinned," Leo said. "Isn't that how it goes? Where's your car?"

He opened the driver's door of Father Dowling's car and told him to get in. When he was behind the wheel, the door slammed. With a flick of his finger he could have locked all the doors. But he waited for Leo to go around the front of the car and then get into the passenger seat.

"That bum won't sound the alarm."

"Where is your grandfather buried?"

"Resurrection." Leo laughed. "Do you believe all that? These bones will live again?"

"Yes."

"Well, if it's any consolation."

Father Dowling started the car and pulled away. His Oldsmobile could have found Resurrection Cemetery by itself, it had been there often enough, when he didn't ride with the undertaker. But he preferred driving his own car to the cemetery; it was better afterward. He would say a final word to the bereaved and then as he drove away see the little band drift off toward their cars, perhaps feeling for the first time the definitiveness of their loss.

It was late morning now and Father Dowling thought of the noon Mass. Why hadn't he included his destination in his note to

Marie? She might have been worried and called Phil and help would be on the way. But he felt more concern for Leo than for himself.

"Leo, nothing you've done is unforgivable. Think about it. You have taken human life. That was the first crime after Original Sin."

"Oh, come on. Just drive."

"Were you raised Catholic?"

"Drive!"

He drove through the busy streets, out of downtown and through a residential area, and finally into the country. Eventually they came to the entrance gate of Resurrection. Old Heidegger might notice his car, it would be familiar enough to him, but there was no sign of the sexton when they passed the gatehouse or as they moved along the quiet, tree-lined road.

"Where is his grave, Leo?"

"Take a left at the next fork."

"You know it pretty well."

"I told you. I used to visit him and tell him what I thought of him."

A charming scene, a resentful grandson muttering over the grave of a grandfather he had never known. "That's it," Leo said. "The houselike thing on that little hill."

They got out of the car and walked side by side across the lawn between the graves. The mausoleum was an impressive structure with the word CORBETT displayed across the front. It had a greenish door with huge iron hinges. The names of the buried were etched in the door.

"Is that your father's name?"

Leo nodded. "It was when he was buried that it first hit me."

"What?"

"My grandfather built this pyramid to rot in and left me with nothing. I had just learned that what my father had been given ran out when he died."

"Perhaps you'll be buried here, too."

"Come around to the other side, away from the road."

"The car's pretty obvious."

Leo thought about that. "Give me your keys."

Father Dowling gave him the keys. He was waiting for something; he wasn't sure yet what is was. Leo wasn't such a monster when you got to know him a bit. Leo started toward the car, then turned.

"You going to run?"

"Would you want me to?"

Leo tried to smile. "You're a strange man. You didn't have to get involved, you know. It's not my fault it's ending up like this."

"No."

"I'll catch you if you run."

"I'll wait."

Leo started off slowly, but then he began to hurry. When he got to the car, he didn't get in. He went to the rear and unlocked the trunk. When he closed it, he had a lug wrench in his hand. He came swiftly back across the grass to Father Dowling.

"You should have run."

"I'm not much of a runner."

They stood facing one another, Leo with the wrench dangling from his hand, the priest facing him.

"I don't want to do this."

"Then don't."

Through the trees, Father Dowling saw cars on the road. Some of them parking. He spoke to Leo with new urgency.

"Leo, you're at the end of the trail. Think of what you learned when you were a child. I can hear your confession."

Leo laughed. "You want to hear my confession? Okay. I put an ax in that priest's back, I drowned Charlotte. Is that what you want to hear?"

"I already knew that."

Figures were moving toward them, from tree to tree, keeping out of sight, but getting closer.

"Give me the wrench, Leo."

"Sure. Where would you like it?" He lifted it menacingly, holding it aloft, glaring at Father Dowling, And then a shot was fired.

Leo spun in pained surprise, the wrench dropped, and his hand went to his shoulder. He looked accusingly at Father Dowling, but then the police converged on them. It was Phil Keegan who wrestled Leo to the ground.

"It's all right, Phil. He's harmless."

"He is now."

❧ Coda ❧

It was perhaps a sign of the times that public sympathy for Leo Corbett rose as the memory of his crimes faded. The brutal murder of Nathaniel and the drowning of Charlotte Priebe in her bath were eclipsed by a long interview with Leo in his cell by Monique Parle of the *Tribune*. Monique had hitherto written indignant essays on the various ways Fox River disappointed her, usually featured on the fourth page of the second section, but her interview with Leo catapulted her into the front ranks of journalists. At least onto page one of the *Tribune*.

"Was he always so fat?" Marie asked, frowning at the paper.

"I think he may have lost weight."

On Monique's telling, Leo was a victim of callous parents— an eccentric father, a mother guilty of substance abuse. As for the heartlessness of Maurice Corbett, words failed Monique.

Leo, spruced up for the occasion, looked soulfully at the camera. There were no pictures of the body of Nathaniel at the grotto or of Charlotte in her tub. Leo seemed to be confined to a cell for vague and nameless reasons while Monique told the litany of his grievances.

"They'll find him guilty," Phil Keegan said to allay Marie's fears. "He could spend ten years in prison."

"Ten years! They should lock him up and throw away the key."

Marie's thirst for justice was currently out of vogue and often confused with a desire for revenge. Of course, justice can be hungered for out of less-than-exalted motives, but it did seem basic that Leo Corbett should pay the price for the murders he had committed.

Charlotte's successor at Anderson Ltd., a slim, bald, boyish man who moved with the grace of a ballet dancer, floated the suggestion that Leo had authored the message found on Charlotte's computer in a libelous effort to divert suspicion from himself. More grist for Monique's mill. The powerful and mighty could not leave Leo alone.

The trial was postponed for a second time in an effort to have it moved to another jurisdiction. Meanwhile, the wedding of Rita Martinez and Michael George was center stage at St. Hilary's. An ecumenical compromise had been reached. There would be a nuptial Mass said by Father Dowling and at the reception Father Maximilian would bless the happy couple.

"But what of the children?" Marie wanted to know.

"Sufficent for the day are the compromises thereof," Father Dowling murmured.

"She'll make a Catholic out of him," Marie decided, her solution to the Great Schism.

The visit of Stanley Morgan to the rectory put Marie's diplomatic skills to an ultimate test. Here was a man whose praises she had initially sung but whose subsequent behavior had placed him in her doghouse. Stanley showed up unannounced at the kitchen door putting Marie into a momentary fluster. His manner was deferential, his smile engaging. Marie asked him in.

"I'll never forget the day you gave me tea here," he said. "It seems a lifetime ago."

"I'll put some on now."

"No. No. Thank you, Mrs. Murkin."

"Marie," she corrected.

"I just wanted to stop and say good-bye."

"Good-bye?"

"I'm returning to California. At least for the time being."

"Well, after what you've been through . . ."

"It was my own fault."

"I never really thought you could have done such a thing," Marie lied. Her memories of Stanley's first visit to her kitchen returned, and with them her benevolent feeling for him.

She ignored his refusal, putting on tea. And there was peach pie as well. She sat across from him, watching him eat.

"Is Father Dowling here?"

"Not at the moment. Stanley, anything you want to say, you can say to me."

"You're very good."

"Goodness has nothing to do with it. It's my job."

"Well."

So he told her of his stay at Marygrove, and of his hope to confront Nathaniel. He spoke ruefully of his time in jail. And they were as one in lamenting the reaction of the Georges, father and son. But now Nathaniel was dead and Stanley free.

He stood then and with his hands on the back of the chair, gave Marie's kitchen a valedictory look. Suddenly he leaned forward and kissed her cheek.

"Good-bye, Marie."

And he was gone. From the doorway Marie watched with tear-blurred eyes as he went down the back steps. Hers was a tough and thankless job, by and large, but there came moments that made it all seem worthwhile. But where was he going?

Marie stepped out on the porch and could see Stanley hurrying along the sidewalk in the direction of the school. A frown came over her face. Was he going to say good-bye to Edna Hospers, too? Marie turned, went back inside and pulled the kitchen door shut with a bang.

Father Dowling and Boniface were on the path that led to the grotto at Marygrove. How much had happened in the weeks since Father Dowling had made his retreat here. But somber as many of those events had been, Boniface was in an almost jolly mood. The cardinal had approved the battle plan for the resurgence of the Athanasian Order. The two priests were discussing publicity for clerical retreats to be offered at Marygrove, a project good in itself but also a means of reacquainting the local clergy with the Athanasians.

"And vocations?" Father Dowling asked.

"Just this morning I received a very serious inquiry."

"Ah."

"I put him off. A person needs time to ponder so serious a move."

"Is it anyone I know?"

"Stanley Morgan."

Well, Our Lord had recruited tax collectors and fishermen. There was nothing to prevent a financial advisor from being called to the altar.

"Was it his stay here that put the idea in his head?"

"That and his time in jail."

Father Dowling looked at Boniface, but there was no irony in that serene countenance.

"I suppose there are precedents."

"I have been trying to think of one. St. Paul won't quite do."

"No."

"Morgan could start a trend."

"Yes. Perhaps, in the fullness of time, Leo Corbett will knock on your door."

Boniface threw up his hands. "May the Good Lord spare us that. *Parce nobis, domine.*"

They came to the grotto and knelt, Boniface having whispered that the prie-dieu on which Nathaniel's body had been found had been relocated. Flames of vigil lights danced against the blackened wall of the grotto; the smell of burning wax was sweet in the nostrils. Father Dowling prayed for Nathaniel and for Charlotte Priebe and for all those who had been involved in recent events. It was a pleasant thought that Nathaniel's old partner might take his place among the Athanasians.